BBQ AND STFU

BBQ AND STFU

THE UNBELIEVABLE MR. BROWNSTONE™ BOOK
TWENTY-TWO

MICHAEL ANDERLE

DISRUPTIVE IMAGINATION

LMBPN Publishing
PMB 196, 2540 South Maryland Pkwy
Las Vegas, NV 89109

First US edition, May 2020
ebook ISBN: 978-1-64202-918-5
Print ISBN: 978-1-64202-919-2

BBQ AND STFU TEAM

Special Thanks
to Mike Ross
for BBQ Consulting
Jessie Rae's BBQ - Las Vegas, NV

Thanks to the JIT Readers

Dave Hicks
Diane L. Smith
John Ashmore
Peter Manis
Dorothy Lloyd
Jeff Goode
Deb Mader
Kerry Mortimer
Jeff Eaton
James Caplan
Paul Westman

If I've missed anyone, please let me know!

Editor
Lynne Stiegler

To Family, Friends and
Those Who Love
to Read.
May We All Enjoy Grace
to Live the Life We Are
Called.

I f asked, Kalath would admit to amusement as he strode to the center of the dark cave. It wasn't the cave that had brought his mirthful mood, but his unassuming appearance, including a loose brown robe around his soft, gangly Light Elf body. Of the various shapes the ancient dragon had worn throughout the years, his current one appealed the most, but it still was ridiculous. Disguises had their uses, but he preferred his true form.

Two other absurd fakes stood in the cave waiting for him, one of whom appeared to be a beautiful Light Elf woman whose face was barely visible beneath her hood. The withered face of the remaining guest was locked in a scowl. The intense pressure of their combined magical energy would have been the first hint they were far more than three Light Elf hermits.

What sort of creature would be brave enough to risk coming closer and finding the truth? He might never know. Most Oricerans wouldn't dare risk entering the dangerous and magically unstable mountains nestled in that corner of their world. The disguises might be unnecessary, but it didn't matter. There wasn't enough room for all three of them to assume their true forms. While their combined power would be more than enough to defeat most enemies, any long-lived being understood that small measures of caution were often worth more than the strongest magic. They needed to conserve surprise given the importance of their task. Their pride in their abilities might not be misplaced, but the history of Oriceran was a history of powerful beings falling to surprising magic. That might be their fate if they didn't act soon.

Makkora, the dragon in the woman's shape, tilted her head, a curious expression on her face. "Why have you summoned us here, Kalath? It's earlier than we agreed, much earlier. It's not like you to waste our time."

They didn't need to talk, but the wards surrounding the cave automatically converted their words into something benign. It'd be far less suspicious than if somehow, a powerful magical watched three of them come together and never utter a word, and it required less magic than full illusions or blocking them entirely. Sometimes, though, Kalath wondered how much they did it for security, and how much they did it because on some small, petty level, they enjoyed the incongruity.

Cerj, the last member of the triad, gave a curt nod. His eyes blazed bright blue as he surveyed the area. "She's right. The last time we got together, we agreed to not do so again for five more years. You were the one who was most insistent on that point."

"I admit to all of that, but I called you here to discuss the prophecy. I wouldn't have risked contacting you otherwise." Kalath spread his arms. "It's as I feared last time. One of the prophecy gems has shattered."

"Those gems aren't without their flaws." Cerj frowned, and the light left his eyes. "The mere destruction of a gem doesn't mean the prophecy is growing closer. We also agreed on that during the last meeting."

"But it could, which is why we all agreed to use them despite their irregularities." Kalath raised his palm and summoned a swirling image of cracking bright-green rocks. "And this is not one of the prophecies we can choose to ignore. The gem cracked when I checked the status of the most dangerous of the prophecies."

"You speak of the threat to the two worlds?" Cerj asked. He sounded unconvinced, but some of the arrogant dismissal had left his voice.

"Are you sure we can't ignore it?" Makkora lowered her hood, her smile soft and inviting despite the truth of her huge, dangerous self. "Many prophecies come to pass, but some end up never coming to fruition, as we've encountered more than once the last few millennia. Consider the many creatures who concerned themselves with Tessa's prophecy about the fate of Oriceran. It led to unnecessary suffering and tension, and even bloodshed, but none of us put stock in it, and we avoided adding to the chaos during a difficult time in Oriceran history."

"We had our reasons for taking that gamble and believing in that possibility concerning Tessa's prophecy." Kalath cut through the air with his hand. "Just as we have our reasons to believe this one is true. Ignoring it isn't a risk we can take. The implications are too great."

"Even if we could be certain of the convergence of the probabilities," Makkora began, "we can't be sure of the interpretation. Our wisdom and knowledge have led to misinterpretations before."

After a nod, a swirling web of sentences written in different ancient Oriceran languages appeared above her. Many were no longer spoken by any living community on the planet, and some were impossible for most of the species on the planet to attempt to speak without magical aid.

"It doesn't matter," Cerj replied. "The gems aren't reliable enough to push us into action in and of themselves. When we move, there are consequences. We must remain mindful of that. And can we be so sure about this prophecy?"

Kalath shook his head. "It's not like most. The Orb of Convergence has never been wrong. Isn't that why we all agreed to share it and deny its wisdom to others? Its scope has been arguable, but name one time in the past five thousand years it has been wrong? When others, even ancients of our kind, plotted in fear of Tessa's words, we knew to hold the course because of the Orb. Will we now turn away from it out of fear when it may be our salvation?"

Makkora dismissed the complicated web of prophecy floating above them with a flick of her wrist. "Perhaps. That doesn't change the fundamental issue. The gems might be useful, but Cerj is right that they are questionable. The destruction of one could mean the prophecy's fulfillment is coming soon, but it might not occur for another century. We can't allow ourselves to act in a hasty manner. We might set things in motions that can't be easily undone, and all our efforts will be for nothing. I would not pass from this existence, knowing I failed Oriceran because I acted in haste."

"We might also draw attention to the Orb," Cerj growled. "There are more threats now, with the Earthlings probing Oriceran more each day. They are combining technology and magic in ways that are difficult to counter. If they were to get their hands on the Orb, it would be a disaster."

"The child born of two worlds," Makkora intoned, citing the prophecy in question. "Destruction comes in his wake. He will consume Oriceran and Earth. The threat hides in the land that opposes demons."

"The prophecy is clear," Kalath murmured. "I believe the gem cracked because the child of the prophecy was recently born. Fate is giving us our chance to intervene and strike him down before he can rise to his true power and threaten both worlds. If we do not act, who will?"

Makkora sighed and raised an arm. Hundreds of translucent images of different beings from a variety of races appeared, everything from graceful Light Elves to hulking kilomea to smirking gnomes to exotic insectoid species whose names couldn't be produced by anything with a normal tongue to floating intelligence clouds.

"The child born of two worlds." Makkora shook her head in disbelief. "Oriceran and Earth. Even before the end of the travel restrictions between the two worlds, the blood of Oricerans has co-mingled with that of the people of Earth. We've been investigating that for millennia and have found nothing, despite all the candidates." The hundreds of images converged into a dark-haired human-looking woman. "We even thought once to interpret the prophecy widely enough to include Leira Berens, but with everything that happened concerning her, it was fortunate that we didn't press our attentions against her and avoided drawing any attention to ourselves. It could have ruined even us and threatened our plans."

Kalath sneered, something that came far too easily in his current form. Perhaps that was why he preferred it. "I didn't summon you here only because of the gem. I've also come across information that changes the scope of our pursuit and makes clear why we've failed before now. I believe once you have this information, you'll change your opinion on our course of action."

"What information could be so useful?" Cerj asked. "Simply identifying a candidate isn't enough."

Kalath let out a low chuckle and summoned another magical picture, a towering creature clad in silver-green armor, the helmet eyeless, a long blade extending from his arm. "I was surprised to learn that King Oriceran and his minions had taken great measures to keep certain truths from the rest of Oriceran, even us." He pointed at the creature. "This was the one who invaded Oriceran and destroyed the Light Elf town during our long slumber. It was that same attack that awakened us prematurely. I trust you recognize what this is."

Makkora narrowed her eyes. "That is the armor of James Brownstone. You're saying James Brownstone destroyed a Light Elf settlement?"

Cerj scoffed. "He's powerful, as his recent intervention

into the Drow matter proves, but he's not that powerful. The Light Elves could have stopped him. That is nonsense."

"This isn't James Brownstone, but I have no doubt he could do it if so inclined." Kalath nodded at the armor. "This is a creature called a Vax that invaded Oriceran, however briefly. It's not from Earth or Oriceran, and its abilities are not completely magical in nature."

"What are you saying?"

Kalath offered a cold smile. "Don't you see? James Brownstone isn't a human who uses magical artifacts. He wasn't born on Earth or Oriceran, but on another world far from either." Kalath stared at the image. "Although the attempts to conceal the existence of the other worlds have failed, there remains much that has been successfully concealed, even from us. The creature that attacked Oriceran was just a scout of his people. It left Oriceran to go to Earth and summoned more of its kind. Earth forces and James Brownstone repelled the assault, but they've kept it secret, as have many on Oriceran who were aware of the truth. The Vax are a vicious and dangerous race, but those who lead Earth and Oriceran would conceal their truth out of short-sighted fear, rather than giving the information to those who need it."

"It doesn't matter." Cerj gestured at the Vax. "Even if what you say is true, James Brownstone doesn't fulfill the prophecy. He's not a child born of two worlds, he's a child born of one world who traveled to another. There might be other prophecies relevant to Brownstone, but not this one."

"Think this through. His current mate is human." Kalath smiled thinly, his eyes glowing. "And he has a child.

If he's not from Earth, and his wife is human, and they have a child together, what does that make his child but a child of two worlds? That is what we've been missing. That is why we could never find what we sought—because we shouldn't have been looking for a half-Oriceran and half-Earthling male child."

Makkora lowered her gaze. "How can you be sure you're right? We might not have intervened with Berens, but there are other cases in which we have, and we've been wrong. We've destroyed innocents unnecessarily."

Kalath scoffed. "We've destroyed innocents to save everyone. You're surprisingly sentimental, Makkora. You know what is at stake. The sacrifice of a small number of lesser creatures is inevitable."

"It's not sentiment to not sink to the level of our enemies. I would prefer to be sure rather than merely inclined to believe."

"We must test the child," Cerj insisted. "Then we can be sure."

"But we no longer have most of the original artifacts. We can't test as we have other recent candidates." Makkora circled beneath the Vax image with a slight frown. "We'll have to find some other way of testing him. We should send our agents to find useful artifacts."

"No, that is unnecessary," Kalath replied. "We can use the ritual."

Makkora froze in place, slowly craning her neck toward Kalath. "But that would require…"

"The sacrifice of the child?" Kalath raised an eyebrow in challenge. "It's as you've said, Makkora. We've already spilled innocent blood. We can't shrink from our task now, not with so much at risk. What is one more sacrifice when weighed against the safety of billions?"

"We can't risk exposing ourselves. Being powerful is not the same thing as being immortal. If we do this, we will make powerful enemies, and not just James Brownstone. If our identity is exposed, the Drow will hunt us, too. Their queens will demand it. There will be war."

Kalath laughed, his eyes turning red and a vertical pupil appearing before his disguise reasserted itself. "You've slept far too long, Makkora. You fear the lesser races so much? The Drow are nothing compared to us."

"A single Drow isn't a threat, but we can't defeat an entire race, and we've made a mockery of many restrictions put in place by King Oriceran. If the Drow draw attention, we might have to face the Light Elves, too. We can't defeat two of the more powerful Oriceran races by ourselves." Makkora spun, the hem of her robe flaring. "We must be certain. If we fail and enemies converge on us, we might not be in a position to track down the true threat if we're wrong about Brownstone's child. If we are slain, all we have worked for might be a waste."

"Of course. I understand your concern, but we no longer have the luxury of waiting." Kalath floated off the ground, slowly rising toward the roof of the chamber and a small path leading to a different level. "I will make arrangements for my agents to collect what we need, including the child, but we cannot shrink from our task, no matter the sacrifice. The risk is too great."

"What about what I just said?" Makkora called.

"So be it," Kalath told her. "Perhaps we should call attention to ourselves on purpose."

Cerj scoffed as Kalath arrived at the opening. "Perhaps you're still half-asleep."

"No." Kalath shook his head. "It's time to set out the right bait. It's been useful in monitoring potential threats, and it has informed us about possibilities, but the time for patience and restraint is over. The Child of Prophecy is but one threat. For now, it doesn't matter. The Brownstone child will be tested."

Kalath stepped into the cramped passage and headed toward an exit on the other side of the cave. Hiding and operating through minions was useful for the years they spent in slumber, but the first of the great prophecies had already come to pass—the reopening of the gates. They'd planned and prepared for the day, but they'd fallen into the habit of focusing more on self-preservation than using their power and abilities to accomplish their destinies as guardians. They'd bound themselves with ancient magic in millennia past, and now it was time to show the two worlds their power. That didn't mean they would boldly stride into the world, but less caution was warranted.

Some lesser beings might fall. Such was the state of nature. The powerful consumed the weak. He didn't seek victims for idle amusement, but to save many others. That might be difficult for some of the lesser races to accept, but he'd made the choice before, and he'd make it again, no matter who or what he needed to destroy.

The passage widened, daylight streaming in from outside. Soon, Kalath would take to the skies in his true form and provide some fodder for rumors. His kind shouldn't live in fear. The lesser races should. The alien invaders with no connection to Oriceran or Earth should fear him most of all.

One small concern lingered. James Brownstone and his kind might be powerful, but the invasion had been defeated on Earth. That thought bothered Kalath. What could possibly be so special about this half-breed child that he would threaten both worlds?

CHAPTER TWO

James slammed the door to the F-350 shut. A stiff wind filled his nostrils with the salty scent of the ocean and a rotten egg stench from the piled seaweed lining the nearby boulder-strewn San Diego beach. There were plenty of beaches in Los Angeles with their share of seaweed and dead fish, but he could smell the subtle difference, no matter where he traveled. This wasn't the stench of the City of Angels.

Engage and terminate target with maximum efficiency, Whispy sent. James had already bonded the symbiont on his way to the target site. Wizards had too many tricks, and he needed to be careful, even after how much his basic body had been modified.

If all goes well, we'll kill this fucker and get out of here before nightfall, James thought back.

May Wu and Keller approached from behind, both in the standard agency black suits, so dark they almost blended in with the black SUV behind them. He hadn't worked much with Keller. The wizard had joined the agency in the last couple of months, but Maria had good things to say about the man, but he was less interested in the staff than their clothes. James couldn't help but grin.

The more shit changes, the more it stays the same. I figured there would be a lot of bitching by now.

"What's with the face?" May asked, looking him up and down. "You're not normally such a jolly guy, James." She shuddered. "And a Jolly James scares me."

He grunted before nodding toward her suit. "The clothes. That shit started because Trey didn't want his boys to look like gang members, but now everyone wears it like a uniform." He shrugged. "It's funny."

"Technically, when you make all your people wear the same kind of clothes, it *is* a uniform." May reached into her jacket and pulled out her wand with an arched eyebrow. "A suit's better than everyone wearing *that*." She gestured with her wand at James' duster and jeans.

Keller laughed and grabbed his own wand. "I like the cowboy look. I could have rocked it. We could have a Cowboy Squad."

"Cowboy?" James frowned and looked down at his clothes. "I wasn't going for cowboy. I was going for functional. You can fit a lot of shit in these pockets. It's not like I wear a cowboy hat."

Keller patted his head. "Now I'm dying to get a cowboy hat. I can ride around on a unicorn."

"Sure. Giddy up, pardner." May raised her wand and performed a series of intricate movements while chanting quietly. Nearby boulders cracked, their component rock flowing and swirling, then reformed into squat, vaguely human shapes. They weren't the quality of statues May typically trafficked in, but they would do for the job at hand.

Keller ran his wand up and down his body, chanting a shield spell. "You sure you want your monthly *community outreach* to be this job, James? From what the bounty information says, he's a level four. May and I can handle him fine, especially with it being a dead-or-alive."

"It helps more when they aren't fives or sixes." James patted his chest. "If I show up for the easier shit, it sends the message I want to send, and it cuts down on fuckers with delusions of grandeur thinking they can move into LA. The big boys have always bought a clue."

Keller wrinkled his nose. "Which is why we're in San Diego. You see the numbers, James. It's hard to get more than petty bastards to come into LA anymore. There is such a thing as being too good at our jobs."

"World's not gonna end because you had to fucking drive to San Diego, Keller," James rumbled. "Don't be a pussy."

May scoffed. "Come on, James. Don't be like that."

He shrugged. "What? That offend you?"

"Yes, but not for the reason you think." May inclined her head toward Keller. "Remember, James, a pussy takes a pounding. It's tough. Not like Keller."

"Hey, I'm a pussy!" Keller blinked. "Wait. No. I'm not." He groaned as May and James laughed.

Cease jocularity and engage and terminate targets, demanded Whispy. *This engagement strategy is not demonstrating maximum efficiency.*

This shit builds morale and leads to better fighting and shit, James responded. *You got someplace better to be?*

Maximum tactical efficiency unnecessary for projected power level of targets.

James snorted. All those years together and Whispy Doom was still a pain in the ass. The symbiont might not be a true Vax tool of mass destruction bent on the conquering of the human race anymore, but that didn't keep him from being a petulant asshole most of the time. A couple more decades might calm him down.

"We sure about this location? I don't want the local cops all pissy about us messing up a tourist spot."

James sniffed and rubbed his nose.

Fucking San Diego seaweed.

May nodded. "Our boy screwed up, and the tracking spell led here. He's here, all right, and I checked when we parked. We've got no one within a couple of miles up or down the beach. Even if you go all...*you* on it, we're fine, and I'm sure you can write a check or two to calm the city down."

James surveyed the area. All he saw was sand, water, and lots of rocks, both spread out and piled into the seawall leading up to the road. The beach location made sense with the bounty stressing the wizard's life magic specialty and manipulation of local sea life, but there were no obvious signs of his presence. Hiding or invisible magicals weren't new to him, but they never stopped being annoying.

Barbeque is so much more straightforward.

"There!" Keller shouted and pointed as another large boulder rose and turned into one of May's soldiers. The massive magical construct was impressive, but the tunnel underneath was the real find.

16

"I thought that boulder looked a lot larger than the others around here." May nodded, a satisfied smile on her face. "I'll give him credit, I didn't detect it in my initial sweep. He's a little better than I thought. Just a little."

"Magic shit?" James asked.

"Since you don't care about the details, yes, we'll just say magic shit." May tapped her wand in her palm. Her small army of stone men, some knee-high, others towering over James, formed a circle around the entrance. "But a guy sloppy enough to get tracked is a guy I'm not worried about, even though he had a good ward over the entrance to his hideout."

Keller twirled his wand and tossed it into the air like a drum major's baton. He caught it and spun it one more time before shoving it forward and shouting a spell. Lines of white energy cracked across the tunnel opening.

"What the fuck was that?" James frowned.

"Defensive spell. I disrupted it. He almost certainly knows we're here now."

"Big fucking deal. It's better when my outreach guys sweat a little." James drew his gun. He ejected the magazine and shoved it in his pocket before fishing out a magazine containing anti-magic bullets from another pocket and slamming into the weapon. "I'll take point, but I don't feel like wasting a Shay snack on this asshole yet."

Keller shrugged. "Hey, stand in front and take all the explosions. Good for me." He saluted. "Show them what you're made of, James Brownstone." He withered under the glare of his employer.

"We have the statues too, remember." May pointed her wand, and the rock men small enough to fit into the tunnel marched toward it. The larger ones reverted. There was no reason to strain herself unnecessarily for something they couldn't use inside.

James fell in behind a rock man. "I don't get half the shit people do these days. They have magic, but they're sitting around in some underground cave making sea monsters? What's the fucking point?"

The tunnel widened after only a couple of yards. A light sphere winked into existence above James and glided forward, matching his pace. There were advantages to having a wizard and a witch along on a bounty. The path angled steeply downward, and the soft crunch of their footsteps filled the air. May's rock statues trundled forward, no souls, no fear to worry them. James might not be worried, but he was surprised.

Shit. I thought this wizard asshole would put up a bigger fight. He's coming off as more a three than a four right now.

After the path leveled out, the sand gave way to black metal on the walls and a large door blocking the end. With a loud buzz, a green ray blasted from the ceiling through one of May's statues, putting a hole through his chest. The magical construct collapsed in a pile of rubble. The team stopped their advance.

Keller grimaced. "Ow. That would have hurt."

James grunted. "Better him than me."

May aimed her wand at the ceiling and muttered an incantation. Intricate glowing wards appeared on the ceiling and the walls. They lined the passage all the way to the door. James recognized a couple of the patterns from what Alison had shown him.

"Good power level, but not the most elegant spells. No

wonder our boy has to hide." May motioned toward the wards with her wand. "If we'd charged in with a group of non-magicals, it would have been nasty. The average bounty hunter doesn't even use an anti-magic deflector."

"I'd hope someone without a deflector wouldn't go after a wizard," Keller replied.

"You'd think." May shrugged. "But there are a lot of idiots out in the world."

Increase exposure to defenses, demanded Whispy. *Moderate adaptive potential.*

James cracked his knuckles and holstered his gun. "We might need all your toys, May. Let me take the hits."

May frowned. "James, I know you're tough, but you can't be sure you can take everything he might throw at you."

"I bet I can." James frowned. "And I'm not asking, I'm telling."

"It is the Brownstone Agency and not the Wu Agency." May's shoulders slumped.

James put his gun away before he took off his duster and holster and handed them to Keller. He had a closet full of the same coats, but he didn't want his gun and ammo to be destroyed if he could help it. He planned to shoot a wizard soon.

"Like Keller said, we have to assume the bounty knows we're coming." May inclined her head toward the door, an annoyed look on her face. "And he'll be ready to attack us once we get through the door."

"Good." James advanced. "It saves us the trouble of having to track his ass down, and it's more reason for me to take point on these traps."

A lightning bolt shot from the ceiling, the sound deafening. The trap struck James in the chest, burning a hole through his shirt. The blast knocked him backward, his skin blackened, and he growled at the pain spreading through his chest.

Near maximum adaptation to attack type reported achieved, Whispy reported. *Armor layer necessary for maximum protection. Minor damage sustained. Regeneration in progress.*

"James!" May shouted.

Flat on his back, James grunted. "I'm not dead."

"You sure about not armoring up, James?" Keller called. "That looked like it hurt a lot."

"That shit?" James sat up. "If it doesn't blow a hole through or tear off an arm, it's not serious."

"I think you and I have very, very different definitions of serious." Keller patted his arm. "And I'd prefer not to know firsthand what it feels like to lose an arm."

"It hurts like a motherfucker."

Keller nodded slowly. "Yes, I kind of figured."

James stood up and waited a moment for Whispy. His additional steps ended with a fireball exploding around him. The trap seared away what remained of his shirt and reddened most of his upper body, but most of the damage from the previous attack had already healed. He took a deep breath and waited until his blisters and the pain receded and new skin covered the minor burns, replacing the reddened flesh. Then, he advanced, his pants still on, but Whispy embedded deep in his chest, the tendrils obvious. He might keep his secret from most people, let alone bounties, about his true nature, but he didn't care if they saw the amulet. They all assumed it was magical, and it only added to his reputation, and that was the main point of his community outreach jobs.

Wait a second.

"Fuck." James kicked at the ground with his boot tip. "I forgot. It's community outreach."

Keller shrugged. "So? Doesn't that just translate as 'Beat down some bounties so people remember not to screw with James Brownstone?'"

"Yeah," James replied. "But it means we should try to take him alive. It's better if we've got someone to spread stories. When I just kill them, people don't talk about them as long."

"Oh. Sure thing." Keller glanced at May, who shrugged, disinterest on her face. "It shouldn't be hard for the three of us to take him alive."

"Let's get this trap shit over with." James bowed his head and charged toward the door. More fireballs and lightning exploded around him, blasting up sand and rock. Another green ray carved a small crater in his shoulder, but it didn't blow a hole through him like it had the statue. "Fuck. That actually hurt."

Smoke filled the passage, obscuring his view of the others. His shoulder and chest throbbed from his injuries, but he was now only steps from the door. A low, long growl escaped his throat.

This fucker is really starting to piss me off. I don't like this game shit. He should have come out and fought me like a man.

Near maximum adaptation to existing attack types already achieved. Sufficient power for transformation, Whispy reported. *Recommend engaging transformation for maximum defensive potential and enhanced regeneration.*

Do it.

Silver-green metallic tendrils sprouted from the amulet and enveloped his body, encasing his limbs in matching armor. The pain from the earlier attacks ebbed as his new layer of protection finished covering him. He grew claws and extended a blade from his arm as the helmet grew around his head. His vision darkened for a brief moment before returning, his range of vision now wider.

"You okay, James?" Keller asked.

"Yeah, I'll be fine. It's all healing. I'm just annoyed."

Ignoring his rapidly diminishing pain, James marched to the door and stabbed through the side. He carved around the edge of the door, then slammed his armored foot into the metal. The blow sent the huge slab forward. It crashed into the hard-packed sand that was the floor for the vast chamber beyond.

"What the fuck?" James rumbled.

A wizard stood on the opposite side, his wand at the ready and a shimmer around his body. His presence wasn't surprising, and he matched the bounty description, but even with the briefing, James wasn't prepared for the large number of sharks standing on thick, mottled gray legs filling the room. Their eyes glowed with a pale blue light. Their long arms ended in three clawed fingers, but there was nothing humanoid about their extended mouths and the teeth inside. It was as if someone had sewn a shark head onto a muscular gray humanoid body.

James didn't find it horrific. It was far, far different. A deep, low laugh built and spilled out like a threatening rumble of distant thunder. May's rock statues marched into the chamber and spread along the front wall. Keller and May followed them in with their wands up.

Minimum adaptation potential, Whispy sent, his thoughts tinged with weary resignation. James wasn't the only one not impressed by the quality of the local cannon fodder. *Terminate all enemies with maximum efficiency.*

The wizard shouted, "You think this is funny?"

"I think you're not gonna conquer the world with a bunch of monsters that look like shit my son draws." James cut through the air with his blade. "Keller, May? What do you think?"

Keller chuckled. "They do look kind of weird. I don't know whether to be scared or laugh."

May stared at a monster, her brow knitting in confusion. "I don't get why you made sea monsters if you're trying to conquer the land. Why not just create a three-headed bear? That would make more sense."

The outraged bounty gnashed his teeth. He went by "Sea King," according to the bounty notice. James hated the bounties with stupid nicknames.

"You have no idea what we've done," Sea King shouted. "I've created servants with inherent anti-magical power. They'll carve through your beloved armor like nothing."

"Keller, May, stay back. Remember, we need Sea Dick alive," James called.

"That's 'Sea King,' Brownstone, and you will bow to me before you die."

"Yeah." James shook his head. "Guys calling themselves King This or That who say that shit to me don't have a good record. Look it up."

Sea King's nostrils flared. "You have no idea what I've

done. This is your only chance to depart with your life. Leave now, or die."

"Keep going, and I'll call you Limp Dick instead. If you thought you could kick our asses, you wouldn't be giving us the out, fish shit." With James' expanded vision, he didn't need to turn his head to keep all the sharks in his line of sight. "I'm gonna give you one fucking chance here, but you need to know your bounty is dead-or-alive. I want to try to keep you alive, but no guarantees unless you surrender right now."

"I will kill you." Sea King sneered. "And I'll enjoy watching the light leave your eyes as my creations shred your armor and flesh with their teeth and claws. I wonder if eating James Brownstone will give them power?"

"If they manage to kill me, I damned well hope so, but I'm glad I can fucking entertain you." James widened his stance and gestured for the sharks to attack with his left hand. "But return the favor. Let's see if your fish can impress me, Limp Dick."

CHAPTER THREE

A hidden chamber full of shark abominations and a wizard with a dumbass nickname proved why James needed his monthly community outreach. More directly, the lack of such a hidden chamber in his home city demonstrated the effectiveness of his efforts. It didn't bother him that the Brownstone Effect didn't extend from Los Angeles to San Diego. One man, even a Vax, was not going to bring an entire world to heel, but that didn't matter. As long as people in LA weren't causing him too much trouble, he could spend most of his time with his family or at the restaurant without worrying about bullshit in the back of his mind. He didn't need more mobsters showing up and asking for favors.

We have normal-ass sharks in LA. None of this arms and glowing eyes crap.

James expected growls or hisses—at least something from the monsters. But the sharks silently eyed him, not advancing and swaying slightly where they stood. The whole scene was more surreal than intimidating. That annoyed him.

If this is what it's going to be like, I need to get this shit over with, so we can hit up Phil's before heading back to LA.

Sustenance is of minor concern, Whispy replied.

Remember what I said about you talking shit about barbeque?

Rapid extermination of enemies will facilitate secondary recreational activity, Whispy responded. *And maximum tactical efficiency was already recommended.*

Yeah, that's what I thought.

James slammed his fists together. "Come on," he roared. "You're supposed to be the Sea King. You've killed other bounty hunters who have come after you. Show me what you've got. I've got shit to do that doesn't involve dealing with your ass."

Keller and May exchanged confused glances. Neither said anything as they turned back to await the Sea King's response.

"Yes. You will be my greatest victory. It's like you offered yourself up in tribute." The Sea King nodded. "Kill him!"

The sharks surged forward. Their teeth emitted a light red glow. They still didn't growl, their only sound the plodding thud and scratching of their two-toed feet as they advanced. May's less horrific creations formed a wedge to protect her and Keller, but the enemy force focused on James. Some charged around his sides as if a rear attack would keep them alive.

Nice try.

James almost felt a little sorry for the dumbass fish. The

low-hanging ceiling didn't provide enough space for jumping, so he jogged toward his left side and the enemies trying to flank him there. It was time for a demonstration of his own.

Low adaptation potential, Whispy reported.

Yeah, that's what I figured. This guy wouldn't be hiding under the beach with his shark toys if he could accomplish anything real. Let's get this over with.

James stabbed the closest abomination through the head. His blade pierced thick flesh with ease, splattering blood all over the ground, and he yanked it back out. In spite of the grievous injury, no howls of pain followed, no threats from the monster. The shark collapsed to the ground and thrashed. The glow in his eyes faded, and he stopped moving. His allies ignored his plight and took the opportunity to bite and claw at the armored form. A small number broke away and scampered toward Keller and May.

Maximum adaptation already achieved against existing attack type, Whispy complained, greater annoyance coloring the thought. *Destroy with maximum efficiency.*

James wasn't surprised. If he'd had his armor on from the beginning, the earlier traps would have barely scratched him. All the previous damage had already regenerated, and it was obvious that the current bounty wasn't going to pull a surprise Brownstone-killing ancient artifact out of his ass. It'd take a level five for him to begin to worry, but these days, even most level sixes had almost no chance. Considering all the creatures and magic he'd faced over the years, he wasn't even sure what might present a legitimate threat when he was in extended advanced mode.

Whatever that threat might be, he knew it wasn't going to be a room full of ridiculous-looking shark-men.

The claws of a shark bounced off the armor, not leaving a scratch. Two more monsters tried to clamp down on James' exposed limbs, cracking their teeth for the effort. They stumbled back, and James decapitated both with one wide swing.

"Yeah, nice try, fishies." He snorted. "I don't know what I was expecting, but it was more than that."

"This can't be happening." Sea King's eyes darted around, taking in the carnage. "Your magic will run out soon enough, Brownstone, and then you'll die."

"Keep telling yourself that. Maybe you'll get lucky. I doubt it, but stranger things have happened."

May and Keller advanced behind the statues. The latter pummeled and kicked the nearby sharks. Unlike with James, the sharks managed to sink their teeth into May's creations. The afflicted constructs headbutted and punched their tormentors, losing portions of their solid bodies but not knowing fear, and also not having any internal organs or blood to lose.

The sharks staggered back under the constructs' assault. Keller whipped his wand back and forth, launching fireballs to finish off whatever sharks survived the blows of the statues. The monsters continued to fall to the ground with no sign of regeneration, giving James hope they could finish the bounty quickly. Community outreach was a necessary chore, but like his current battle, it often involved delusional assholes or psychos. There was something about the criminal brain that made them stupid.

James continued slicing and dicing through the

surrounding enemies, not bothering to growl or roar. Sharks piled on top of him and clamped their jaws, but their teeth could find no purchase on the biometallic armor protecting his body. James' victims filled the chamber, so it was now clear enough that Keller could toss fireballs at the bounty. The enemy wizard responded with a spectacular flashing orb that exploded against one of May's constructs and shattered it into hundreds of pieces. The others filled the hole in the formation.

The Sea King fell back, chanting under his breath and ducking. The shimmer of his shield intensified. The remaining sharks clambered over the bodies of their fallen brethren, not wavering in the slightest despite their horrific losses. There was no hint of fear in their aggressive movements or their glowing eyes. They continued their desperate attack against a predator far more frightening than anything on sea or land. Their persistence wasn't rewarded; James sliced one in half and ripped out the throat of a second with his claws.

"You're ruining months of effort," the wizard shouted. "Do you know how much time and resources I've placed into creating my army?"

"Yeah, I do that kind of shit a lot. Ruin it." James offered an easy shrug, the casual motion at odds with his blood-soaked armored alien appearance. "It's easier for everybody involved when you fuckers just surrender, but there's always some guy who thinks he's gonna be the one to finally take down James Brownstone and become some sort of underworld hero." He pointed his blade at the advancing rock constructs. "I'm only here because I need to put in face time. My people would have whooped your ass even if I wasn't here, you stupid limp-dick piece of shit."

"You can't win. I won't let you win." The Sea King lifted his wand and cut through the air with quick movements and louder incantations in a strange, guttural language. A translucent white sphere surrounded him, and hatred contorted his face. His remaining sharks rushed forward, snapping their jaws.

James, Keller, May, and the stone army marched forward and continued their slaughter of the remaining shark men. Unlike with James, the claws and bites shredded and dismembered the stone tormentors, but that also didn't stop the statues from punching into or ripping limbs off the attacking sharks. Attrition favored May's forces, leaving a couple of statues and one remaining shark near James. He finished the last monster with an overhead slash that cleaved the beast in half and added another layer of blood to the front of his armor.

Huh. This was a little fun. Not exactly spearfishing, but it's kind of similar.

"You understand yet, fucker?" James rumbled and raised his blade. "You could have had ten times that many freaking fish, and you still would have lost. You're going down, and the sooner you realize that, the sooner you stop embarrassing yourself."

"I don't care either way," Keller added, "but he wants to take you alive. I know he's not going to lose any sleep if he doesn't, though. You're a killer and a freak. The world would be better off without you, which is why they have a dead-or-alive bounty on you."

"I know I don't care." May stared at the bounty, her

wand at the ready. The remains of her statues covered the area in piles of rock and dust. She wrinkled her nose.

I'm glad I can't smell much in this thing. Those shark bastards must be rank. Did you kill my nose?

Unnecessary distraction, given current tactical environment. High levels of non-dangerous volatile organic compounds are present, Whispy reported. *None present a risk at this time.*

That your way of saying it smells like ass in here, and you don't want me gagging in the middle of the fight?

The Sea King stared at James, slack-jawed, his eyes wide. "I..." He shook his head. "Those teeth and claws could go through steel. I trained them on cars! I've seen them shred old power armor. How can you be barely scratched?"

May's remaining statues crowded near the bounty. The obvious escape route behind the wizard remained unobstructed, but the man hadn't made any move to leave. He hadn't even looked behind him. He stared at James, ashen, his eyes wide with panic.

Is he going to run, or is he going to collapse this place or some shit like that?

Terminate the target to decrease probability of non-optimal tactical event, Whispy insisted.

I told you already. I need this fucker alive, so he can talk about me in jail and shit. I think he might be ready to give up. I just need to give him a push.

"Guess that means I'm harder than steel." James wiped his blade on a nearby body. "So, we can continue this shit, and I can carve you up or have May's rock guys bash your skull in. If you like it better, Keller can fry your ass. Or you can drop your fucking shield and wand and put your hands up."

Keller sniffed at the air. "Fuck. It smells like a whale died in here and exploded. Come on, Sea King. Cut us a break. I want to get out of here sooner rather than later."

May tapped her nose. "You could just use a spell, so you don't have to smell anything."

"Oh, yeah." Keller laughed. "But he still needs to surrender."

James grunted. "Yeah." He pointed at the bounty. "Because I'm not gonna sit here and pick my nose waiting for you. You ever see me blow through someone on one of those internet videos? It's not like we need *all* of you. I'm sure half your body will be enough for the bounty."

The Sea King's lip quivered before he lowered his wand. The sphere surrounding him vanished, along with the shimmer. He tossed his wand on the heap of shark corpses and dropped to his knees, putting his hands behind his head.

"I surrender," he whimpered. "Please don't kill me. Take me to the police."

Keller grinned. "See? That wasn't so hard, was it?"

CHAPTER FOUR

S wallowing a yawn, James pushed open his front door. Pauline stood in the living room, smiling down at Thomas, who was running in circles around the dog of the same name and whooping. The dog, for his part, lay curled up, snoring, oblivious to the rambunctious child.

It's good to be home.

Shay looked on from the couch, her hands behind her head. "That's not the same shirt you wore down there, and your pants have holes in them."

"Sh…" James shrugged. "Stuff happened, but we got the guy."

Thomas skidded to a halt and pivoted toward James, charging him with his hands outstretched. "Daddy!"

James scooped him up and hugged him. "Did you miss me?"

"Daddy beat down bad man?" Thomas asked.

James chuckled. "I had to beat down some shark guys, but the bounty gave up, and he's in jail now."

"The bad man gave up because Daddy's so strong!"

Thomas did his best impression of a roar. "Daddy's the strongest dad."

"Probably."

Shay smirked. "Really?"

"No reason to lie to the kid."

James had long since stopped caring that his eight-month-old son could run around with ease, had excellent manual dexterity, and was speaking in full sentences. Thomas was also in the ninety-ninth percentile for height and weight for his age. The average person might easily mistake him for a two-year-old. There was obviously some sort of Vax and human genetics interaction involved in his accelerated growth and language proficiency, but James found it convenient. It was easier to talk to a kid who knew more than two words and didn't need a diaper.

Technically, although the boy was unusual, he wasn't yet displaying any traits that were clearly superhuman. Whispy had asked James on a couple of occasions about bonding the boy, but James made it clear that wasn't going to be happening for a long time, if ever. If he had to choose between his son and the symbiont, he would choose his son, even if it meant tossing Whispy into a volcano.

That shit probably wouldn't work on him anyway.

James set Thomas down and patted his head. He turned to Shay. "You're home early."

"I just got here, but so are you," Shay replied with a wink. "I thought you wouldn't be back for a couple of hours."

Thomas skipped over to the dog and knelt by him to stroke his fur. Pauline stood behind the boy, her hands folded in front of her. She offered James a polite nod.

"My guys did a good job of tracking the bounty down this time." James shrugged. "It's not like they need me for that anyway. I'm just putting in an appearance, so people remember I'm in the game. What about you? You solve all of history?"

"I'm not home in spirit. I have a dozen papers to grade. I'm going to pound them out tonight so they aren't hanging over my head." Shay groaned and laid her head back on the couch. "I love every part of my job except for grading papers."

"What about meetings?" James asked.

"Oh, those are easy. I just tune them out. It's kind of like a free nap during the day." Shay hopped up and stretched her arms above her head. "Any problem with the boy today, Pauline?"

The nanny shook her head. "He's rambunctious, but nothing I couldn't handle. He does want to go to the zoo again soon, but I told him he might want to do that with you."

Shay waved a hand. "He can go with you and us. We bought that annual pass, so we might as well use it. I think he has more fun when he goes with you anyway."

Pauline's brow wrinkled in confusion. "Why would you say that?"

She inclined her head toward James. "It's hard to go anywhere with this one without somebody coming up and asking for an autograph or to arm wrestle or regular wrestle." She rolled her eyes. "Remember that guy who demanded a best two-out-of-three Greco-Roman wrestling match with you? Who does that? Why so specific?"

"It wasn't a big deal." James grunted. "I told him to f..." He glanced down at Thomas. "I told him I was busy and asked him to leave. He got the point and left. I'm sure he went to some other famous bounty hunter and challenged him."

Pauline tapped her bottom lip. "I worry about you two at times."

"Us?" James walked over to his recliner and dropped into it. The chair groaned under his weight. "Why do you worry about us?"

"You're both so busy, and you have a new child." Pauline sighed. "And it's not like you ever truly have time to yourselves."

"Time to play with my bear!" Thomas stood and ran toward the stairs. He scampered upstairs to his room before James could even think to shout a warning about being careful. When he'd rebuilt the house, it was designed with external security in mind, not protecting wild children from themselves. There was only so much child-proofing could do when your kid was unusual.

"It's not a big deal," James rumbled. "We have you."

"Yes." Pauline gestured toward the stairs. "But he is a handful because he's so full of energy. I know you love him, but it's not wrong for parents to want some time for themselves, and I don't mean a couple of hours at night after the boy has gone to bed. It's best for your sanity."

Shay looked at James. "If I think about it, it *has* been a while since we took a decent trip together." She held up a hand. "I'm not complaining about your road trips. I'm the one who usually tells you to take one, but it'd be nice to do something, just you and me."

"A relaxing vacation." Pauline smiled warmly.

Shay shook her head. "Well, relaxing in a certain way. I was thinking more his-and-hers ass-kicking."

Pauline arched an eyebrow. "I see. I didn't realize you were so inclined. Not that it is my place to judge."

James groaned and scrubbed a hand down her face. "She doesn't mean any freaky shit. She's talking about going on a tomb raid together, or a bounty combined with a tomb raid. That kind of thing."

Pauline's mouth formed an O and she nodded, her cheeks coloring.

"Exactly." Shay rubbed her hands. "Not a bounty, but it's been a while since I faced any enemy except petulant undergrads and arrogant graduate students. It's good to keep my skills up. I might not have a big reputation to maintain, but I'm getting soft."

"I'm more than happy to watch Thomas for as long as you need," Pauline replied. "If I'm not being too forward, let me also suggest it's good for him to get used to spending time away from his parents. It will help with independence. I've seen this in other children I've cared for."

"That makes sense, and the books all say that kind of thing." James furrowed his brow. "We can combine shit. Barbeque road trip."

Shay rubbed her temples. "I don't want to go on a barbeque road trip. I want to go on a tomb raid. Come on, James, work with me."

"I'm just saying we'll pick up some barbeque along the way." James shrugged. "Though with my luck the last few times, some alien car thief will show up and take a town hostage until I give him my F-350. You can get in some practice then."

Pauline laughed and clapped once. "Oh, that would be a delicious sight. I would enjoy watching you destroy an extraterrestrial thief over your vehicle. It would be...thrilling."

Shay leaned forward, peering at James with her eyes narrowed. She nodded. "Okay. We can do a road trip with barbeque along the way, but not *only* barbeque. I married you and I love you, and we even had a child together, but that doesn't mean I agreed to become the Barbeque Queen."

James sighed. "Nobody's perfect. I've learned to look past it."

"Very funny." Shay stood. "Now I'm even more moti-vated to pound through those papers. I'm sure I can scare some people into giving me time off as long as nothing major is hanging over me. There's no reason to wait."

"Yeah. I'll need to get shit figured out at the restaurant and make sure the agency's okay with me being gone."

Shay frowned. "Why would the agency need to be okay with it? You barely work bounties as it is." She motioned toward the window. "If it hadn't been for Stonelink roughing up mobsters, you wouldn't be going back to your 'community outreach.'" She made air quotes around the last two words and rolled her eyes.

"Sure, but that's the problem." James reached under his shirt and pulled out his amulet. He dropped it outside his shirt. "If people know I'm not here, they might get ideas. I just want everyone to be prepared for that."

"It's not like you're going to send a press release about

being gone." Shay shrugged. "And the last few times you went on a road trip, it's more that trouble followed you rather than waited until you were away to screw with LA."

"True." James chuckled. "But make sure you're well-armed."

"We're going on a tomb raid. Of course, I'll be well-armed." Shay strolled toward the hall leading to their bedroom. "I'm going to head over to Warehouse Five and check out the possibilities. Since it's going to be a road trip, I'll pick something we can drive to in less than a week, maybe even a couple of days."

"Are there tomb raids that close?"

This is going to be a good thing. Quality time with my wife.

Shay stopped at the entrance to the hall and grinned over her shoulder. "You'd be surprised."

"Nothing surprises me these days."

Shay sauntered back into the living room, leaned down, and wrapped her arms around James' neck. "We deserve a trip together, a little excitement that can be shared."

"And if someone fucks it up?" James asked.

Shay stood back up, a dark scowl covering her face. "I pity the fucking moron who takes both of us on when we're pissed off because they fucked up our vacation."

Yeah. That's the woman I fell in love with.

CHAPTER FIVE

Trey licked the tangy God Sauce off his fingers and patted his stomach. He might not be a true barbeque fanatic like James, but it was hard to be a brother and not have a decent appreciation of the fine art of grilling meat. No one could eat at Jesse Rae's every day, but damned if Trey hadn't come close in his time in Las Vegas.

Sometimes I think the big man made a mistake by not retiring here, but he probably didn't want to compete with his idol. Shit, even I'm not sure if James is better than Mike yet.

Trey chuckled quietly and shook his head. Las Vegas was not LA, and the Brownstone Agency's efforts continued to push decent bounties farther afield. Having magicals on the payroll who could portal helped, but the bounty hunters still needed to find a bounty before they could travel to them, and that often meant bringing their vehicles along. Magic might be impressive and do wonders, but it still couldn't solve every problem, even if it'd helped the Brownstone Agency make a lot of money.

I could retire today if I wanted. I have more money than I ever thought I'd have, even when I was running the gang and thinking I was big shit.

He wasn't sure what he wanted to do with his future. James had barbeque, but Trey didn't have a great hobby passion, and as much as they loved him, Zoe and Little Zoe would probably stab him in the eye if he hung out around the house all the time. Sometimes a woman needed to be left alone with her daughter and man-eating magical plants to do her own thing.

"You look like you're having a good time."

Trey slowly turned his head toward the sultry voice. A voluptuous blonde woman in a tight blue dress stood behind him, a knowing smile on her face. He adjusted his tie and offered her a nice smile. It wouldn't be the first time a fangirl showed up. He hated breaking their hearts, but he would never cheat on his wife, and not just because she might feed him to a monster plant.

"Barbeque for lunch is always a good time," Trey replied. "Especially at Jessie Rae's." He nodded toward the counter. "But you're here, so you already know that, or is this your first time?"

"This is my first time, actually." The woman held a tray of ribs in her hand. "You're Trey Garfield, right? The bounty hunter?"

"The one and only." He fluffed his lapels. There was nothing wrong with soaking up admiration as long as he kept his limits clear. He gestured to the seat. "I'm leaving soon, but if you want to chat, I'm free. I can't give you proprietary company info, and I can't talk about the bounties we're currently going after."

"I understand." The woman extended her hand. "I'm

Vina."

"Nice to meet you." Trey gave her hand a firm shake, and she sat down. "You're not a reporter, are you? We've got a PR person to handle that kind of thing."

Vina laughed and shook her head. "No. I'm far too impatient for that kind of work. I'm more a kind of adrenaline junkie." She leaned forward. "That's why I'm interested in people like you."

Trey put his left fist to his mouth and coughed in an effort to display his wedding band. "People like me?"

"Everyone knows how dangerous your job is, and you're no normal bounty hunter." Vina licked her lips. "You take on very dangerous people. You're licensed for class five work, and you're not even a magical. That makes sense, I suppose, given who you work for."

"I've got some nice toys." Trey shrugged. "And you're right. The big man helped me a lot. I'd be just another dead punk without his help."

"The big man?" Brief uncertainty flashed in her eyes. "Oh, you mean James Brownstone? Is that what you call him?" She tucked a stray strand of hair behind her ear. "I suppose I brought him up first."

"Yeah. I call him James most of the time, but that doesn't mean he's not still the big man."

Is she trying to learn more about him? No reason she needs to know the truth, and that's assuming she's not a reporter sniffing around trying to get me to confirm it.

"But he's not here." Trey gestured around the restaurant. "He doesn't get to Vegas much these days. He's too busy with his new kid and his restaurant."

"That's right. He's semiretired." Vina frowned. "But I

thought I read he came out of retirement?"

Trey shook his head. "He's just doing the occasional bounty here and there, but he's a pitmaster first, a bounty hunter a distant second. Idiots just don't know to leave him alone."

Vina sighed. "I didn't come here to talk about James Brownstone." She reached toward his hand, but Trey yanked it back. "I came here to talk about you." She leaned forward to provide him a better view of her cleavage.

"That's fine." Trey frowned and focused on her eyes. "But we need to get something straight upfront if this conversation is going to continue."

"What's that?" Vina asked.

He splayed his hand and wiggled his ring finger. "I'm spoken for, and I took vows before my wife, Nana, and God. I love and fear all three even more than I fear the big man, and that's saying something."

"Wait. I get your grandmother and God." Vina rolled her eyes. "But you're afraid of your wife?"

"I said I both love and fear her." Trey picked up his mostly empty glass of water to take a sip. "But it's not just that. She's the hottest wife ever, and she's been great for me in every way I could want. I've got no reason to ever cheat on her, and that's before I think about that vow before Nana and God. And she's given me a great daughter. But…"

"But?" Vina sounded curious.

"She could turn me into a frog if I pissed her off." Trey shrugged. "I don't think it's all that smart to piss off a beautiful, loyal wife who can also turn you into a frog. I'm not a dumbass."

Vina laughed. She leaned back with a sigh and shook her head. "Oh, well. You can't blame a girl for trying. I noticed the ring, but I was half-hoping she was a shrill harpy you hated."

"My player days are long over, Vina." Trey set his glass down. "You're years too late."

"A kid." Vina shook her head. "I'm impressed you have a kid. You have such a dangerous job. I'd be worried about leaving my kid behind."

Damn. Right to it, huh?

Trey took a deep breath and slowly nodded, thinking about what she'd said. It wasn't something he'd ignored.

"It's not the safest job, for sure, but there are a lot of jobs out there that need doing that aren't safe. I've got all sorts of fancy artifacts, but the average cop or firefighter doesn't. These days, nothing's safe. Hell, you could be sitting there minding your own business when some crazy-ass wizard shows up and blows up the city block. LA used to be that way before the big man made his presence known." Trey pointed out the window. "Vegas has had its share of trouble, too."

"I guess you're right." Vina stared into the distance. "I'm too young to remember what it was like before magic was out in the open. I've read about it, but it's hard to imagine."

"Hey, I'm not much older than you," Trey replied, but in truth, he probably had a good ten years on the woman, judging by her appearance. "It's the same for me, and I was born and raised in LA. If I lived in Laramie or something, it might have been different, but Oricerans and magic were all over LA in a big way from early on."

"This is going to sound weird, but..." Vina sighed. "I'm

curious because you mentioned Brownstone."

Trey scoffed. "Girl, don't think you can get James Brownstone to stray. He's more Catholic than the Pope, and his wife is even scarier than mine. I don't think it's just 'til death do them part if you know what I'm saying."

Vina waved her hands with a pained expression. "No, no, no. I'm not interested in James Brownstone that way. He's not my...type, but I can't help being curious about the guy. He's pretty famous."

"That's one way to put it."

"I saw a story on the news that said you were one of his oldest friends."

Trey chuckled. "That's kind of true. He didn't have a lot of friends back in the day, but I always respected him, and he respected me, and that grew into something real. That's how James works. He's all about respect, always has been. You can be a senator, or you can be a Mafia boss. You respect him, and he'll respect you."

Vina nodded slowly, barely concealed hunger in her eyes. "There's a lot of power in that kind of relationship. Think about it. You're friends with a demi-god."

Trey grimaced. "Don't be talking like that." He shuddered. "If James heard that, he'd get angry. He's a tough guy, but there's one man he respects more than anyone." He pointed to the sky. "The ultimate Big Man."

"I wasn't trying to offend you." Vina's cheeks reddened. "I'm just curious about him. I mean, it's weird enough thinking about you having a kid, and the idea of Brownstone having a young son is even weirder."

"But he already had a kid before Thomas." Trey shrugged. "Alison."

"I've read about her. She was a teenager, and she spent all that time at boarding school." Vina rolled her eyes. "And well, look where she is now. It's not like she needs her dad's help.

What? She jealous of the queen now?

"I'm just saying James had years of a kid before Thomas." Trey shrugged.

"I know," Vina replied. "But I can't help but think about the future. Questions like 'Will Brownstone's son follow in his father's footsteps?'"

Trey laughed. "I hope not."

Vina blinked. "You do?"

"Yeah, I don't know if the world can handle two Brownstones on the job. Alison did her own thing, and even that got pretty crazy. It's probably a good thing she's on Oriceran half the time these days." Trey inclined his head toward the TV in the corner of the room. "Those Brownstones can take a lot of people down, but when you've got that kind of strength, it can send the wrong idea to troublemakers who think they can prove something by taking you down. I feel for Thomas if he becomes a bounty hunter. I think criminals will go after him so they are the one who took down the son of James Brownstone. It'll be twice as hard for him as it is for his dad."

"What about you?" Vina asked. "Isn't there someone who wants to become famous by being the man who took down Trey Garfield?"

"Probably. I just haven't met him yet." Trey leaned back and shot the woman a lazy grin. "But I don't worry about that. I don't doubt my skills, but I know who I am and what I can do compared to James. No problem with being a local celebrity, but the big man, he's an interplanetary celebrity. It's a headache."

Vina stood and smoothed her dress. "That's interesting. I hate to leave so abruptly, but I remembered something I'm late for."

"No problem." Trey gestured toward the ribs on his plate, long stripped of meat. "I was finishing up when you stopped by, anyway."

"Sorry about the flirting." Vina placed her palms together in a placating gesture. "Don't tell your wife, please. I don't think I'd look good as a frog."

"I won't." Trey laughed. "You take it easy."

Vina wiggled her fingers and sashayed out of the restaurant, smiling back at him one last time. Trey took in a deep breath and stretched. He loved his wife, but it was nice to be reminded he still had it. A frown crept onto his face.

Something's off. I can feel it, but what? Wait...

Trey reached into his jacket and patted around. His gun, wallet, and phone were there. He patted his other pocket. His artifact gloves were there, too. Vina wasn't some sort of magical pickpocket. He focused on her tray across the table. She hadn't touched her ribs.

Did she come in here just to hit on me or pump me for information?

He shook his head. It was hard to be in the business and not end up paranoid, especially when a random beautiful woman chatted a man up, but that was the price of taking down scum, magical and non.

Oh, well. It's probably nothing. It's not like she learned anything people don't already know.

CHAPTER SIX

Tarik leaned against the brick wall of the abandoned storefront, his arms crossed, the illumination dim since all the nearby streetlights were broken. To the average human, he'd looked like a pale-skinned member of their species in a jacket, t-shirt, and jeans—nothing of note. He didn't find humans as disgusting as some Drow did, but he preferred his own appearance. There was something unsettling to him about his people's ability to shapeshift with ease. It was if they were always meant to hide their appearance. That offended him on a fundamental level.

We should never have to hide what we are. That's the cowardice of the weak.

He looked up at the moon. That was another thing that always unsettled him about Earth. Something was deeply unnatural about only one moon hanging in the sky. It was arrogant, just like everyone on Earth. The planet was infested with short-lived humans who inflated their self-importance.

A bearded man in a gray suit strolled down the darkened street, a confident swagger in his step. He whistled a happy tune, some Earth song Tarik didn't recognize, but the Drow could sense the magic radiating off the new arrival's clothes, marking him as a wizard. The bearded man slowed and focused his gaze on Tarik. He stopped whistling and turned toward the nearby alley. Tarik had warded it extensively in preparation for this meeting. The man matched the description he'd been given, but a shapeshifter understood all too well how pointless it was to place much stock in surface appearance.

"I need something," the bearded man declared, his voice steely. "I'm wondering if you could sell it to me."

"It depends on what it is," Tarik replied. He stepped away from the wall. "What are you looking for?"

"Cigars," the man replied. "Gnomish cigars."

Tarik nodded toward the alley. "I know some suppliers, but they aren't good for you."

The wizard nodded back, suspicion on his face. He stepped into the alley, disappearing from view. Tarik followed him, passing through the obscuring wards. The wizard waited, his eyes narrowed in suspicion.

"You're John?" Tarik asked.

"I go by many names, but that's what I'm going by this week." The wizard's fingers twitched as if he wanted to reach for his wand. If he tried, Tarik was more than prepared to strike him down.

"We're safe here." Tarik motioned around the alley. "Queen Alison couldn't see through these wards without me knowing."

"I don't care about Drow royalty, and I don't care about

you getting caught." John smiled. "I do care if you have what I asked for because I'm under some time pressure."

"I might." Tarik looked him up and down. "If you have what I asked for."

John slowly reached into his jacket. He brushed his holster but didn't go for the wand. He stuck his hand into a pocket, pulled out a small black velvet drawstring bag, and held it in his palm.

"Let's see if I wasted my time." Tarik grabbed and opened the bag. Six small twinkling yellow crystals lay inside. He didn't care about them in and of themselves, but he had a buyer already interested in the crystals and willing to pay a premium. The Drow stuffed the bag into his pocket.

"What about what I need?" John asked. "You have a good reputation. I hope you can live up to it."

"I earned my reputation." Tarik nodded to a moldering cardboard box behind the wizard. He lifted his hand, and with a couple intricate motions, he removed the illusion to reveal a tiny hinged silver box. "Open it. I've canceled all the wards."

His lips pursed, John opened the lid and stared into the box with a smile. "Excellent. With your help, it's been far easier than I thought. It's almost like the universe wanted me to find this." He chuckled. "You're an impressive man, Tarik. I'm sure my associates and I will be able to push a lot of business your way, depending on upcoming needs."

"You know how to find me now." Tarik nodded toward the mouth of the alley. "And I hope you find the artifact satisfactory."

"You don't want to know what I'm going to do with it?" John asked.

Tarik scoffed. "I buy and sell artifacts. I don't care about the why. You can blow up King Oriceran's palace for all I care."

"All the more reason I think we'll have a long and profitable relationship." John tucked the box into a pocket with a smile. "Until next time." He strolled out of the alley and headed down the street.

Tarik waited an interminable five minutes before canceling the wards around the alley and stepping out. He looked up and down the street. A couple of cars drove past, but no one paid him any attention. There weren't any drones around. John was nowhere to be seen. The deal was complete.

The Drow headed down the street at a casual pace. That was the problem with doing deals on Earth. There were too many ways to be observed. He could deal with magic, but technology presented another threat. It wasn't always as simple as using a couple of wards.

Tarik sneered. That was one thing he would give Queen Alison. Her knowledge of Earth technology combined with her magic had made her difficult to deal with. He'd been smuggling artifacts since before Queen Laena was deposed with ease, but now Queen Alison and Queen Rasila were squeezing his business and destroying his supply channels. Change was painful for some.

He arrived on a street corner and waited for the signal to change. When it flipped, he looked over his shoulder before proceeding across the street. There were more people wandering the area and more cars driving past. An

LAPD drone hovered overhead, a constant reminder that people were being watched.

Tarik brushed past an old woman who glared at him. He didn't have the time or the inclination to care about what some weak old human felt. Their pathetic species preyed on each other enough. He wasn't doing anything other than being rude. The hairs on the back of his neck rose. He slowed after a couple of yards and looked over his shoulder. The old woman turned the corner, mumbling under her breath.

He took a moment to survey the area. No one appeared to be looking at him, but his heart quickened. Someone was following him, he was sure of it, but he didn't sense any obvious magic. There were fragments of distant spells, but in a large city, it was hard to avoid them entirely.

Tarik picked up his pace. It might be the Royal Guard. They'd almost caught him a month prior, during a raid where they smashed into the building without magic with the help of explosives sourced by Queen Alison. He missed the Guardians and their divided attention. There was nothing worse for a criminal than a competent government.

The sensation of being followed refused to leave. As long as he was moving, the Royal Guard couldn't easily contain him. A quick portal could get him near a safehouse, and from there, he could return to Oriceran and hide. If they were this close, they knew who he was. He would have to stay away from Drow territory for a while.

Tarik picked up the pace to a jog. The only problem was that the crystals he was carrying dampened magic. There was no way he could conjure a portal while carrying them,

MICHAEL ANDERLE

but tossing them would mean he had just handed over a very powerful artifact to John at heavy risk for no profit. He would also have to explain to the customer expecting the crystals, and he might end up with a powerful enemy far more interested in killing than jailing him.

I should have brought a gun. Queen Alison would have brought a gun in case magic was at a disadvantage.

Tarik crossed another street and then headed down an alley, changing his appearance to that of an elderly human woman, his Drow shapeshifting nature not affected by the crystals. He slowed to a walk and then emerged from the alley, looking both ways with a practiced smile. His disguise in place, he adopted a more leisurely pace, but the feeling didn't abate.

The seconds stretched out painfully as Tarik continued down the street, doing his best to not betray his new appearance with too swift of movement. He didn't know if it was paranoia or a true stalker. The Royal Guard usually lacked subtlety, and he doubted they would follow him for so long without making an appearance. He approached another street corner and considered his options. His eyes widened, and he felt magic.

A young blonde human woman stood there, barely a girl, really, in a dark blue suit, a smile on her face. Tarik slowed. If the magic radiating off her wasn't enough, the faint shimmer of his shield was. She whipped out a wand. "Agent Raine Campbell, FBI. Place your hands in the air and don't move. You're under arrest for artifact smuggling."

CHAPTER SEVEN

"I don't know what you're talking about," Tarik offered in a sweet tone, his appearance still of an elderly human woman. "Smuggling? I don't even know how anyone could do that sort of thing. I've seen it in movies, but that's all."

"Sure." Raine moved closer, circling around but never lowering her wand. The Drow had an advantage over her in that he could cast without a wand. "Don't make this harder than it has to be."

"Maybe I should call my son. I'm confused by all this."

Raine shook her wand, her irritation building with each word coming out of the suspect's mouth. "Don't screw with me, Tarik. You think this is the first time I've gone after someone who can change their appearance? You probably thought you were being careful, but magic isn't the only way to watch someone. If you're going to commit crimes on Earth, you need to prepare better for how things work on Earth."

The old woman's face twitched, and her hands flexed. Raine had seen Drow summon shadow blades without any incantations. She could push out an attack spell before he could close the distance, but she didn't want to have a fight on the street. People milled around, pointing and gesturing, some recording with their phones. It must have been an odd sight, a witch pointing a wand at a little old lady.

"This is an FBI matter," Raine shouted. "Everyone, please disperse for your own safety."

A faint grin spread across Tarik's face. If the bastard tried to hurt innocent people, Raine would take him down. She hadn't wanted to take him on in such a public location, but her tip had paid off better than she'd suspected. Now she just needed to keep the situation under control.

Raine hadn't been in the FBI for long enough to be considered a veteran, but her focus on dangerous magicals made each month feel like a year. FBI culture and the law hadn't fully adapted to a world where magical beings walked openly among regular humans. They'd been far too willing to pass responsibility to the PDA. Sometimes the Bureau didn't know what to do with a witch.

In Raine's time as the FBI's first open magical, she'd arrested numerous suspects, but she'd also made some mistakes. However, she hadn't made one today. Tarik could wear whatever face he wanted, and it wouldn't fool her. There was no way a witch showed up and jammed a wand in some innocent little old lady's face without the woman being frightened or indignant. He needed to improve his acting.

"Don't waste any more of my time, Tarik," Raine barked. "I've been using drones with high-end cameras to keep an eye on you. When you thought no one could see you, I could. So why don't you be a nice little smuggler and surrender? Otherwise, things will get rough for both of us, but I'm the only one with backup."

"Backup? I don't see any backup." The little old lady smirked, looking around. "You're so confident, little witch. If I am who you say I am, I would have thought you'd be smarter than to try to bluff your way through an encounter with me. It won't end well."

"I doubt that, and it's *Agent* Campbell, to you." Raine took a step toward the suspect, her heart pounding. She hoped her mic was still working. "You got cocky, and now you've been caught. If you thought you could win easily, you would have attacked me already. Don't try to feed me the idea that all Drow are unstoppable killing machines. You think I haven't had my fair share of magicals try to kill me? People were trying to kill me when I was still in school."

Tarik wagged a finger. "You know what I think, little witch?"

"That you'll enjoy the wonderful opportunity to explore an American prison? That you're excited to see the cutting-edge anti-magic technologies that have been developed?"

"You talk about backup, but I see only you, little girl." Tarik let out a sinister chuckle, the faint concern fading from his eyes. "Since when does the FBI send one single witch after a Drow smuggler? I think you're full of crap. Is this a case your superiors don't fully support? Otherwise, there'd have been a dozen agents arresting me. You're too young to deceive someone like me."

Well, crap. This is going great.

Raine shook her head, determined not to let him have the upper hand. Her fellow agents weren't the only ones who underestimated her due to her age, and he was only half-right. It was time to turn the conversation around on him.

"Thanks for making this even easier, Tarik," Raine replied. "With that little confession, I won't have to spend as much time justifying this arrest. Probable cause is a real bear when it comes to magic. Now, on the ground, and put your hands on your head. I've just requisitioned some nice new anti-magic cuffs I'd love to try on a suspect. I hope you don't have big wrists. They looked kind of small."

"If he tries anything, should I take a shot?" her partner Clifton transmitted to her concealed receiver. His voice soothed her, but her heart rate didn't slow down. One dedicated partner was worth six agents working a case they didn't believe in.

"Let's keep it calm," Raine whispered. "We can do this without trouble."

She kept her gaze focused on the fake old woman in front of her. Her partner lay on top of a building with a rifle loaded with anti-magic bullets. Just because her field office didn't want to give her full support on one of her hunches, it didn't mean her partner wouldn't have her back. She wouldn't have had as much success throughout her young career without his help.

"You think it's going to be that easy, little witch?" Tarik's form shifted into his true appearance—dark skin, light hair, dark clothing. He looked like he was in his thirties by human standards, which meant he might be decades, if not centuries, older. "You think I'm going to give up because a child witch sticks a wand in my face?"

"I think I've got the drop on you," Raine replied. "And like I said, I've got the numbers."

"Enough!" Tarik yelled. "You want to fight me so badly?"

"No, I want you to surrender. Last chance. On the ground, and put your hands on your head."

Tarik thrust out his hand. A blue-black orb formed and flew toward Raine. She spun to the side, avoiding the magical attack. The orb struck a nearby parking meter, which exploded in a shower of light blue sparks.

Or you could do that.

A nearby woman screamed and the crowd scattered, finally appreciating the danger. Raine twisted back toward him and pointed her wand at him just as he ducked in a nearby alley. She shouted an incantation for a stun spell. A blue ray ripped from her wand and narrowly missed her suspect. She sprinted after him, shaking her head, not surprised but very much annoyed. Criminals were always stubborn. Too bad for them, she was more stubborn.

"I don't have the shot anymore, Raine!" Clifton yelled. "Damn it. He didn't come out the other end from what I saw, but I don't want to pull off the rifle to move the drones."

"Move to cover me. I'm going after him." Raine charged into the alley and skidded to a halt at the sight of eight Drow, including Tarik, who had his hand raised and his palm out. She swept her wand back and forth, unsure if any of the men were real.

Was this why he was confident?

Tarik's grin widened into something more predatory. "You know why you're not dead, little witch?"

"Years of good training even before I left school?" Raine asked with a shrug. "A good partner?"

"Because I don't need the trouble of a dead federal agent." Tarik sneered. "Now leave. I buy and sell things, but I see no reason to kill a stupid little girl who doesn't know better."

"You're bluffing. I'm still the only one here with back-up." Raine kept her wand trained at Tarik. Slight movements of the other Drow men made it difficult to discern if they were illusions, but if Tarik had a posse, there was no way he'd do high-value deals without them present. Her background research on the man didn't point to him having close allies.

"You think I haven't heard of you, Necessary Witch?" Contempt dripped from every word. "A stupid little witch who went to a stupid, disgusting little school. The same school that poisoned our queen and weakened my people. The Drow would be stronger if Alison Brownstone had died years ago, or that horrible school had been burned to the ground."

Raine sighed. She trusted Clifton, and he was fit for a man of his age, but it wasn't like he could leap from building to building. She would need to make a move and stop the smuggler.

"What was the deal, Tarik?" she asked. "I know you moved something big. You're just the first link in the chain. You can probably cut a deal if you cooperate."

"Last chance, little witch." Tarik's voice was low. "I don't have infinite patience."

Raine's stomach tightened as a wave of intense magical pressure erupted in front of her. Two dark portals opened behind and in front of Tarik. She might have been confident about the other men being fakes, but a magical who could open a portal wasn't easily dismissed.

"Clifton, go ahead and call the locals for AET backup." Raine took a deep breath. "We've got major trouble."

"Get out of there, Raine!" he replied. "Just let him go. It's not worth it."

"I'm not letting this guy go after we got lucky enough to find him." Raine's grip tightened on her wand. "I just need to stall him," she whispered. "And call AET."

She'd expected a smug, triumphant smirk on Tarik's face, but blinked at what she saw. The confidence on the Drow's face had vanished, replaced by wide-eyed fear. She could work with that, assuming monsters weren't about to storm through and eat her face. It wouldn't be the first time in the FBI or during school.

They must be customers, not friends, and not nice customers. Was he expecting them or not?

Drow in ornate black armor emerged from the portals, a group of twelve in all. Some held swords or axes. Others lacked metal weapons, instead bearing shadow blades—extensions of pure darkness that seemed to swallow the light around them. Shields clung to their bodies, darkened shells that helped them blend in with the shadows of the alley. A tall, beautiful Drow was the last to emerge. She pointed her shadow blade at Tarik.

"Tarik." The woman's sneer matched her disgusted tone. "How far you've sunk, you pathetic traitor."

The Drow woman spared only the briefest of glances at Raine, continuing to drill into the smuggler with her angry gaze. Her companions kept close to Tarik, several flexing their fingers on the hilts of their weapons. The Drow criminal sighed and raised his arms. His shield disappeared.

"I'm not a traitor," Tarik replied haughtily. "You follow corruption, Zana. There should be no loyalty to corrupt or weak half-breeds pretending to be queen."

Zana placed her blade at his throat. "Speak ill of either of our queens again, and I'll cut your head off and put it on a pole for all traitors to see."

"AET en route," Clifton reported. "ETA eight minutes."

"Things just got more complicated," Raine whispered.

"What the hell does that mean?" He sounded exasperated.

"It means there are twelve more Drow here now, and I don't think they like our suspect very much." Raine lowered her wand. "But I also don't think they're going to cause me trouble."

"Shit." Clifton let out a groan. "They're Drow cops, aren't they? Those bastards are going to take our collar!"

"They don't have the same kind of law enforcement, we do, but yes, I think that's what is going on. I'll see what I can do without starting an interplanetary war." Raine waved and raised her voice. "Uh, excuse me."

Zana frowned and looked her way. "Leave, witch. This is not your affair."

Raine rubbed the back of her neck and smiled. "You see, it kind of is. I'm Agent Raine Campbell, FBI." She nodded at Tarik. "Our mutual friend there has been smuggling illegal artifacts into the United States and other countries for a while, and well, we're in the US now, not Drow lands, so I have jurisdiction. I'm arresting him and taking him in for interrogation."

"He will be punished by his own kind for his crimes both against your people and ours." Zana's mouth twitched. "I can assure you that this is not a rescue. He is a traitor and a scoundrel."

"Not disagreeing with the last part." Raine folded her arms. "And I don't have anything against Drow, but I'd prefer to bring him in after putting in the leg work. I don't know you, so I can't release him into your custody. I'd have to explain it to my bosses, and I don't think they'd look upon it very kindly."

Tarik's gaze darted to the two arguing women. He remained rigid, his arms above him. Despite Zana having pulled back, there wasn't a weapon more than a foot away from him, with some within inches. Any sudden movements would lead to a bad day for the smuggler. Even if he tried to re-summon his shield, there was no way he could win against a dozen Drow and an FBI witch. Even Alison Brownstone might have trouble in this situation.

Raine narrowed her eyes. She'd missed it when the portals had opened, but there was another presence in the alley, scrying magic. Someone else was watching.

"I won't fight you, Agent Campbell." Zana's jaw tightened. "But I will not release Tarik into your custody, either. We need to come to some sort of accommodation that will leave you satisfied and us with our prisoner."

"This isn't the old days." Raine frowned. "You don't just—"

Another portal opened. A young woman stepped out, far paler than her Drow compatriots, even if her long white hair matched theirs. Her low-cut dark gown flattered her athletic body, and it took Raine a moment to notice the human ears and recognize the woman.

"Alison?" Raine blinked.

"That's Queen Alison to you, witch," Zana barked.

Alison waved a hand. "It's okay, Zana. I know her." She smiled at Raine. "It's been a while."

Raine chuckled. "Clifton, cancel the AET. Tell them we have the situation in hand."

"You sure?" he replied warily.

"Yes, Alison Brownstone is here," Raine explained.

"Is that a good thing or a bad thing?" Clifton sounded as uncertain as his words. "We can't beat a Brownstone. We might not even be able to do that with AET or RRAET backing."

"Sure," Raine replied. "I'm not in the mood to piss off someone who is both a Brownstone and one of the two Drow queens, and I'm confident that with a Brownstone here, Tarik's not going to be released on his own recognizance."

Alison stepped through the crowd of Drow warriors toward Raine. She squinted and surveyed the area. "Is your partner nearby?"

Raine pointed over her shoulder with her thumb. "Back a building. I had him on a roof with anti-magic bullets in case Tarik got too...feisty." She looked Alison up and down, uncertain. "New look?"

Alison averted her eyes. "I was about to attend an official function when I was informed my people had found Tarik. There are certain expectations that go with my new position. I don't *always* dress this way. You can imagine it's not all that combat effective."

"You look magnificent, my queen," Zana declared. She managed an elegant bow while still keeping her shadow blade near Tarik's neck. The smuggler nodded his agreement and offered a forced smile to Alison.

"So everyone keeps telling me." Alison gestured to Tarik. "I hate to do this to you, Raine. I know us alumnae need to stick together, but this guy's not just been smuggling artifacts, he's been supplying some dead-ender Drow terrorists who are causing trouble on Oriceran. We've got the stronger claim."

"That might be true, but you still can't come to Earth and snatch up suspects." Raine shrugged. "We will turn him over to you once we're done here. I promise you."

Alison shook her head. "I'm already in contact with the State Department, the PDA, and the FBI over Tarik. I'm surprised they didn't tell you to back off. I'm sorry to have wasted your time."

Raine frowned. Her superiors hadn't wanted her working the case, but no one had mentioned high-level diplomatic pressure. They hadn't actively forbidden her from taking it on, either. It wouldn't be the first time someone up the food chain wanted the glory but was happy to claim plausible deniability if something happened and the wrong parties were offended.

"They all said you get first dibs?" Raine asked. "Even if he's on American soil?"

Alison nodded. "Yes. I'm sorry, Raine. I'll make sure official notifications are sent to you directly, but we don't have time to mess around with bureaucratic games. Some of the artifacts he's been trafficking in are potentially very dangerous in the wrong hands, and I think we can persuade him to give up his suppliers more efficiently than you." She glared at Tarik. "There were some recent high-profile artifact thefts across Oriceran blamed on Drow, and I need to make sure my people don't end up getting blown into the World in Between. We'll be sharing intelligence with the relevant agencies on Earth and groups on Oriceran, but it's not something I feel comfortable talking about in a random alley."

Raine nodded. "I'm not happy about it, but I understand."

"Secure the prisoner, Zana," Alison ordered.

Zana and some of the other Drow began chanting and moving their hands in careful, intricate motions. Raine didn't understand the incantation language, but the spell movements were similar to binding rituals she'd witnessed before. She sighed and tucked her wand into its holster.

"I'd prefer it if he came with me," Raine began, "but I get it. I'm not going to stand up to the State Department, the Drow, the FBI, and the PDA for a single dirtbag." She smiled at Tarik. "Good for you. You get to go home to a land without defense lawyers."

Tarik fell to his knees, his shoulders slumped, wearing a defeated expression. "I'm not a terrorist. I haven't committed treason, and I didn't steal from the Drow. I only took from other races."

Alison snorted. "No, you're not a terrorist. You just supply them." She raised her arm, and a large swirling portal appeared. "It was nice to see you again, Raine. We really need to stop bumping into each other while chasing random scumbags."

Raine laughed and waved. As the Drow stepped

through the portal, her mirth began to fade. She knew Tarik was helping dangerous people, but now she found herself wondering what he'd done to earn the direct attention of a Drow queen.

Why do I have a feeling something really bad is coming down the pipe?

CHAPTER EIGHT

T*hank you, Lord, for creating cows and making them so damned delicious,* James thought as he flipped a steak on his backyard grill. Thomas the boy and Thomas the dog alternated chasing each other, laughing or barking in joy. At the rate he was growing, he probably wouldn't find that kind of game entertaining in a couple of months, but it was nice to see it for now.

Shay was at her warehouse, doing some last-minute research for her tomb raid. He didn't mind going on the raid, and it'd be nice to fight alongside his wife again, but he was going to miss not being on a pure barbeque road trip. At least this one wouldn't involve the CIA or alien bounty hunters. He frowned. The last one wasn't supposed to have involved those either.

His phone rang and he pulled it out of his pocket, looking at the caller ID with a furrowed brow. The person wasn't unwelcome, just unexpected. "Something wrong, Maria?"

She laughed. "That's a matter of perspective."

"Does it involve shit blowing up or people getting turned into monsters?" James asked. "Does it involve me having to introduce my fist to someone's face?"

"No, it doesn't involve any of that." Maria sighed, deep weariness in the sound. "I've been talking a lot to Tyler lately, and it's made me come to some conclusions."

"It's good to mess with your brain cells, but you're the one who chose to marry him. It takes all kinds."

"Look, I don't want to waste a lot of time leading up to this, but since you're going on your trip soon, I figured I should tell you right now. I hate putting off things once I've made up my mind."

James frowned. He cradled the phone with his neck to grab his spatula and flip more of the steaks. Every individual piece of meat demanded perfect timing to unlock the flavor. Amateurs spent too much time thinking of their meat as a unit rather than as unique entities. It was something that had taken him years to realize.

"Tell me what?" he asked.

"I was a cop for a long time," Maria murmured. "And I've been a bounty hunter for far longer than I expected. I'm not you, James. I age, and I think I'm getting a little old to be busting down doors, even wearing power armor and shooting bastards with a rail gun. Tyler's been on my ass to retire for a while, and I'm finally ready to pull the trigger. Real retirement, not moving to another high-stress, dangerous job like I did last time."

"It's not like I'm one to talk." James grunted. "Just because I do a little community outreach, it doesn't mean I'm not mostly retired. I don't think about shit bounties most of the time."

"I'm thinking completely retired." Maria chuckled quietly. "Not mostly. I'm not planning to leave this second, but I wanted you to know, so we can start transitioning leadership at the agency. I'd always thought we might bring Trey back to LA, but I think he's pretty firm about being in Vegas. We've got a lot of good people now. I'm not worried, even if I am a control freak. I think the agency will be fine without me."

"Shit. Should I put off my trip? I'm sure Shay would understand." James turned at loud barking. Thomas the boy was jumping back and forth over Thomas the dog, who was wagging his tail happily. "Stop that," James yelled. "You're going to trip over him and both get hurt, and then your mom's gonna be angry, and I'm gonna be angry."

His son landed and giggled. "Okay, Daddy. No jumping the dog." He returned to chasing the pet in circles. "I'm gonna get you, bounty."

"Everything okay?" Maria asked. "It sounds like things are rowdy there."

"Just a kid being a kid," James replied. "He's precocious, but he's not too much for me yet. I figure that'll take at least a couple more years."

I wonder if she regrets not having kids? She's never said so, but I'm glad I got the chance with Alison and Thomas.

"And don't cancel your trip," Maria insisted. "You two need it, and you've earned it. The agency will be fine without you, and like I said, I want to transition out, not quit tomorrow and sail to Fiji. We'll figure everything out once you come back. This has just been hanging over me, and I didn't want you to feel like I was holding anything back from you."

"You're not planning on moving to Scottsdale or Florida or some shit like that?" James asked, more disdain coming out than he'd intended. "You don't seem like the golfing type."

"No, I'm a Los Angeles woman through and through." Maria let out a quiet laugh. "They call this place the City of Angels, but it's more like a couple of angels fighting a lot of demons. You've made it a better place to live, James."

"I've kicked my share of ass, but no one man can clean up a city. We all have. You did before as a cop, too. Fuck, these days, you're doing a lot more than me."

"Yes, I was a cop," Maria replied quietly. "I was a real bitch to you at first, and all you were doing was taking down scum who needed it. It pisses me off that I was such an idiot back then."

"That shit was a long time ago. It doesn't matter anymore." James squatted to eye the side of one of his steaks. He flipped it with a frown. "You changed. Fuck, I've changed. All that shit might as well be in the Old West, it was so long ago."

"Anyway, I didn't call to get all weepy like a little girl." Maria took a deep breath. "I'm retiring, but I'm not leaving until you're back. I won't be going anywhere else. Tyler has his connections here. I've put my time in beating down bad guys, and we've got a new generation of cops and bounty hunters to take over. I think I'm going to take it easy. Take up painting, but not golf."

"You've earned your retirement, Maria," James replied. "You don't have to justify it to me. You don't have to justify it to anyone."

"I know. I think I'm trying to justify it to myself. I'm being self-indulgent."

James let out a chuckle to lighten the mood. "I'm cooking steaks. It's not like I am taking down a level six here."

"The last thing I want to do is stand between you and a dead animal." Maria's voice sounded lighter, more relaxed. "Anyway, I got the news to you. I'll talk to you later. Enjoy your trip. Try to stay out of trouble."

"Sure. I'll try, but you know me."

"That's the problem."

Maria ended the call, leaving James alone with his thoughts. What was retirement? Even before his recent community outreach efforts, he'd done occasional bounties, and if not those, getting caught up in bizarre incidents across the country and the world. He was supposed to be concentrating on his wife, family, and barbeque, but there was always an Oriceran death factory, a crazy-ass necromancer, or a weird-ass alien showing up to cause him trouble.

He could stick Whispy in a vault and dump it into the ocean, but that was the coward's way out. It was also an insult to his parents. They had sacrificed their lives to save him from being a slave to the Vax war machine, and paying them back meant using the modified symbiont to protect his new home as necessary. That was the best way to honor his father and mother.

I wonder what they would have thought about all this shit? Earth's not a peaceful planet, but at least it's not sending crazy-ass super-soldiers around the galaxy trying to fuck people up.

He grunted at the sound of more loud barking. His son

had resumed his dog-hurdling game. James watched the boy's ease of movement and jump height with a mixture of fascination and concern. There had never been a Vax-human hybrid before. Even without Whispy Doom, Thomas would end up far from normal. Not just far from normal, but also powerful and strong. And that power, strength, and his name would bring him enemies. Between Alison and Thomas, there would be a Brownstone legacy.

The metal spacers adorning the back of James' amulet rested against his chest, a constant reminder of the potential locked deep within him—a potential that could be used to destroy an entire world or to save it. The years of modifications, tinkering, and sacrifice had honed him into the ultimate weapon, as his people desired. He'd simply chosen to use the power in a different way. He patted the amulet. No, he wouldn't be getting rid of it.

At least I'll never get bored.

Shay stood by their bed, her arms outstretched in a dramatic welcoming pose. "I give you…the Underworld Cave."

James had been reading recipes on his phone while Shay was in the bathroom. When she emerged, she looked as excited as someone who had been constipated for weeks and finally found relief. He offered his most stunning and well-thought-out response, based on his current knowledge of the situation.

"Huh? Underworld Cave? What the fuck is that, other than an underground cave?"

"Great analysis, James." Shay sat on the bed and held up her phone. "It's the tomb raiding portion of our little road trip. Everything I found that was interesting was too far away, and I didn't want to hear you bitch about being on a plane for hours. Then something came up earlier today, confirmation of stuff from a few days ago."

"You found something that quickly?" James asked, surprised.

Shay nodded. "I still keep my ear out for possibilities, and there's a rumored cave system in southwest Wyoming. It might include the so-called Underworld Cave, which was supposed to have had a direct link to Oriceran once upon a time." She waved a hand. "I'm sure that part is bullshit, but I'm interested because some people believe the Eye of Pluto is there."

James frowned. "Poor dog."

"Not the damned cartoon dog." Shay rolled her eyes. "I don't know if you're serious or not, but I'm talking about the ancient god. Now, I don't give a shit whether there *was* a Pluto, or it was Oricerans pretended to be him, or if he was a Nine Systems Alliance alien road tripper having a little fun at the expense of the stupid locals." She waved a hand. "I do care that there has been a Mycenaean crown said throughout the centuries to possess the ultimate power in binding magic. In some of the legends, it's even used to bind the actions of the gods by forcing them to agree to specific mortal demands." She frowned. "I don't like the idea of anyone but me having something like that, and I've always thought it'd be cool to own for my collection."

"The one you keep locked away in a hidden warehouse that almost no one ever sees?"

"I see it, and that's what is important." Shay frowned. "Besides, you're not the only one who's learned from the bullshit that's happened over the last couple of years. If the Eye of Pluto is real and in that cave, I'm not the only one who might find it. We're planning to go on a trip anyway, so we might as well head that way and grab it, so no one can use it against you."

"Whatever works, as long as you weren't lying about getting some barbeque along the way. Jessie Rae's, but other places too. At least one a day."

"We'll get barbeque." Shay shook her head. "I'm talking about artifacts thousands of years old that might steal your abilities, and you're concerned about the best barbeque joint in Wyoming."

"Got to have priorities. Some fucker's always planning to screw with me, but not all barbeque joints survive. Most restaurants fail." James shrugged, his expression unapologetic. Marriage was about compromise.

"Sure. I'll keep that in mind, but I've been interested in finding this thing since I first read about it." Shay scooted up the bed and placed her phone on her nightstand before slipping under the covers. "But I've never had any good leads before. Most historians and tomb raiders believe even if it was real, it has long since been destroyed. There are conflicting legends about powerful magical beings fearing it and seeking to destroy it."

"Yeah, that's what I'd do with that kind of shit."

Shay narrowed her eyes. "You're going to break my crown?"

"Not unless I have to." James leaned over to turn off his bedside lamp. "This all sounds fine to me, but from what you're saying, a lot of people will want it. What if we show up and there's a line?"

Shay offered him a vicious grin. "Then you do a little community outreach there, too. If they're not total dipshits, they'll back off once they realize James Brownstone and Aletheia are there."

"Not going to be a relaxing vacation." James laid his head on his pillow. "You sure about this? I don't care about beating down anyone who comes at us, but it's gonna be closer to my last couple of road trips than some spa day shit."

"It'll be nice to have quality adult time." Shay shrugged with a soft smile. "Our quality adult time just happens to sometimes include shooting people and punching them through walls."

James chuckled. "And if we don't find your crown?"

"Then at least I won't ask myself about what could have been." Shay shut off her lamp. "This is going to be fun. Thomas loves Pauline, and he was fine with the idea of us going. This could be a good thing for the future. We could alternate parents-only and family trips. I wish Alison could come, but she's kind of busy these days."

"That's a big assumption," James replied. "Even if we don't think about Alison."

Shay shifted to her side. "What's that?"

"That this trip won't turn into a big clusterfuck involving aliens, the CIA, or shit like that." James grunted in irritation. "Sometimes I think I need more than one type of community outreach."

"It'll be fine." Shay let out a contented sigh. "Even if someone comes at us, it'll be good practice. Anyone stupid enough to come after both of us at the same time won't last long." She leaned over to squeeze his hand. "This'll be fun. Goodnight, James."

"Goodnight, Shay."

Yeah. She's right. If we find the cave, it'll be the dumbass tomb raiders who will run away the second they realize who I am. We've got nothing to worry about. Who would fuck with me at this point?

CHAPTER NINE

Alison rested her elbow on the edge of the long, dark wooden table filling one of the many conference rooms in the palace. She didn't understand why they had so many in the palace. The tables all dated from before the Guardians, and Laena wasn't a woman who had staffed a Drow bureaucracy. She could think of more impressive ways of displaying wealth and power, but she would be the first to admit that she didn't think like a typical Drow.

I'm supposed to guide them into a better society. Damn it. It's a good thing I'm going to live centuries because this is going to take a long time, given I don't even understand excessive Drow furniture tastes yet. Laena spent centuries twisting her subjects, too.

Rasila sat at the other end of the table with a slight knowing smile. There was a certain absurdity having the women sitting so far apart, but as Alison grew into her new role, she continued to accept that protocol was its own strength. She considered her co-queen—her friend— and accepted Rasila's argument about being regal in different ways. She couldn't shape her people if she didn't respect them.

"We're overstaffed." Alison managed a smile. "I keep thinking that."

"Overstaffed?" Rasila's eyebrows rose. "What do you mean?" She looked around the room, but no one else was there.

"We're both, uh, queening full-time lately." Alison chuckled. "It wasn't what we originally planned or intended."

"These are challenging times, and they require unorthodox solutions." Rasila raised her hand and conjured a small illusion of Tarik. "We both knew there would be additional difficulties following our rise to the throne. No one can dare challenge our power directly, and we've won the respect and hearts of most of our people, but it might take years to fully quell discontent." Her mouth twitched into an evil smile. "The Guardians never managed it. If Laena had, she wouldn't have ended up deposed, would she? I don't intend for us to share their pathetic fates."

Alison stared at Rasila, unsure how to respond. She trusted the other woman with her life. That sometimes led her to forget how ruthless Rasila could be. Their initial meeting had been a rainy-day ambush. That ruthless nature served the Drow well in battles, but Alison sensed she'd need to keep her co-queen in check in the coming decades. The Drow wouldn't survive more centuries of self-centered, bloodthirsty rule.

"Damned Tarik." Alison gestured to the image. "He was kind of pathetic."

"Pathetic?"

"Yes. I was expecting more. He couldn't stand up to the persuasion magic that well. I'm kind of surprised given his chosen line of work, but based on Zana's last report, we've swept up most of what remains of his network among our people. I don't think they were prepared for such quick follow-up raids. We'll have to reach out to our contacts across Oriceran about some of his clients, but I'm more concerned about Drow trouble than what some dwarf or Light Elf might do. That said, I'm really worried about some of the artifacts that ended up on Earth and are unaccounted for."

Rasila waved a hand dismissively. "I think you're too focused on the artifacts. If you're worried about those precious human governments blaming us, they'll be in a weak position to do so, given their own failures. We both know how many artifacts illegally flow around Earth. Your family's personal encounters are proof of that. Besides..." She sneered.

"Besides what?" Alison hoped the next sentence didn't involve a situation where she'd have to explain why a brutal massacre wouldn't be an appropriate response. She wasn't above using force where necessary, but moderation never hurt.

Rasila lowered her hand, and the image of Tarik disappeared. "None of the artifacts are weapons. Most are of minor importance. There will be no carnage, no breathless human reporters standing in a crater to speak of the dastardly Drow and our porous borders delivering death to their poorly defended city. We've only managed to trace defensive artifacts, and most didn't even go to Earth. I'm dubious too much damage can be done on Oriceran with such artifacts."

Alison nodded slowly. "I understand where you're coming from, but them being defensive artifacts worries me more. It might just be that it's easier to traffic in those kinds of goods, or it might be pointing to something larger. That's what my instincts tell me, and while I might not be a full-time security contractor anymore, those instincts served me well."

"Really?" Rasila laughed, a hint of mockery in the sound. "The enemies we have left, Alison, are not like those we've faced before. They are the detritus of worthy foes. They hide because they know they cannot stand up to their queens. This pathetic smuggler is the same thing. He hasn't granted some grand foe of the Drow or humanity the ultimate weapon. He stole and lied his way into a source of revenue, and his greed led him to get caught and punished. What has he done? He's traded away walls."

"A good wall is as much of a weapon as a sword." Alison considered the artifacts they'd yet to track down. "And you're not thinking things through. Using some of those artifacts, like the Dagger of Kaladon, they could seal the palace from the outside and attack while cutting us off from reinforcements. They might have sent it to Earth, but they might be getting it back, or they could be planning to do the same to the White House or the Kremlin, or a stadium filled with tens of thousands of fans. Even if you don't care about the humans, we can't be sure the recipients on Earth and Oriceran weren't intermediaries for rogue Drow."

Rasila snorted. "If they used such a strategy, they would

cut themselves off from reinforcements as well. And to what end? They can't hide an entire army, though it might be about defending a base of operations after conducting another operation." Her brows knitted, a pained look of irritation taking over her face. "I do see what you're saying. The Dagger would prevent them from portaling out, though. That's assuming whoever took it, whether they care about the Drow or not, has any grand plans other than collecting ancient and powerful artifacts. That's not an impossibility."

"Nobody collects powerful magical artifacts for the fun of it. Not even my mom. These aren't damned Faberge eggs." Alison sucked in a breath. "It's not enough that we've destroyed the smuggling ring. We need to secure the artifacts. Otherwise, any deaths that occur are on our heads."

"I have no problem seeking those who would mock our rule and destroying them, regardless of species," Rasila declared. "But don't overburden yourself, Alison. It's not our duty to save every creature that exists. Other races need to be able to protect themselves, and those who survived the Great War or the brutal wars on your planet have honed their ability to do just that."

I need to turn this around in a way she'll agree.

"If the Drow are letting terrorists and criminals operate with impunity, we'll look weak." Alison stood, bracing her hands against the table. "And as a queen and a Brownstone, there is no way in hell that I'll let myself look weak. That will invite more challenges, and we won't be able to lead our people back to greatness."

Rasila smiled, but it didn't reach her eyes. "You do raise a good point, but we're still limited in our options. We don't have authority over any land on Earth. And now that the smugglers have been arrested, I doubt the US government will be as accepting of our agents operating without closer coordination with them. Even with your contacts, they won't be comfortable with that. You've told me that yourself."

"Things have gotten more difficult since I assumed the throne." Alison dropped back into her chair and groaned. "Damn it. You're right. I'll reach out again to my contacts in the government and see if I can push them in any way. We can present it as a continued investigation into the final destination of the artifacts. If we let them take the lead on this but offer our aid, we can continue tracking things down. And Tarik might have been out of the loop. There still might be rogue Drow at the other end we can find and identify."

"Understandable, but what will we do if we're too late? What if some grand plan succeeds with these artifacts, but we only find out after the fact?" Rasila looked unworried about the possibility. "I won't feel too much concern, but how you present yourself to the others will influence things."

Alison locked eyes with Rasila. "If that happens, I'll do what my father taught me to do in this kind of situation."

"Which is what?"

"Make a very public example out of someone," Alison replied, her voice a near growl.

Rasila threw her hand back, laughed, and clapped. "Excellent. Sometimes I think it's a cruel joke that James Brownstone wasn't born a Drow."

"I still can't get over John," the witch offered in a merry tone. "Why do you choose that name out of all the choices available? Even an Oriceran name wouldn't have bothered a Drow."

The wizard leaned over a small wooden crate, inspecting the artifacts laid out inside: a jeweled dagger, a pendant, a cracked bone, and a flute. "It's useful in its anonymity. Vina is not a grand name, either."

"But it has a certain charm." The witch ran a hand through her long blonde locks. "As does this current appearance. The master has so little regard for humanoid appearance. I'm grateful to serve him, but it's refreshing to spend so much time among lesser beings."

John lifted the dagger and nodded approvingly. "Remember our task then, *Vina*. The master's request for quick resolution has forced us to take dangerous risks. Our enemies are closer to us than we think. Fate doesn't always bend in the way even the master desires. We can't allow anyone to disrupt his plans, no matter the cost."

Vina circled the table, her hands clasped behind her back, smiling at the artifacts. "And what have you done to ensure we carry out the master's plan?"

"I killed the others who provided me the artifacts," John explained. "I used different methods and disposed of the bodies in different locations. It's unlikely that anyone will connect the killings."

Vina nodded. "I expected as much. You're always efficient at this sort of thing."

"But I wasn't able to take care of all loose ends."

Vina's smile disappeared. "You weren't?"

John shook the dagger. "I was following the Drow who sold me this. An FBI agent interfered. A witch. I was preparing to kill them both when other Drow arrived in numbers, then Alison Brownstone came." He gnashed his teeth. "The coincidence worries me. We were so careful, but now she's so close."

Vina's eyes widened. "Do you think she knows of the plan?"

"She's given no indication, and how could she?" He scoffed as much to convince himself as the witch. "The smuggler doesn't even know who I really am, but I don't like the fact that she now knows he successfully sold off the dagger. There is more risk to the plan. Our other efforts haven't been directly connected, and there's no evidence otherwise. We cannot fail the master."

"We won't, and we haven't. Alison Brownstone being near one of our suppliers is irrelevant. She and her allies haven't been near any of the others, correct?"

John nodded. "Yes. I doubt she would have allowed me to dispose of them if that were the case."

Vina stopped and tilted her head, taking a long look at the pendant. "Sealing, amplification, observation, suppression. We already have the necessary artifacts, and all evidence points to no Brownstones having a clue about our true plan." She chuckled. "I've been in contact with many of James Brownstone's close friends." She ran her finger along the edge of the crate until she neared the pendant, then traced its form with her finger. "It's charged sufficiently with the feelings and connections of his friends to work for our purposes."

"Are you sure?"

"Yes," Vina replied. "Don't you see? It doesn't matter if Alison Brownstone or her father even figure out that the same people have all four of these artifacts. They won't understand the connection or the plan." She stood, her eyes narrowing. "And how could they figure it out? Only the dagger came from a Drow. It's not as if they're watching every artifact smuggler on Earth. What occurred was an unpleasant coincidence, nothing more."

"It may be as you say." John took a deep breath and let it out slowly. "Then, are you prepared to move forward? We do this for our master, but once we do it, we will become an enemy of one of the strongest men on Earth. The risks aren't insignificant."

"Strongest on Earth?" Vina chuckled dismissively. "I don't care if he's a strange creature from another world like the master told us. James Brownstone isn't used to true power. Earth is nothing before Oriceran, and he's nothing before our master."

"Is everything in place for the distraction?" John asked.

"Of course. That's why I'm not worried."

"Then we gather our forces and prepare." John closed his eyes and took a deep breath. "The master's will be done."

Vina bowed her head. "The master's will be done."

CHAPTER TEN

James shoved the last of Shay's pile of suitcases into the back of his F-350, which was in the garage. "You used to travel the world, going to caves and underwater and shit. I know you can travel light, so why do you have to bring so many suitcases now?"

Shay leaned against the wall beside a tool rack, her arms crossed. She had a knowing smirk on her face that made James wonder if this trip might be a mistake.

"This is a vacation featuring a tomb raid, not just any tomb raid." Shay drummed her fingers against her arm. "There's no reason to pack light. If the tomb raid goes well, we'll have plenty of time to relax and do other things, and some of the things I brought, we'll need for other things."

Huh? What the fuck does that mean?

Pauline stepped into the garage, saving James from having to think too deeply about the implications. "Ah. You're loaded. Shall I wake Thomas from his nap?"

"No. We'll do that right before we leave. I still need to take a shower." James furrowed his brow in thought, looking at the truck and the nanny. It wasn't like he'd never taken a trip since the birth of his son, but this was the first time their son wouldn't see either parent for days. He couldn't ignore that.

"Are all the special measures in place?" Shay asked, looking at Pauline. It was the first time since they'd discussed the trip she sounded worried.

Glad I'm not the only one.

The nanny nodded with a coy smile. "I've added additional wards and spells on top of what Alison had in place. The boy will be fine. You two should concentrate on your time together."

Shay marched over to Pauline until she was inches from her. "And if someone comes for him?"

"You know what I'll do."

"Not good enough." Shay narrowed her eyes. "Say it."

"If someone comes for Thomas, I will kill them." Pauline's words came out casually. Determination burned in her blue eyes. "You have my word."

"Don't fucking play games with them. No cutesy shit to show off, just kill them. We might not be in a position to get to you easily."

James thought that over. The most likely scenario, given his past trips, was that someone would attack him on the road. That could delay their return home, but he wasn't worried about anyone targeting Thomas. He'd made sure the locals understood what that meant, and the LA underworld had gone out of its way to make clear it wouldn't be tolerated. Despite all that, it was nice having a lethal nanny around as backup.

Shay took a step back and blew out a breath. "I don't

care who they are. I don't care about the political implications, or if it'll start a gang war that will make the streets run red with the blood of everyone in LA. If anyone shows up and so much as frowns at our son, you kill them. I give you my solemn vow that we'll protect you after that."

Pauline laced her fingers together and bowed her head. "I have never allowed a child under my care to be harmed, and I won't as long as I draw breath. Many of my spells will persist even after that."

James rubbed his forehead, agitation building. "Damn it, you two. You keep talking like that, and I'm not gonna go. Fuck. You're making it sound like World War III is going to break out the minute we hit the road."

Shay winced and averted her eyes. "I just wanted to make sure we're all on the same page. This is my first time being away from our boy. I'm still getting used to the idea."

Pauline smiled softly. "Don't worry. No one but your closest friends knows you're going on a trip. There will be no risk other than Thomas crying a lot."

Shay sighed, her cheeks pink. "I think I'm having more clinging issues than the boy. This is pathetic. The old Killer Me would have slit my throat."

"I think a woman prepared to defend her child is a greater killer."

"Just go get him." James nodded toward the door. "Screw the shower. Let's give him a hug and kiss and get out of here before Shay stabs half of LA."

"It's good to get out as parents," Zoe purred. She brushed her dark hair behind her ear, smiling at James.

Fuck. All these years, and I still can't tell if she's flirting with me.

Shay and James were passing through Vegas, so they decided to have lunch with Zoe and Trey. Jessie Rae's was the obvious choice. James was already digging into his second tray of brisket and ribs. Something about a road trip with his wife made him want to eat five times as much barbeque, not that he needed an excuse. Shay might not share his passion for barbeque, but she did appreciate quality like their current location.

"What about you?" Shay looked at Zoe. "You're comfortable with your babysitting situation? You've had a little longer to get used to it."

Zoe laughed. "Our daughter is older and yes. I don't think our babysitter has the lethal pedigree of Pauline, but she can handle herself well, and anyone who might come to the house who hasn't been properly scented might find some of my creations to be troublesome." She licked her lips. "I'm dubious police would think to investigate my plants."

James swallowed some brisket. "We can't get killer plants. Thomas would probably rip up their roots." He paused for a moment before adding, "My dog, not the kid, but the kid probably would, too. He's so damned full of energy right now."

Trey wiped his face with a napkin. "Zoe's right. It's good that you're getting out. It took me a long time before I could bring myself to go on a vacation without Little Zoe, but I'm glad I did. It helps keep the fire alive and reminds me that I'm a husband and not just a dad and the world's second most badass bounty hunter." He laughed and shook his head. "Damn. I can't believe this. Hell."

"What?" James looked around for a source of trouble, his hand inside his coat, resting on his .45. He'd signed autographs upon arrival, and everyone else knew to leave him alone at the owner Mike's request. Anyone who dared fuck with Jessie Rae's would learn the meaning of fear, just as a thief had years prior.

Trey gestured to James and then himself. "Listen to us, big man. We're all sitting here talking about babysitters and nannies for our kids. I remember when you used to roll up in your F-350 in our old hood, before it was nice, to ask my boys and me if we'd seen anything like bounties and missing dogs. I never thought I'd be working for you, married to a beautiful witch, and have a daughter. Shit. I didn't think I should have a kid. I thought I'd be dead by now."

Shay snickered. "So did I." She tapped her chest. "I mean, I thought I'd be dead. It's weird when your mistakes mean you live longer."

"You two are depressing," James rumbled. "How can you be talking like that?"

Zoe let out a quiet laugh. "To live is to struggle. It is in struggling that we appreciate what we have. All of us have suffered adversity, and because of that, we understand the simple beauty of our current lives all the more."

"I guess." James shrugged. "I do what I have to do, but it doesn't mean I love it. If fuckers come out, I put them in the ground. Most fuckers now know not to come at me."

"If you're doing more these days with community

outreach and shit, that changes things with Thomas, doesn't it?" Trey eyed James, a glint of curiosity there. "And his future?"

"How?" James reached for a rib, having demolished the last of the brisket. "He's still a little kid, even with his fast growth and crap. I'm not bringing him on any bounties anytime soon."

"I know. I know." Trey waved his hands. "I just always figured you would spin being a bounty hunter down, you know what I'm saying? Go all the way to becoming the Big Man of Barbeque and hang up your gun. You were doing fewer and fewer bounties, but now you're doing your community outreach and all that. Monthly motherfucking Brownstone. It's almost like the old days." Trey chuckled. "You weren't a daily guy even before you settled down, and so now I'm wondering."

"Wondering what?" James asked.

Trey leaned toward him and lowered his voice. "We took a blind girl and trained her to fight. Yeah, she got artifacts later, but I keep going back to that. How long before Thomas learns the family trade? When he's twelve? When he's fifteen?"

Zoe inclined her head toward Shay. "He could be interested in history and archaeology. He might have little interest in violent pursuits."

"Sure." Trey rubbed his lip. "But Shay's into all that and can still take care of herself."

Shay took a drag off her beer bottle. "We're not pushing anything for a while. Even if he's growing faster than we anticipated, it's not like he's going to be an adult anytime soon. For right now, he doesn't need to worry about how to kill people."

Trey grinned. "For now. But it sounds like you're planning to teach him and planning to turn him into a full-on Brownstone in a way you couldn't with Alison."

James shrugged. "The name means he'll be targeted no matter what he wants to do. He'll need to know how to take care of himself. Once he's older, we'll know his capabilities better, and we can get the artifacts and training he needs. After that, I don't care. He can do anything. He can be whatever he wants after that except a vegetarian. Fuck that shit."

Trey barked out a laugh. "Some things never change, huh? Any thoughts about the…family heirloom?"

"Not for a long fucking time," James growled. "At the end of the day, *he* still has his own agenda."

"Gotcha. I hope you two enjoy your trip. I enjoyed our first trip without Little Zoe, but it was hard the next time. It got easier after that, but it's not like we're going on couples-only trips every weekend."

Zoe peered out the window, a distant look in her eyes. "That's true. We've taken family trips, of course, but it can be difficult to leave your beloved child behind. I know you think you're used to it because of Alison, but it's a different situation."

Shay smiled. "I don't think we're planning on doing this all that often, but I'll keep that in mind. We'll see how this trip goes. I think we're in for a pleasant surprise."

"I'm sure you'll have no problems." Zoe smiled warmly. "After all, who would be foolish enough to harass you two, of all people?"

CHAPTER ELEVEN

The entrance to the cave was unassuming. Porous limestone surrounded a passage large enough for a man, even James Brownstone, but the natural curves and forms suggested it was a product of nature, not careful design. They'd hugged the southern border of Wyoming and entered the national forest following Shay's directions. The roads in the forest gave way to simple dirt paths, but the trees soon became impassable, and they had to park the F-350. Three hours of backpacking with the help of GPS had brought them to the cave. Rays of light cut through the densely packed trees and their branches, highlighting the entrance like a celestial flashlight.

That shit looks more pretty than mystical.

Shay rubbed her hands together before reaching up to pull her AR goggles over her eyes. "It's great when everything comes together. I was worried that we might not get here in time, but it doesn't look like anyone else has come this way in years. It might have been fun to kick tomb-raider ass, but I probably shouldn't be picking up new enemies since I killed all my old ones."

"You're saying it's better to be lucky than good?" James asked with a grin.

"Or you can just be me and be both." Shay winked and murmured a command to her goggles under her breath. "But just because no one's come this way in years, it doesn't mean there isn't any risk. I expect traps and something in there. Probably nothing alive, but an explosion isn't alive."

Low probability of adaptation potential, Whispy complained. James had bonded him once they began the hike, reasoning that a cave with a powerful artifact would be dangerous. Based on what Shay had told him, there was also a good chance that other tomb raiders might show up.

Happy wife, happy life, James sent back.

Logic accepted.

Shay crept toward the cave, slowly looking around. "I came across some information this morning that, if true, would really make my day." She held up a hand. "I'm not going to go into it yet. I don't want to get too excited in case I'm wrong. If the crown's there, that'd be enough to make my year."

"You care that much?" James asked. "You used to sell off most of the artifacts you collected."

"This one's different." Shay took another step toward the cave, now moving her head up and down, the goggles concealing her eyes and much of her facial expression. "A lot of artifacts are about power. They don't have such an important link to history, like the crown. I've always been interested in it more academically than as a tomb raider because it might help shed light on the nature of Greek mythology and its relationship with Oriceran." She side-stepped and now was only a yard from the entrance to the cave. "But I wasn't sure it was real. Shit. I'm still not sure, but this is the first solid lead I've had in years. It's like the crown *wants* me to find it."

James frowned. "Can they do that? Want you to find them?"

Shay laughed. "I'm being metaphorical here." Her smile vanished. She crouched and grabbed a small stone from the ground. She flung it toward the side of the cave entrance. Jets of flame shot out from all sides and charred it.

"Huh." James let out a grunt of surprise. "Definitely not a normal cave. That's good, right?"

"You could say that." Shay backed away. "That's some aggressive trap bullshit. I thought we wouldn't have to worry about it until we got deeper inside." She laughed. "This is where having Lily would have been handy."

"You want to go on a couples vacation with her?" James frowned.

"I'm just saying." Shay flung her hand up in a dismissive gesture. "The thermal signature is almost back to normal, but it's hard to tell. Before, I detected slight differentials, but the trap could still be active. I'll have to be careful about it."

"You're saying we're going to have to crawl through this cave because of traps?" James asked, annoyance building. He wanted to spend time with his wife doing fun things like eating barbeque or smashing through monsters, not edging forward two inches an hour, worried about traps.

"That's just part of the raid." Shay shrugged. "The good

news is, based on my background research, I have little reason to suspect there are traps that will bring the entire cave down. But considering what I think's in there, there's every reason to suspect it's going to be filled with deadly bullshit, and I think most of it will be magical. I don't have enough artifacts with me to disable every trap, so we'll have to be careful. This is the part of tomb raiding I always hated."

Inefficiency in mission timeline risks emotional equilibrium of mate, Whispy suggested. *Happiness of wife unlikely. Subsequent happiness of life is additionally unlikely.*

Fuck that. I don't want to be here for three days, either. I've got an idea.

"So, the real problem is there will be a bunch of killer traps spewing death." James motioned to the cave. "But nothing that'll bury us. That about sum it up?"

Shay nodded. "Based on background research, yeah. This isn't a sacred tomb or anything like that. It's the equivalent of an ancient storage locker. I think whoever stored the crown here meant to come get it eventually, but shit happened along the way." She lifted her goggles, peering into the cave with narrowed eyes. "They might have even put it in here before the gates closed the last time. That's the only way they could have powered the traps. That's what's confusing me."

"Couldn't they just have absorbed magic like kemanas?" James asked.

"Anyplace that can store a decent amount of magic is a place where magicals would have already set up shop." Shay shook her head. "But you're right. The traps might work now because the gates are open, but they would have had to bring along some method of charging magic in-between. Or they just got damned lucky." She gestured at the thick undergrowth and the trees. "It's like no one has been here in a long while."

"That confuses me." James knelt and ran his hand through a bush. "This isn't Antarctica. No one's ever come hiking this way? They have satellites and shit that can spot caves from orbit."

"Maybe they did." Shay shrugged. "You'd be surprised how easy it can be to miss something unless you know exactly where you're going, but it might support something I read the other day. There's some suggestion that the cave had magic to hide it, a spell that can turn a person around in the woods without them realizing it."

"But we found it, and wouldn't that take magical power?"

"Yes, because we knew exactly where to go." Shay sighed. "But it has occurred to me that's pretty lucky, too. I see your point. There are a lot of questions about this."

"What are you getting at?" James asked.

"Now that we're talking about it out loud, the timing of finding this information and the information I found makes me suspicious." Shay glowered. "But I couldn't pass up the chance of getting the crown."

James growled. "You think it's a trap?"

Shay nodded. "Yes, but not in the way you think."

"Then I don't want to waste a bunch of time tiptoeing through fucking traps." James reached into his pocket and pulled out a small warm toothpick, a Shay snack. "I'm not going to waste all day while we go through the traps from some dead asshole from thousands of years." He scowled.

"You want the crown, right? If it's about you getting a thrill out of the traps, fine, but otherwise, I'm gonna suit up and go right through them."

"That's one way to do things." Shay nodded toward the cave. "It's not nearly as fun."

"You *like* nearly getting killed by traps?"

Shay smirked. "'Nearly getting killed' implies it would have been close."

"Yeah." James walked toward the cave mouth and slipped the artifact under his shirt. "Don't worry. I'm sure there are some ghost shits down there."

"A ghost shit? Is that like the ghost of shit? How does that work?"

James growled. "You know what I mean."

"Just armor up, James." Shay tilted her head. "Your wife needs a new crown."

CHAPTER TWELVE

M*aximum adaptation achieved against existing attack type,* Whispy reported. *Regeneration in progress.*

James shook his arms with a grunt, flicking acid from the extended advanced mode armor onto the walls, where it sizzled and carved a channel into the limestone. The minor pits in his armor vanished within seconds. It had been the seventh trap on the trip through the cave. The plan had worked. He moved forward, with Shay well behind. The resulting traps only hurt him, and barely at that. Fire, ice, some sort of necromantic death ray from what he could tell, and even good, old-fashioned spears. He would give the ancient designers credit for variety, but he'd yet to run into anything new. While he wasn't expecting a nuclear bomb to go off in an ancient cave, he'd expected something more.

Shay walked over to his side. She adjusted the straps of her backpack before tapping her AR goggles and peering around. The silver glow from her defense artifacts remained undimmed. "I'm starting to see density differences. I think we're getting close to something important. Or something more important than all these damned traps."

"Or something that's not a trap, can move on its own, and is going to try and kill us." James poked his blade into a small hole bored by the acid. "You know they're going to have something else."

"Something has already been trying to kill us." Shay gestured to the acid burns along the wall and cave floor. "Something that can move. It's just not been doing a very good job of it." She pointed to the top of the cave. "Huh. That's new, as in the last couple of seconds."

James craned his neck upward. Dimly glowing curvilinear sigils stretched throughout the low-hanging roof of the cave. They didn't resemble any language he was familiar with, but that didn't mean anything. Despite his memory, he hadn't spent any significant time studying foreign languages from either Earth or Oriceran. Disinterest or laziness, he would admit to both depending on his mood.

"These look a lot like the arcane language of some of the allegedly lost ancient Mesoamerican tribes that maintained better knowledge of magic following the closing of the gates." Shay rubbed her chin. "It's just like in the article I wrote a couple years back. Huh. That's kind of odd, but I think we're past the traps."

"I thought you said everyone ripped you over that article." James' review of the symbols didn't accomplish anything. "They said you were full of shit. I don't get that. I mean, all of history was mostly full of shit for thousands of years."

"It's still a controversial theory. Just because Oriceran's a thing, it doesn't mean everything's true." Shay shrugged. "But I believe in my theory, whatever those tiny-dick reviewers had to say. And sure, it's admittedly based on big assumptions about circumstantial evidence, but that doesn't mean those assholes are right. They are all fuckers who would have laughed away anyone who suggested magic was real in the past." She snorted and flung her hand toward the cave roof. "But this proves I was right. Fuckers. I'll have to indirectly arrange for a dig here. It's my lucky day. Shit, it's my lucky week. I can get an artifact and bolster my reputation. I can get all sorts of papers out of this place."

I remember when she only cared about money, and now she cares what a bunch of professor assholes has to say about who was right about shit that happened before either of us were born.

"What does it say?" James asked. He might not be that personally interested, but he was happy Shay was excited.

She shook her head. "I'm not all that fluent in the relevant languages, but I'm pretty sure it's a warning against trespassing. Something about a curse."

"Yeah. That sounds about right. Abandon all hope and all that shit. Just once, you'd think you'd end up in one of these places and they'd be all like, 'Congratulations, you're the hundredth person who has attempted to steal from here! You win a special prize.'"

"That would be nice." Shay snickered. She patted her holster and her sheath. "But I doubt anything's still alive around here, based on what we've seen, so if we're through the traps, we're probably safe. There's a chance they might reset, so you'll have to take the lead on the way out, too."

She gestured to her body and the silver glow surrounding it. "Not that I don't trust this, but we both know who is sturdier."

"Fine by me." James continued forward, resisting the urge to scrape his blade against the wall. He'd already caused a lot of damage setting off the traps, and if his wife was going to come back and dig it up for science, it needed to be as untouched as possible.

Something bothered him about the tomb raid, but he couldn't figure out what it was. It'd been a while since he'd last accompanied Shay on something like this, so he hoped that was the reason and not some deep part of his bounty hunting instincts warning him. He hoped it was as simple as wanting more barbeque.

Background alternative energy levels high relative to average exposure planetary baseline, Whispy reported. *Magical energy levels consistent with levels observed previously in kemana locations.*

Yeah. That makes sense. Something's had to keep this place safe, and that means they needed some way of storing magic. Maybe we were wrong, and this place just slipped through the cracks. Weirder shit has happened, and those traps weren't all that impressive.

Upgrading adaptation probability to low from very low, Whispy replied. A note of disappointment made it through the mental link.

A rumble echoed through the cave. Another came moments later, followed by scratching and a low, resonant hum. It was reminiscent of a high-voltage power line. James didn't spot anything in either direction, but the sound was so faint, he wasn't sure how close its source might be.

"You hear that?" he asked.

Shay took a deep breath and pulled out a dagger with her left hand and murmured an activation incantation. Flames burst from the blade as she yanked out her pistol with her other hand. "This is what happens when I don't go on raids enough. I knew this was too easy."

"Other tomb raiders?" James didn't believe it even before the words left his mouth.

"I doubt it." Shay knitted her brows in consternation. "I'd love it if it were, but I think they've got more than passive defenses in this place. I was wrong. Something else is coming, not just traps."

"This isn't going to be some sort of ancient demon prison shit, is it?" James growled, remembering a mess involving Alison. His plan to preserve the cave wasn't going to work if he needed to fight. A swarm of monsters might require his cannon.

Structural integrity of cave system is unknown, Whispy observed. *Recommend against energy discharges.*

I'll do what I need to do to kill the fuckers, but yeah, I get you. I won't bury us all alive.

"I've not read anything like that about this place." Shay didn't sound convincing with her weapons out. "If it were some sort of prison, it would have made it into at least one rumor or story."

"But it's holding a death god artifact, right? Maybe the real Pluto was a bitch-ass necromancer back in the day. There could be a whole zombie horde shuffling toward us."

Shay looked back and forth, an eerie glow coming from her AR goggles. "That's not impossible, but the Eye of Pluto isn't that kind of artifact. It's not necromantic at all."

"Doesn't mean he didn't use zombies to guard it," James replied.

The hum grew louder, the rumbling closer. Something was coming. James sliced through the air a couple of times with his blade in anticipation. He didn't fear zombies if that was what was coming, but their existence offended him. That fueled a desire to destroy them as quickly as possible. Too bad whoever had created them had long since turned to dust.

Background alternative energy levels increasing, Whispy reported. *Unusual phenomenon.*

"What the fuck? Whispy's saying there's magic flooding in here. Magical energy, not actual spells."

Shay took a couple of slow, deep breaths. "It sounds like the magical version of emergency backup power just turned on. The big question is what it might be powering. We've got their attention now."

"This cave gonna go up?" James asked.

"That can't be it. They didn't store something here this long just to blow it. Damn it."

Shay pointed her weapons upward. Circular holes opened in the ceiling, the rock pulling back to reveal long, smooth tubes. The rumbling ceased, but the incessant hum became louder. The sigils flashed in sequence.

James stepped in front of Shay and brought up his blade. He might not know shit about ancient artifacts, but he knew when something was about to spit out trouble. He grinned under his helmet. All barbeque, all the time might have been more entertaining than a tomb raid, but kicking ass with Shay was a fun date, too.

Men in polished suits of bronze armor, holding small circular shields and long, round-tipped swords, fell from the tubes bathed in a yellow glow. They landed on one knee with loud thuds. They lifted their heads adorned with conical helmets to reveal glowing red eyes staring out from inky but otherwise featureless darkness. The same shifting inky darkness formed their arms and legs. They weren't men, more like shadows wearing armor.

More bronze warriors fell from the tubes. Their movements rigid, the initial arrivals stood, raising their shields and swords. Now that they were right in front of James, he could source the hum to their glowing armaments.

"Well, look on the bright side." Shay pointed her pistol at the closest enemy and shrugged. "At least they aren't zombies."

James let out a long, low growl. "What the fuck are they then? Ghosts?"

"I don't think so." Shay wrinkled her nose. "I'm guessing there's an artifact somewhere just powering up armor and swords to kill intruders. I don't feel like digging for it, but these guys are between the Eye of Pluto and us."

The rate of new arrivals increased. Bronze warriors now filled the area. They continued to stand and spread out, but they didn't advance on the pair.

"Are they gonna stop coming or what?" James asked.

"Who the fuck knows?" Shay shrugged. "At least they're not doing anything."

"Yeah, they're probably waiting until there's a million of them."

Dozens of the warriors now stood in the cave, all staring at James and Shay with their glowing red eyes, their combined hum sounding more like the buzz of an angry swarm of zombie bees. No matter how many things James had fought throughout the years, he always managed to run into something new. All the wonderful creations of the world were eager to present themselves for death and destruction.

"Let's see how anti-magic bullets do." Shay fired twice into the head of one of the warriors, and it jerked back, misty darkness gushing out like a leaking gas. "That could have gone better."

The warrior charged, and James sliced where its throat would be. The helmet flew off, and the darkness collapsed to the ground in a spreading cloud that dissipated seconds later. The helmet, armor, and shield clattered to the ground, the glow slowly fading. The remaining enemies spread out to block the cave, forming several overlapping ranks of defenders, but they didn't advance or charge as a group like he expected.

"They aren't very smart," James muttered.

"But there are a lot of them."

Destroy all enemies, Whispy demanded.

You know you don't have to tell me that shit when they're trying to kill me.

Acknowledged.

Shay holstered her pistol and gripped her flaming knife with both hands. A lopsided grin spread over her face. "This is going to be fun. I'm going to treat it like a workout."

"You sure?" James asked. "It looks like they aren't gonna

fuck with us if we don't try to get through. I don't give a shit, but it's your raid."

"If I wasn't convinced there was something worth grabbing before, I am now." Shay tossed her knife between her hands a couple of times. "We just need to get through the magical rent-a-cops here and get to the good shit."

"If we start busting shit up, it might make a mess if you come back here later on a university dig." James shrugged. "Especially if I have to go all-out."

"I can live with that, and you won't need to do that." Shay pointed to the left. "I'll take that side. You take the rest?"

"Works for me." James examined his blade for damage or stains, but it was untouched.

Shay charged toward the warriors. The enemy readied their swords and lifted their shields. James barreled toward the other side of the formation, roaring. His loud attempts at intimidation didn't appear to accomplish anything. All the bronze warriors remained in their overlapping ranks, awaiting the arrival of their attackers.

James eschewed subtlety or careful strategy, instead opting to crash into the front line and knock enemies over. He swung his blade and cleaved a warrior in half. The gaseous shadow fled the armor as it had with his earlier attack.

Good. That makes shit easy.

He sliced and swung with little regard. His blows cut through the armor and shields with ease. The warriors surrounding him stabbed, sliced, and thrust with their glowing blades, but the attacks bounced off his armor with barely a scratch. It was like a group of toddlers trying to take down a heavyweight boxer.

Maximum adaptation achieved against existing attack types, Whispy confirmed.

Shay dove right in, thrusting her flaming blade in a feint before slicing through the neck of a warrior swinging at her. She ducked the stab of one of his allies, pivoting around him and decapitating him. Another warrior offered a half-decent thrust, and the blow connected with her side. She grunted at the sting and jumped back, her silver sheen diminishing, but not disappearing. A jump kick knocked another warrior back while she finished removing the head of the who'd just struck her.

The density of the formation provided constant targets for Shay to flank and kill and James to stomp through. The discarded pile of now inert armor, weapons, and shields grew. A falling sword bounced off a shield with a loud clang. Shay spun that way, distracted for a moment before spinning back to finish off her latest foe. She'd carved deep into her side. James' efforts sent him deep into the center of the formation.

Yeah. Whatever these are, they aren't fucking ghosts. It's like fighting dumbass robots who don't know when to give up.

James slammed his fist into one of the warriors, knocking the helmet off. The armor collapsed, and the shadowy essence fled. He whipped out his blade and ripped through two other enemies. Their nice earlier formation had collapsed and been replaced by uneven piles of equipment, a cluster of enemies surrounding the armored James, and another trying to down the fast-moving Shay with no better success.

The couples' efforts thinned the dozens to a dozen. The rate of destruction increased, Shay cackling in delight as she sidestepped a clumsy warrior's slash and finished off her attacker. James shoved his blade through the chests of two warriors before yanking his arm back and knocking their heads off. He shook off the armor and sent it to join the burgeoning pile.

Shay leapt back from her latest kill. "Sometimes, I regret giving my best sword to Alison."

"She and her people have gotten a lot of use out of it."

"Sure, but it was so damned fun." Shay shook her knife. "Not that a flaming knife isn't."

As an experiment, James bisected an armor vertically. The enemy didn't get back up, and he nodded in satisfaction. He lifted his blade, ready to destroy more, but there was nothing left but inanimate weapons and armor.

Shay wiped the sweat off her brow before deactivating and sheathing her blade. "And I have grown attached to this knife." She kicked a helmet against the wall. "That said, do you ever get the feeling someone's mocking you?"

"Huh? A bunch of walking shadow warriors tried to kill us. They weren't tough, but they would have killed most tomb raiders. I don't think they were trying to fuck with you that way."

"That's not what I'm talking about." Shay squatted by some armor and picked up the sword. "This armor and these weapons aren't quite right. I think they're supposed to look ancient Mycenaean, but it's more like a costume designer saw a picture in a book and then made something they thought looked cool."

James shrugged, not ready to mention his earlier

concerns, unsure if he had just been expecting a threat like the warriors.

"Does the gear have to be accurate for magical defense?" he asked.

"No." Shay stood and shook her head. "I suppose it doesn't, but I might be overthinking things." She nodded toward the other end of the cave. "Let's keep going. I want to leave this place with something more than a bronze sword."

CHAPTER THIRTEEN

The defeated armor pile disappeared behind them as they continued forward, and the passageway widened the deeper they moved into the cave. An increasing glow from the walls ahead pushed back the darkness, rendering Shay's goggles and James' current night vision adaptations unnecessary. Shay pushed up her headgear and squinted into the distance.

Minimal adaptation potential, Whispy sent.

Remember, this is supposed to be about Shay, not you.

"The cave's connected to something else." Shay crept toward one of the glowing walls and ran her hand along the pale blue crystalline surface. "I wonder if this is the battery that was keeping our guards ready and able to slice people up. It's impressive for a place sitting around for thousands of years, but it's not enough to support a full kemana. That might explain why no one was ever here."

"You'd know better than me. This place seems like hell."

Shay turned to James, a curious look on her face. "Really?"

"No kitchen," James explained.

"Maybe they didn't need to eat."

James let out a grunt of disapproval. "Then it really is hell."

They continued their exploration, the crystalline hallway continuing for some distance before connecting to a brightly lit round chamber. A trio of floating light orbs swirled around the center of the room, over a golden chest lying in the center. James and Shay watched the lights with caution for over a minute, but they didn't move from the center of the room. If they were part of the defense system, they hadn't recognized the intruders yet.

"Whatever happened to hiding shit?" James pointed at the chest. "Shouldn't you have to solve some riddles or trace some hieroglyphics? It always seems like that's how the raids I went on with you before went."

"You do realize you've probably been on like five percent of my tomb raids?" Shay offered him a playful smile.

"Just saying."

"And the answer to your question is no, especially if you're depending on a bunch of magical armor and swords to kill people. There are some fascinating differences in the kind of defenses you see, depending on time period, but I'm thinking you don't want the lecture."

James considered the question for a couple of seconds before asking, "Will it help me kill anything better?"

Shay shook her head. "Probably not."

"Then, yeah. I don't want the lecture."

"But all that said, I'm with you. This is too easy for the"

type of artifact we're trying to recover." Shay frowned, suspicion in her eyes. "There must be final traps in the central chamber." She lowered her goggles and tapped a couple of times for magnification. "I'm not detecting any major density differences. Fuck. Could it be that easy? Okay, the chest does appear to be pre-Shaft Mycenaean."

"That's a good thing, right? Isn't that what you were looking for?" James asked. Her earlier comments questioning the authenticity of the warriors remained in the back of his mind. When it came to magic, a man could never be too paranoid. He didn't want their road trip to end with them getting turned into statues as warnings to others.

Shay nodded. "It is what I'm looking for, but it's not consistent with the writing we've otherwise been seeing. There's just a lot going on?" She lifted her goggles and scratched the side of her head. "There might be an interesting story here, or it could have been as simple as someone portaled the artifact over here a long time ago to keep with some locals. Still..."

"Still what?" James asked, not following her academic logic. Finding a powerful artifact was straightforward enough. He didn't know why the historical details mattered that much in this case.

"Don't worry about it." Shay smacked her lips. "There's something I'm still working out, but let's find the Eye of Pluto first." She gestured to the chamber ahead with a grin. "If there are traps, I'd prefer you trip them. No reason to test my ring and pendant to their limit."

They crept closer, the light from the orbs growing

brighter until they stood right outside the circular chamber. Unlike the crystalline walls of the hallway or the natural limestone of the cave, dark green metal covered with intricate whorls and connecting lines formed the walls and floor. The ceiling stood so high its details were lost in the darkness.

James took a single step into the chamber, waiting for the lethal trap. No death rays, explosions, poison darts, acids, or deadly beasts assaulted him. There was no hum or rumbling.

"That was kind of anticlimactic." Shay chuckled.

"You prefer I get blown up?" James rumbled.

"Unless they have a star hidden in here, I doubt there's anything they **could** do to mess you up."

"Is this more Mesoamerican or Mycenaean stuff?" James pointed toward the patterns on the walls.

Shay shook her head, gingerly entering the chamber with a deepening frown. "This resembles something else entirely. A couple of things, actually." She frowned. "It's like this place is an archaeological grab bag."

"Isn't that how shit works? Oriceran crap and all that?"

"Sometimes, and it's not impossible for this kind of mix to happen in Oriceran and magic-related sites, but it's still weird." Shay sucked a breath through her teeth. "There's a reason the false history lasted for as long as it did, occasional out-of-place artifact aside. But I've never read about a site this diverse at the same strata."

James was only a little surprised when the entire chamber shook. A stone slab dropped to the ground and sealed them inside. Shay drew her blade and activated the fire aura. She spun and sought an enemy.

"I'm not seeing shit," he complained. "You?"

"Nothing yet." Shay widened her stance. "But you don't trap someone if you don't intend to kill them."

"They could plan to starve us out."

"People with enough power to get through their armor could get through a door, given enough time," Shay growled in frustration. "Just get it over with already!" she yelled. "I want my damned crown."

The chest lid flung itself open, accompanied by a familiar hum. A gold crown rose, gold spikes rising from the top. Differently colored gemstones covered in red vein-like striations formed a curved line across the body of the crown. A massive head of shadow and smoke formed beneath the headwear. Like with the warriors, glowing red eyes appeared, providing the only distinguishing feature. Streams of smoke condensed into a massive shadowy body. The shadow king's body continued to grow until he loomed over James and Shay.

"This is more what I was expecting," James commented.

"Just fucking kill it already," Shay shouted, motioning to the shadow king. "But be careful. That's not just a crown. That's the damned Eye of Pluto!"

"I thought you said it wasn't necromancer shit?"

"It's not." Shay waved her flaming blade. "It's not like the armor and swords were necromancer artifacts either."

The shadow king batted the chest out of the way. It flew to the side of the room, crashing so hard against the wall, the lid wrenched off. The pieces fell to the floor. Other than the loud redecoration, the creature produced no other noise. He took a silent step forward, his glowing gaze fixed on James.

Let's just get this shit over with.

James marched toward the shadow king. "I don't know if you're Pluto or just another magical rent-a-cop, but this is kind of a special day for my wife. So, sorry, fucker, you're going down. If the best you can do is throw shit, this will be over quickly."

He crouched and leapt into the air, bringing back his blade. The shadow king swung his arm, which connected with James. With a grunt, he crashed into the wall.

Minimal damage, Whispy reported, disapproval flavoring the thought.

"That all you got, bitch?" James roared.

He rushed toward the shadow king, who took another swing. James pushed off, launching over the massive enemy's arm. The shadow king yanked his arm back, but it was too late as James arrived at his throat. His blade cut through the tenebrous form with almost no resistance, and the body disappeared into the nothingness from whence it had come. The shadow king's crown shot up with a crackling pop while James fell to the floor, landing with a loud, echoing thud.

The crown fell. Shay sprinted toward her prize. A last-second jump, tuck, and roll saved it from colliding with the hard floor. The silver aura from her defensive artifacts flickered for a moment.

Neither of us got a scratch. That works.

No adaptation achieved, Whispy replied. *Minimal tactical usefulness from encounter.*

James ignored the whining symbiont and nodded at the huge smile on his wife's face. There were some things a man couldn't buy, like the joy he could give his wife by cutting through a giant shadow man with his alien armor to steal an ancient artifact.

Shay lifted the crown with both hands and let out a whoop of joy. "Nice. Very nice. Now let's get the fuck out of here before an entire army of shadows shows up."

James stared over his shoulder at the cave in the distance. Their trip out had been trivial. There had been no more traps and no more enemies. He wanted to attribute that to the cave understanding it couldn't win, but the slowly building scowl on Shay's face suggested something else. He'd not managed to get rid of the nagging in his gut that told him something was wrong.

"I don't get it," he finally admitted. "Why aren't you happy?"

"Because I get the distinct feeling some asshole has played me, and I'm trying to figure out the fucker's angle," Shay growled and kicked a pebble out of her way. "Everything about that cave was both too perfect and not perfect enough at the same time."

James furrowed his brow. "What the fuck does that mean?"

"It means I've wanted this artifact forever, and it conveniently shows up right when I'm about to take a trip, my first trip alone with you in a while? The archaeological details were off in the cave, and sure, I had you with me, but the level of defenses for something this important was pretty low. Too low. There's no way an artifact like the Eye of Pluto would be that badly defended. Yes, we're tough, but a lot of tomb raiders or teams could have made it through those guys."

James had been grateful to have released Whispy and not have to listen to the continued complaints about lack of murderous efficiency, but now he glanced at his chest, wondering if that had been a smart move.

"What if they ran out of power? If nobody was maintaining this place, they might not have had much magic." He frowned, considering the possibilities. "But that doesn't explain what Whispy felt. If anything, it seemed like there was more background magic than in a normal place or even a kemana."

"You might have been right the first time. There could be all sorts of explanation for the magic." Shay's eyes darted around. "I'm out of practice, and I might just be seeing screw jobs behind every shadow. It could be that the magic was there, but the spells weren't maintained well enough. The sigils might have faded from their original design. I don't know. I wasn't checking that closely." She patted him on the shoulder. "What am I doing? We went there, and we got a nice artifact, and I'm bitching about it being too easy? When did I turn into a difficult wife?"

"Before we first met?" James replied.

Shay smirked and pointed her thumb at her backpack. "I'll let that go because of the nice accessory you got for me."

"Not trying to be a paranoid bitch, but are you sure someone didn't use you to get the Eye for them?"

"If they could do all that and know all that about me, why not just get it themselves?" Shay ran her tongue inside her cheek as she thought. "But it's a possibility. There might have been spells that didn't go off because of who we were. Specific defenses against particular Oriceran races. I've seen that before. Shit. I hate this feeling."

"The good news is if they were gonna jump us, it would have made sense to do it already." James patted his chest. "And if they were watching, they know I'm not armored up right now. If this is some sort of set up, we're probably fine until we get back to the truck."

"True," Shay replied. "We also might be thinking this through too hard. I keep thinking about some dangerous witch or tomb raider having it in for me, but it might have just been some rich asshole who had the money to know about the Eye of Pluto, but he didn't have the people to get it. I did a good job of keeping my tomb-raiding identity secret, but some people knew."

"You think you're going to get a call where someone's asking to buy it soon?" James asked.

Shay nodded. "That's one possibility, and it'd explain a lot, though it doesn't explain why some of the cave features…" She sighed and waved a hand. "It doesn't matter. We've got the Eye of Pluto, and for now, it's with us. It can't get much safer. Once I get it back to the warehouse, it'll be practically impossible to find. Let's just head back to LA so I can lock it up and have some peace of mind. I'll figure out everything else later."

"Back to LA? You sure?" James shrugged. "It's gonna be a pretty short trip. I mean, we hit Jessie Rae's and the R&R

in Salt Lake, so I can't complain about barbeque, but I thought you wanted to be gone longer?"

"It's not a big deal. Once I secure it in the vault, we can spend a couple of days in a hotel in LA." Shay waggled her eyebrows. "There's more than one way to have fun without your kid around."

CHAPTER FOURTEEN

"Slow down, Thomas," Pauline called with a soft smile. They were heading back to the house after a trip to the park. The boy wanted to bring his canine namesake, but the elderly dog didn't always move as fast as the nanny preferred in public, and he could use a rest from the attentions of the overeager child.

Thomas stopped skipping ahead and stuck his tongue out at her. He was a marvel. No one would be able to guess his true age from his appearance and capabilities. That didn't surprise her, given his parents, but that didn't make it any less special. She was honored to help raise him in her own small way. So much of her early life had been steeped in blood. It soothed her soul to focus on the next generation and not on ending lives, even when well-deserved. She wasn't sure how long the Brownstone family would employ her, but she would savor the opportunity for as long as she could and do her part to make Thomas a good person.

A powerful pulse of magic passed through the area. Her

heart rate sped up, and she swallowed. It'd been a long time since she had sensed something that strong. Her hand inched toward her purse, where she kept her wand and pistol.

No one would be foolish enough to attack the son of James Brownstone. She kept telling herself that. There would be no hiding the person who dared. The authorities would be aided by the underworld. Only pain, destruction, and death would follow. James had made that very clear on multiple occasions.

Pauline's jaw tightened. She'd witnessed plenty of insanity and evil in her short life. With a casual, slow motion, she drew the wand from her purse. Thomas alternated between skipping and walking slowly, but he wasn't looking back at her. There wasn't anyone else on the street, but she wasn't worried. Everyone in the neighborhood knew she was a witch. The kind of people who didn't fear James Brownstone were unlikely to fear a single witch. They expected his friends and family to be colorful.

She moved her wand in quick, tight lines and chanted her spell. Thomas clapped as a faint glow surrounded him. He waved at her and grinned. She layered a shield on herself, wrestling with whether to grab him and run. If she were wrong, she would terrorize the child unnecessarily.

Pauline slowed her pace as a fog settled over her thoughts. She stared down at her wand. What had she been doing? She couldn't remember. Something about Thomas? The nanny hissed in frustration and raised her wand. She quickly cast another spell, summoning walls not for her body, but her mind.

Her mind cleared, and the intense magical sensations

around her were unmistakable. She raised her wand to protect Thomas' mind, but he'd stopped and was looking at her.

"Why you stop?" he asked with a frown. "I wanna go home and chase the doggie."

Pauline blinked. Whatever mental manipulation spells were soaking the area, they didn't seem to affect the boy. He'd never demonstrated innate anti-magical defenses before, but it'd never occurred to her to attempt a mind spell on him.

She jogged over to him and took his hand. "Then let's go."

Thomas cheered, happy to speed up as his nanny power-walked him down the empty street. A neighbor standing behind a window raised his arm to wave, only to collapse. Fortunately, Thomas didn't see, but Pauline's stomach tightened in anticipation.

The neighbor was a young man. She doubted he'd suddenly suffered a heart attack, and the level of magic in the area had moved from intense to oppressive. The last time she'd felt something like this was when she'd been helping to defend a team of wizards disarming a magical WMD in Lyon.

The Brownstone house wasn't far now. There was no one outside, no vehicles other than her small blue Hyundai sedan. Once they were within, the wards would equalize the situation.

"Why you sad, Pauline?" Thomas cocked his head to the side and looked up at her.

"I'm fine, *mon petit chou*," Pauline offered with a forced

smile, her grip tightening on her wand. "I could never be sad when I'm with you, no?"

A secure basement. Pauline's wards. Shay's artifacts. Multiple layers of defensive spells cast by Alison, Rasila, and other magical allies. The Brownstone home might appear unassuming from the outside, but it was a fortress when properly manned by a magical.

Pauline let out a sigh of relief as they arrived at the small, well-kept front lawn. Once she was inside and secure behind the house's defenses, she could call for reinforcements. She might be overreacting, but she'd rather be mocked than risk the boy's safety.

"I need you to stop," called a man from behind her.

Keeping her grip on Thomas, Pauline spun and pointed her wand forward. A bearded man in a suit she didn't recognize stood behind her. A wand hung from a belt holster.

"Who are you?" Pauline asked.

"You can call me John. I believe you are Pauline, correct?" The man's smile was infuriatingly pleasant.

"I don't know you, *John.*" Pauline kept her tone smooth for Thomas' sake.

"You know me now." The wizard nodded toward Thomas. "You're going to hand over the boy. We've been looking for him, this boy in the City of Angeles."

"I think I already know the answer, but I'll ask anyway to help us avoid trouble." Pauline narrowed her eyes. "You do know who he is, correct?"

"Yes, Thomas Brownstone, son of James Brownstone."

"That's me!" Thomas waved at John with his free hand. "My daddy's super-strong! Strongest in the world!"

"This world, maybe." John clucked his tongue before returning his attention to Pauline. "Given your haste to return home, you are surely aware of how precarious your situation is." He pointed up. "If not, take a look."

Pauline didn't raise her head. He might be trying to distract her and draw his wand. Instead, she looked past him to the sky in the distance. The color was off, a slight green. She hadn't noticed in her haste. A bird flying overhead vanished.

"What have you done?" She let go of Thomas' hand and cupped his ears, the wand making it awkward. "If you've harmed anyone in this neighborhood, you will die. Do you understand that? You will pay in ten times the blood."

John sighed. "My master has no desire to harm anyone in this neighborhood. I was given specific instructions to minimize unnecessary casualties. Don't worry, none of them are hurt. To ensure their safety, we've put them to sleep for now, but as I think you've figured out, we've also encased this entire area in a magical shell." He tapped his wand. "There will be no communication out, magical or otherwise, and only lesser animals lacking true intelligence can travel freely in and out of the shell. Everyone nonmagical in this area is unconscious, and I suspect any other magicals are as well. I applaud you for applying a counterspell so quickly. It's almost unfortunate that you're so competent. That makes this whole thing more unpleasant and complicated."

Thomas' eyes widened. He stared at the sky, looking more curious than frightened. Pauline wished she had his innocence, but lacking that, she would do her best to preserve his. He didn't make any move to remove her hands.

"Your arrogance will be your undoing, John." Pauline removed her hands from Thomas' ears. Stepping in front of the boy, she tossed her wand into her left hand and reached toward her purse with her right. "Do you really think you can use this kind of magic in the middle of Los Angeles without anyone noticing? The PDA will come. The police will come with AET. The Brownstone Agency will come."

"You'd be surprised what can happen with the appropriate artifacts. It's not like we didn't carefully plan this." John gestured toward the sky. "And yes, they'll notice sooner rather than later, but by then, it'll be too late. We'll have what we need." He inclined his head toward Thomas. "Now give me the boy."

Thomas stuck his tongue out at John. "You a bad man."

John chuckled. "That's your prerogative to believe, young man, but if you don't come with me, I will kill your nanny in front of you."

Thomas growled. "You leave Pauline alone! I'll bite your butt."

John wrinkled his nose in disgust. "Don't you see, witch? That boy is unnatural. He's growing too fast. His father is not of this world. We're doing this planet a favor."

Pauline couldn't stop the gasp that escaped. John nodded slowly, a knowing smile on his face. Thomas did his best imitation of his canine namesake and barked at the wizard.

"We know more than you could possibly imagine, witch," John offered.

"I've killed far more impressive men than you," Pauline snarled. She stepped in front of Thomas. "You will not have this child."

"The only reason you're not already dead is that my master wishes to minimize harm to innocents. You're not like the criminal scum we've dealt with before." John let out a long sigh. "I'm not at liberty to explain our reasons, but know that he only does what is best for your world and Oriceran. If you won't respond to reason," he raised his finger in the air and made a circle, "maybe you'll respond to force."

The air shimmered behind him. A blonde witch in a hooded gray robe appeared, a triangular pendant hanging around her necklace and her wand already in hand. Moments later, more witches and wizards appeared, all attired similarly.

Thomas tried to step in front of Pauline, but she pushed him back. The boy glared at John, but he stopped growling.

"Remember, *mon petit chou.*" Pauline squeezed Thomas' hand. "It's time for the special game of hide and seek I told you about."

Thomas nodded eagerly, but uncertainty clouded his eyes. It pained Pauline to see him frightened, and she was slightly consoled that he clearly didn't have a total understanding of the situation at hand. He didn't need to see what would come next.

John took a step forward. "Do you understand now? Do you think we haven't done our research? I understand how dangerous you are. That's why they have you watch the boy, but you can't win against all of us." He motioned to the small army of magicals. "And no one is coming to save you.

If you oppose us, you will die for no reason. If you surrender the boy to us, you will live, simple as that. Why die to delay the inevitable?"

Pauline yanked her gun out of her purse. "Shay gave me specific instructions before she left. She told me, and I quote, 'If anyone shows up and so much as frowns at our son, you kill them.'"

"A pity." John reached for his wand. "I assure you this will bring me no pleasure."

Pauline shot him a vicious grin. "I assure you, for me, it will."

CHAPTER FIFTEEN

Pauline shouted an incantation. Her wand had already been moving before she finished her last sentence. Dirt and dust blasted from the lawn to form swirling dust devils. It wouldn't stop the kidnappers, but it only needed to distract them. A fireball tore through the dust cloud and slammed into Pauline. She hissed in pain and staggered back, her shield absorbing most of the blow.

Ignoring the sting, she tossed her wand into the air, stuck her hand into her purse and pulled out a small vial. She popped the top with her thumb and shook the fine powder inside all over Thomas before grabbing her now-falling wand. Another couple of fireballs struck her, and she stumbled back.

"Pauline!" Thomas shouted. The dust around him sparkled. A moment later, a portal opened behind him, and Pauline shoved him through. The portal snapped shut. Step one of protecting her charge was in place. Now she could fight without concern.

John flicked his wand to the side and hissed an incantation. Pauline's dust devils dissipated, the dirt and rocks inside raining on the ground. She backed away, sweeping the area with her gun while keeping her wand pointed at John.

He golf-clapped. "I admire your poise under pressure, but you've accomplished nothing."

"He's safe now," Pauline yelled. "You'll never find him."

"No, he's not safe." John inclined his head toward the house. "I'm sure he's in there somewhere. Come now. The spells we've set up prevent portaling to or from this area, so I know you've sent him somewhere inside, and logic dictates it's the house. I'm sure you and Alison Brownstone have set up all sorts of interesting wards, but I have an entire team here to get through them."

Pauline edged toward her car. "Every second I delay you raises your risk. Leave now before you die."

"Oh, it's fine." John tapped his wand against the side of his head. "It'll probably be a good half-hour before anyone realizes what's going on here. We've put more than a little thought into it." He nodded to one of the witches. "Vina, come with me. I'll need your help. The rest of you kill her."

Pauline pointed her gun at John and fired three quick shots, but her bullets bounced off with flashes. He ignored her and continued toward the front porch. A rain of fireballs and ice lances forced her back. She vaulted over the hood of her car and fired more rounds. Fireballs exploded against the side of her car as she ejected her current magazine and slammed in the anti-magic bullet magazine she kept in her purse.

She stayed low as the magical barrage continued. The windows of her car shattered, showering her with glass. A moment later, her car lifted into the air. Pauline rolled to her side in time to avoid a converging blast of fireballs and a dark brown ray that sliced into the pavement. A jump to the side saved her from having her car crush her. She pointed her gun toward the closest wizard and fired twice at his head. His shield slowed her bullets, but not enough. The man screamed and fell backward.

Not taking any time to savor her victory, Pauline jumped to her feet and ran into the street, squeezing off rounds. John and Vina had already entered the house. She hissed in frustration. If she were inside, she could make better use of the wards. She needed to finish off the other witches and wizards.

Chunks of the sidewalk ripped up and rearranged themselves into a rough shield for the surviving magicals. Pauline managed to land another shot in the chest of a witch before they hunkered down behind their concrete barrier. She shoved her wand forward, rapidly chanting. Asphalt peeled off the street and coalesced into three barriers spaced a couple of yards from each other. She ran to the first, pinning down a wizard with a couple of shots. He dropped behind his barrier, and her bullets bounced off with a spark.

She took a deep breath and started moving her wand, the intricacy of the gestures building with each word of her incantation. A spin took her to her next barrier, where she finished the spell. The concrete barrier exploded on one side, knocking some of the enemy to the ground. Pauline took her opportunity and emptied her magazine into the downed magicals. The enchanted bullets ripped through their shields and bodies.

An arc of electricity crackled from a nearby powerline and struck her in the back. She cried out and fell to the ground. Her empty gun flew from her hand as her vision swam. Crawling, she kept her wand in hand. A quick roll saved her from another electrical attack.

Pauline pointed her wand at herself and spat out a speed spell. She jumped up, ignoring the pain and ringing in her ears and sprinted in a zigzag motion toward the surviving enemy. Only one man managed to keep enough discipline to fire off another spell, this time a web. She ducked, allowing the web to fly over her while reaching toward a hidden knife in her boot. The piercing enchantment served her well since the weapon ended up in the throat of a wizard before she'd returned to her feet.

The survivors of the enemy group stood scattered among the fallen bodies of their comrades, unsure of themselves. Pauline ran toward the wizard she'd just killed, rapid-firing flame bolts toward her attackers. She snatched the knife off the ground, spun, and tossed it into a nearby witch's throat before blinding the group with a flare spell. Magical power and variety could be useful, but battles weren't often determined by fancy, complicated rituals, but instead, the simple maneuvers reinforced by training and executed with muscle memory. That was the problem. Whoever these kidnappers were, the main group didn't strike her as highly trained battle magicals.

Not hesitating, Pauline again retrieved her knife, but this time, she didn't throw it. She sprinted between the stumbling wizards and witches, shoving the blade in their hearts and throats with quick, practiced motions. They collapsed, gurgling and clutching at their wounds, their blood splattering over the lethal nanny. A final pivot brought her to her last enemy. His eyes screamed for mercy, but they'd made the mistake of coming for Thomas. There would be no mercy. She slashed his throat and spat on him.

Taking deep breaths, Pauline tried to ignore the pain in her back and sides. She'd taken more hits than she would have liked, but she'd finished off almost the entirety of the enemy. Now, she only needed to take down the arrogant bastards who thought they could waltz into James Brownstone's home and get away with it.

As if willed by her thoughts, the door flew open. Vina stood there, her wand outstretched and a wicked smile adorning her face. A mass of small floating blue orbs of pulsating light blasted from rapid-fire a spinning array floating in the air. Pauline tried to jump out of the way.

The first barrage stung as they exploded in blue flame over her body. Pauline's shield failed after the second wave. She screamed in agony as the third wave pierced her body. She fell to her knees, pain suffusing every part of her and a pool of her blood forming beneath her. It wasn't until her head hit the ground that she realized she'd dropped her wand.

Vina sashayed forward, pointing her wand at Pauline. "It's unfortunate. If you'd agreed to surrender, you might have been a good recruit to serve our master." She sighed and shook her head. "You killed many, but it accomplished nothing in the end. That was why we tried to talk you out of it."

John emerged from the house. He walked over to the

fallen witch and pushed his heel down hard into a wound. She cried out.

"Where is he?" he demanded. "Tell me, and all this is over. We'll even heal you enough so you'll survive until help comes."

"Having trouble finding him?" Pauline managed a weak grin. Darkness clawed at the edge of her vision. "I think you needed this to happen quickly," she added weakly. "Quicker than you hinted, but by the time you unravel the wards to find him, you'll be fighting half of Los Angeles off. I just killed all your people. Do you think you two can win against the others who are coming?"

"No one will come before you die, witch." John ground his heel into the wound. "I don't do this because I enjoy hurting people. I do this to protect people."

"Fuck you. I do this to protect one person!"

John knelt and put the tip of his wand against her forehead. "You just killed a lot of people. Good men and women. I'd be justified in killing you."

"I killed monsters who came for a child." Pauline hocked bloody spittle on his jacket. "You can tell yourself whatever stories about what you do that let you sleep at night, but I know if I had handed Thomas over to you, he would have been hurt."

"Tell me where he is, witch." John narrowed his eyes. "Or you die."

Pauline closed her eyes. "God, please watch over little Thomas," she whispered in French.

She held her breath. Her pulse pounded in her ears. Somehow, dying in defense of a special child seemed appropriate. A loud thunderclap shook the area. She shivered in pain and opened her eyes.

Pauline gasped. The green color of the magical shell sealing in the area was retreating, peeling away as if being eaten by an invisible creature.

"I told you," she wheezed. "They're here. You should not have sealed this area off. The second that happened, an alarm was sent."

CHAPTER SIXTEEN

"Unfortunately, it's time for the backup plan." John glowered at Pauline. "If only you hadn't been so stubborn."

"Stubbornness is a useful trait when dealing with children." Pauline coughed up more blood. "You have to have more willpower than them."

"This isn't about raising children now, witch. Your stubbornness has cost a lot of lives today, including yours." John flourished his wand, and portals opened. "But you're not the only one who can bring reinforcements now. More blood will be spilled, and it will be on your head."

"I...think you're the one who started this."

More hooded figures poured through the new portals, some with the hints of pointed ears, others carrying wands. The diversity was less important than the fact that easily three times the number who had participated in the initial assault emerged from the portals. Moments later, four-armed monsters with sharp talons loped through the portal. Pauline had heard of the Zain and James' encounters with the magical mercenaries, but she'd never seen one before.

She blinked her eyes, trying to ignore the pain and fight off the urge to give in to it. If he was there harassing her, he wasn't in the house seeking Thomas. John had miscalculated. She could tell. They hadn't anticipated her trick with the portal dust.

The sky continued its return to its normal color. The intense magic accompanying the shell faded, along with the green. Eerie quiet gave way to the roar of engines. Dropship silhouettes crossed the sun and grew closer with each passing second. It could be the agency or the LAPD. Either would do.

Across the street, another portal opened, this one much darker in hue. The tip of two shadow blades appeared first before their wielder, Alison, emerged, her face a mask of pure rage. A group of armored Drow followed her out and spread out along either side of her. They didn't look as angry as their queen. They stared at the robed interlopers with obvious eagerness to test their skills on their faces. It didn't matter why they wanted to fight, just that they would.

John's nostrils flared. He pointed his wand at Pauline's head. "You attack us, the witch dies."

"You kill Pauline, you die," Alison replied, her voice tight.

The Zain snarled and snapped their jaws toward the Drow. The elves sneered at the mercenaries, the curiosity and eagerness they'd shown toward the wizards and witches gone. Fighting for a cause was one thing, but fighting for pay was beneath them.

The dropships screamed overhead, their backs already open. Sunlight glinted off the power-armored men and women inside as they leapt from the backs of the dropships and kicked in their jet packs to slow their descent. The new arrivals trained their railguns on the gray-robed army before landing on the ground beside the Drow force.

One of the power armors stepped forward, and a familiar voice sounded from its loudspeaker. "This is Maria Hall of the Brownstone Agency to the mixed Zain and humanoid party. You will stand down immediately, or lethal force will be used. We don't give two shits that you probably don't have bounties."

Transfixed by the power armors, Pauline hadn't noticed the smaller figures who leapt out after them, a man and a woman. They glided gently to the ground, streams of light flowing from their backs and limbs. It was May and Keller.

The magicals didn't offer any immediate verbal threats as they landed and moved to add to the burgeoning Brownstone Army. Keller aimed his wand at John, but May pointed her wand at an empty part of the street. Asphalt and concrete ripped up from the road and sidewalk to form statues. They stomped over to stand in front of May and Keller. The newly arrived Brownstone Army was as absurd as it was impressive in its variety. Magic, technology, and honor-bound warriors had gathered to defend one unusual child.

John clucked his tongue and shook his head at the new potholes created by May. "Rather destructive, aren't you?"

She glared at him. "I'll fix that later, along with the rest of the mess you made. I think my creations will be able to crush the skulls of your rental monsters."

The Zain snarled and scraped their claws in challenge. One of them pointed its claws at the Brownstone agency witch. Despite the pain wracking her body, Pauline smiled, now confident in the victory of her allies. She'd done what she needed to do—stall and protect Thomas. There was no way the attackers could win.

John sighed and shook his head. He pointed his wand at Pauline. "So many wasted resources and lives today. No one else has to die. Do you all understand that? There's no way that we fight now without death. The Zain barely tolerate the concept of trying to take a prisoner alive. I didn't want to have to rely on them, but this witch forced my hand."

Alison glowered at him. "You honestly think you can win against all of us? You're either insane or stupid, but that's not going to save you."

"I admit it's unlikely, but it doesn't matter."

"Why is that?"

John smiled. "Because I know you can't win without additional casualties. I'm prepared to die." He motioned to the other robed figures. "We're all prepared to die. Every one of my group has pledged ourselves to our master, body and soul. And the Zain, well, they've pledged themselves to fight for money. So, Queen Alison, you're going to have to ask yourself how many lives are you willing to sacrifice for one? Are you willing to face foes who will fight to their dying breath? And for what? I don't know how the witch got you here, but you don't understand the situation."

"You think we didn't anticipate someone might cut this place off?" Alison's gaze dipped to the wounded Pauline, her lips curled back. "We've had a long time to set up all sorts of nice little relays using wards and artifacts. The minute you locked this place down, you alerted us. Your little spell slowed us down, but let's just say I've had recent experience with that sort of thing, and I'm pretty sure I know how you generated it." She jerked her head to the side and glared at Vina, who had been edging back to the house. "You try to go in there, and I'll make sure you're the first to die. If Pauline's on the ground like that, there's only one reason. You came here for my brother, and you'll have to kill me to get him."

"We fight and die for our queen!" the Drow shouted.

"Our boss wouldn't like it if we let his son be taken," Maria added.

"Loyalty is commendable," John replied. "Even if it's unfortunately misplaced in this situation."

Another portal opened in front of Alison. Pauline let out a quiet chuckle even as it became harder to remain conscious. The army was a foretaste of the true threat.

"You're already dead, John," she murmured. "You were dead the minute you came for the boy. If you run now, you might live longer."

"Quiet, stubborn witch," John replied. "You've done your part. Be a good girl and shut your mouth."

A Drow woman stepped out of the latest portal. Pauline recognized her as Zana, one of the Royal Guards. James' massive silver-green armored form stomped out next, long blades sticking out of both arms and claws on both hands. It was a thing of both beauty and terror, something Pauline had only seen briefly in her time working for the family. Shay emerged last, bearing a huge backpack, a silver sheen surrounding her. She held a flaming dagger in her left hand and her pistol in her right. Unlike Pauline, she'd been on a tomb raid. She probably had nothing but antimagic bullets on her. Whatever small sliver of a chance John's force had had of winning the encounter had vanished with the appearance of all three Brownstones.

No one spoke. Everyone focused on James, their expressions running the gamut of curiosity, fear, and excitement on the faces of both forces. It wasn't every day someone got to see James Brownstone in action and unchained in his intensity. He was a force of nature on his controlled days.

James broke the silence with a bone-shattering roar. John and his forces took an unconscious step back. Pauline shivered. Even the Zain backed away, their snarls silenced. A predator recognized a more lethal predator.

"Get. The. Fuck. Away. From. My. Nanny," James snarled, then lifted his arm, his next words coming out like a rumbling earthquake. "You get to choose, motherfucker. You can fight and die now, or you can wait until I track you down, but make no mistake, you're dead. I don't know why you decided to come and fuck with my house, but it was a lethal mistake. Don't even fucking try and tell me you didn't know that."

"I understood the risks quite well." John's face twitched. "And I represent my master, who is more powerful even than you. I will die for him here, and I will do my best to exchange my life for potential enemies, including you, James Brownstone."

"Your master?" James roared. "Where is he? The fucker should be here himself, not sending his pussy-ass piece-of-shit second-rate lackeys. I'll fucking tear him from mouth to asshole and then feed that shit to sharks."

The Drow clustered closer to Alison, concern on their faces. They might serve his daughter, but they'd also witnessed the terror and power of James angry and knew what he could do when properly motivated. Not only had he defeated some of their greatest warriors, but he'd also faced the old Drow queen twice, defeating her with relative ease.

James couldn't manage another intelligible sentence. Growls and snarls came out, and he hunched over, like a beast ready to pounce. The excitement of seeing her employer prepared to destroy the people who wanted Thomas kept Pauline awake.

"Who is your master?" Shay demanded, her finger hovering over her trigger. "If you're just the errand boy, you might be able to buy your way out of this. We can be reasonable." She wasn't yelling like her husband, but the murderous venom in her voice communicated the same emotions.

"I would never betray my master," John replied. "I would die before that."

"You're very close to getting that wish."

"They came for Thomas," Pauline managed to get out. "But he's...safe in his special hiding spot."

With that, her head slumped to the side, and darkness took her.

Exterminate all threats to the offspring! Whispy screamed in

James' mind. *Terminate with maximum force. Ignore collateral damage considerations to protect the offspring! This is your primary operational objective.*

A near-constant growl escaped James' mouth. This was one time he didn't disagree with Whispy. Beautiful, caring Pauline lay in a pool of her own blood, her eyes closed, her body riddled with holes like someone had blasted her with a magical shotgun. The only thing holding James back was his concern for the nanny and the risk of harming innocent people. If the wizard was as fanatical as he was suggesting, the battle might damage the house and hurt Thomas in his hiding spot. For all his fast physical and mental growth, he hadn't demonstrated regeneration ability.

It's time to show those fuckers I'm serious.

Green sparks arced over James' blade. "You have ten seconds to leave. Nine, eight, seven…"

"Gather our dead," John ordered. He slowly lifted his wand and pointed it behind him to open a new portal. The other robed figures picked up the bodies and headed toward the portal as the Zain formed a defensive line surrounding the evacuation. They'd been noticeably quiet since James' last rant.

"Tell your master we're coming for him," James shouted, powering down his energy cannon. "There's nowhere he can hide I won't find him. There's nowhere I won't go to fuck him up. I don't give a shit if he's hiding at the bottom of the ocean in Oriceran. I will find him, and I will kill him. *No one* fucks with my family. You're already dead, mother-fucker. He's dead, too. You're both gonna be less than fucking dust by the time I'm done with you. If you want to live for a few minutes longer, you should run far, far away because anyone who is near him when I get to him is fucking dead."

John bowed over his wand, his face unperturbed. "I'll pass that along, Mr. Brownstone. You should be proud of that one." He inclined his head toward Pauline. "We didn't anticipate she'd be so hard to take down. Alas, if she'd been weaker, we could have avoided all this unpleasantness." With that, he disappeared into the portal. The Zain growled and bared their teeth before backing into the portal. It snapped shut, ending the standoff.

You are fucking dead.

CHAPTER SEVENTEEN

U*tilize local Drow to follow targets,* Whispy yelled in James' mind. *Extermination incomplete. Threat to offspring remains high. Destroy all enemies.*

The symbiont continued his bloodthirsty ranting and raving. James could appreciate the sentiment, but he needed to make sure Thomas and Pauline were all right. Despite his rage, he understood it wouldn't be as simple as following the wizard. The true power behind the attack was hiding somewhere, smug and convinced of their own security.

I will find them, and I will make them fucking wet themselves.

Annihilate the enemy, Whispy replied. *Maximum destruction necessary!*

James took several deep breaths before releasing Whispy. He couldn't keep the symbiont on when he was quaking with rage. Whispy's obsession with Thomas was one of the things they shared, and there was always the chance the symbiont could use that to take full control.

The last thing the situation needed was a Vax going Fore-runner and berserk. The armor receded into tendrils, returning to the amulet. His pants and shirt were tattered rags, but he didn't care. Everyone could see him naked. It wouldn't make a damned bit of difference.

Zana gave James a curt nod. "I will gather the others, and we'll bring your vehicle and your other things here, Mr. Brownstone."

James barely heard her, let alone acknowledged her, even his beloved truck a secondary consideration despite it being parked alongside a Utah highway. He stared at Pauline's body, wondering if it was too late. He ground his teeth. It didn't matter if the wizard worked for King Oriceran himself. No one could be allowed to come to his neighborhood and his home and hurt his nanny and threaten his child. He dropped to his knees and tightened his hands into fists, frustrated there was nothing around to punch. After slamming his fist into the ground several times, he let out another bellow of frustration. Magic could work wonders, but it couldn't bring back the dead.

Keller ran over to the fallen nanny. He knelt and put his finger to her neck. "Damn. She's still alive." He cradled her neck. "Hang on, Pauline. We've got you."

He reached into his pocket and pulled out a healing potion. Gently tilting her head back, he poured the potion down her throat. Everyone held their breath, finally exhaling as some of her more obvious wounds began to close.

Thank God.

Keller scooped the woman into his arms. "I'm going to take her inside and use more healing magic."

"Good." James stood and wiped his bloodied knuckles on what was left of his shirt. Even without Whispy, the wounds would heal soon enough. That wasn't important now.

Shay walked over and squeezed James' arm, giving him a comforting smile despite the worry on her face. "Thank you, Zana. And thank you for getting us here so quickly."

"Of course." The Drow glanced at Pauline, respect in her eyes, before jogging over to join the others.

Alison released her shield and shadow blades and walked to her parents' side. They jogged toward the house, following Keller inside. The wizard gently set the unconscious Pauline on the couch and knelt next to her with his wand out.

The Brownstones ignored his spells and advanced to the locked door leading to the basement stairs, a numeric keypad and a DNA scanner beside it. James tapped in the code before placing his thumb against the silver scanner and waiting for the telltale burn. The lock in the thick metal door clicked. He threw open the door and bounded down the stairs, Shay and Alison close behind. They hit the basement in seconds. Trays and boxes lay upended or on their side, weapons and ammo everywhere. A gaping hole lay in the back wall. The wizard's people had been there. James' stomach knotted. Maybe the bastard had been stalling while one of his little assholes was escaping with Thomas.

Alison walked to a wall, placed her hand against the wood, and murmured an incantation. Bright wards appeared before a couple vanished and a new door appeared, this one simple and wooden. She swallowed, her hand shaking.

Please let him be in there.

James stomped over to the door. He stopped himself from tearing it off its hinges, not wanting to scare his son. With a deep breath, he turned the knob and slowly pulled the door open. Thomas sat inside on the edge of a small bed next to a dorm refrigerator, clutching a stuffed pig, his cheeks red from tears.

"Bad men came, Daddy," Thomas whimpered. "They said bad things to Pauline."

Shay brushed past James and lifted their boy to pull him against her chest. "We know, but it's okay now, Thomas. Mommy and Daddy are here."

James took several deep breaths and forced himself to relax his posture and hands. "Yeah. Pauline stopped those bad men until we came, and now they're gone."

"Are they gonna come back, Daddy?" Thomas whispered.

"No." James kept his voice even, his tone calm. "Daddy is gonna go find them and make sure they never, ever come back."

An hour later, most of the defensive force had departed. Members of the Royal Guard remained stationed around the house at Zana's insistence. May also remained and was finishing up repairs to the road after her repairs to the basement. Shay and James sat in their living room. They'd moved Pauline into the master bedroom. Keller's potion and spells had stabilized her condition, but they didn't need Thomas to see his beloved nanny in torn, blood-soaked clothes. The boy, overwhelmed by the excitement, was now fast asleep in his room. James was grateful for that. There would come a time Thomas would need to understand the horror of battle, but not when he was so young.

Too damned close. If we hadn't gotten here when we did, Pauline would be dead, and Thomas might have been kidnapped by these fuckers or worse.

James frowned at a knock at the door, not bothering to keep his tone polite. He was out of fucks to give. "What?"

The door opened, and a suited man stepped in, a badge clipped to his breast pocket. "I'm sorry to bother you, Mr. Brownstone. I'm Detective Tack with the LAPD. Maria tried to run interference for you, but this isn't something we can just ignore. Whatever the phenomenon was that took out cameras and drones for most of the incident, we did get some long-range video of a group of robed individuals leaving your lawn and stepping into portals after obviously suffering casualties, and there is blood out there." He inclined his head toward the lawn.

"The cops don't need to get involved," James rumbled. He gripped the armrests of his recliner. "I don't even know if those fuckers who attacked us are from Earth. And the ones killed were killed in self-defense. No one's gonna come whining about them. I guarantee you."

Detective Tack raised his hands in front of his chest in a placating gesture. "You're James Brownstone. I get it. Shit happens and follows you, and the LAPD appreciates that you do your best to keep your messes out of other people's lives. Everyone knows we have an easier job in this city because you live here, but we also have an entire neighborhood that spontaneously fell asleep. That means it didn't stay isolated to you." He motioned toward the front window. "We're taking samples for DNA tests, but if those guys weren't from Earth, then you're right. We probably won't have anything on them. We're also reaching out to the PDA and FBI for assistance on this one. I don't think anyone's comfortable with the idea that a group of magicals showed up and messed with an entire neighborhood. I know your rep well enough to guess how you're planning to handle it, but if you know anything that might be helpful, tell us now, so we can at least try to do this the right way."

"We don't know who it is," James replied. "The only thing we know is that the fuckers wanted my son and tried to convince my nanny to give him up. She told them to fuck themselves in so many words, so they tried to take him by force. She resisted to protect herself and my boy, and yeah, she killed a lot of the fuckers, but it was all self-defense and protecting a child from kidnapping. If the cops or the DA have a problem with that, you can all fuck yourselves."

Detective Tack ran his hand through his thinning hair and turned toward the door. He stopped before exiting. "Look, Brownstone. Whatever went down sounds like it's way above what the LAPD wants to get involved with, and I'm not encouraging anything in particular, but given that the only people who ended up dead in this are the assailants and we probably can't even track them down because they're hiding in some castle on Oriceran, I've been told to pass along that if you happen to *solve* this problem your own way without involving your neighbors and away from Los Angeles, no one's going to complain about you saving the taxpayers money." He offered a polite nod. "I'll show myself out, and I'll be in touch if we need anything else, but please be aware our forensics guys are going to be here for a couple of hours. We would have appreciated it if you didn't have your employee alter much of the crime scene, but too late now."

He stepped back onto the front porch, shaking his head with weary resignation. Alison already stood there. She nodded to him, entered the house, and closed the door behind her.

"This is all my fault."

James frowned. "How the fuck is this your fault? You know who those guys are?"

"No, not the gray robe patrol, but..." Alison sighed. "There was a Drow smuggling ring that my people recently busted up." She put her palm to her face. "We've located and recovered at least one of the artifacts that was smuggled by that group, the Dagger of Kaladon. It was responsible for isolating the area. It's how we were able to break through the spell so quickly. We already knew the kind of magic that might be involved, and it's similar to other magic I've encountered."

Shay sighed. She rested her head on the back of the couch. "When you say busted the smuggling ring, do you mean you killed them?"

"No, we caught them and interrogated them. They're now sitting in a Drow prison." Shay cleared her throat. "A different one than the one Dad blew up."

"Did these smugglers give you anything about their customers?" Shay asked. "Anything that might point to the identity of the mastermind? There was obviously a lot of magic involved, but that was a mixed group, so that makes it more complicated."

Alison shook her head. "The smugglers were mostly just profit-seeking scum. There were a few who thought they were part of some Laena loyalist faction, but even they were mostly in it for the money. Unless they were spectacularly resistant to our interrogation magic without us being aware of it, they are what they appeared to be: guys hoping to move artifacts for fun and profit. They don't know the real names of any of the people they delivered artifacts to. They did mention the wizard named John, but it's likely an alias."

"It's worse than that." Shay scrubbed a hand over her face. "I'd already been worried that my tomb raid was too perfect. It might have been bait to lure me away. They might have figured I'd want James with me to retrieve such an important artifact. I'll have to double-check the Eye of Pluto to make sure it's secure. They likely recovered it from another location and then planted it at that location. If they doctored the site, that might explain some of the inconsistencies I noticed. They might have some sort of special tracking magic on the artifact."

James tore fabric from his armrest and growled. "We need to find those fuckers. Can't we use their blood to track them? I should have just followed them right then and there, or killed them."

"You did the right thing," Shay replied. "Pauline

wouldn't have lasted through a fight, and they would have finished her off first."

He gritted his teeth. "She killed a lot of them, but I want that bearded fucker."

"We have to assume if they can portal and gain access to the kinds of artifacts used in the attack," Alison began, "that they know how to cover their tracks, and it's going to be harder anyway. I've already tried some tracking spells, and none of them are working. Not only that, the blood on the lawn and street is from dead bodies, it looks like." She took a deep breath through her nose. "I'll continue to investigate on my end, both through the company and with Drow resources. Rasila is, unsurprisingly, supportive of a bloody campaign of vengeance. I might be in a better position to find something out than you. Whoever these guys are, I doubt they have a bounty or run in those kinds of circles."

"We all push from every angle until we find them." Shay stood, a determined look on her face. "We have resources we can use. No one can mount an attack like that without leaving a trail, even if they're careful. You heard that cop. If we pop over to some dark wizard hidden base in the Alps and take them out, no one's going to come after us or give a shit. I think he's terrified of the idea of having to go after them."

Alison nodded her agreement, but she still looked worried. "And if they're on Oriceran? If it's on Drow land, it'd be easy. I saw a couple of what might have been Light and Wood Elves, but no Drow. The Oricerans might get worried if Dad shows up all Vaxed out. I've received my share of complaints about his participation in the succession battle. I'm not saying we don't do what we need to, and I'll tell any diplomats who show up to screw off, but the US government might get testy and worry about you violating your agreement."

"I'll call Johnston," James rumbled, staring at the floor. "Not for permission, but just to let him know. I meant what I said before. I don't care who that fucker works for. We will find them, and we will kill them. Anyone who has a problem with that better stay the fuck out of our way."

CHAPTER EIGHTEEN

"What have you done, Kalath?" Cerj shook his head, the disappointment palpable on his face. "How can one of us be so rash? You might as well be human to have done what you've done. All our careful plans and preparation are now at risk."

All three of the dragons were meeting in the same location using the same forms, but the air was thick with tension. Cerj and Makkora's servants had informed their masters within minutes of the failed raid. They'd been observing from a distance but not participating, per their masters' instructions.

"What have I done?" Kalath replied. "I've done what must be done, what is necessary. Action because of danger, and what have I done that's so wrong? I thought we all agreed the boy must be tested. I recall us agreeing that sacrifices would be necessary. I won't insult you by asking you if you remember."

"That's not what this is about," Makkora replied. "Your

efforts were too bold. Far too bold. We didn't agree to that scope of action. I had hoped you intended far more subtlety. We share your concerns about the boy, but this!"

An aerial image of Brownstone's gathered army facing off against the second wave of reinforcements appeared. It rotated slowly and shifted to different angles.

"This isn't acceptable," Makkora concluded. "This was too bold. This is not what we agreed to."

"Boldness is called for," Kalath responded with a sneer. "And I was not bold at all. True boldness would have been flying to his house and destroying it myself, not cowering behind my servants and concealing myself on Oriceran."

"A dragon laying waste to a city in Oriceran would be too much," Cerj replied. "A dragon doing the same thing on Earth would end with armies invading Oriceran, seeking to become dragon slayers, or with Oriceran armies looking for us. Our power isn't absolute, Kalath, remember that."

"The risk would have been worth it if it had ended with the death of the boy." Kalath gave a light shake of his head. "I attempted restraint, and this is what happened—a narrowing of the possibilities. Our lives aren't important if the prophecy comes true. We will perish, along with all the lesser races."

"You don't accept that you've gone too far?" Makkora asked. "I appreciate your use of spells and artifacts to minimize the damage to the innocents around in the area, but the plan has still raised attention. The Drow aren't the only ones stirred. The Light Elves are asking questions, too, along with the human authorities. Everyone understands this wasn't some small group of rogue wizards and elves."

"Let them ask all the questions they want." Kalath scoffed. "What we do, we do for Oriceran and Earth. Only we have the vision and power to do what is necessary, as we have done in the past so many times. This was why we all agreed to this so many centuries ago. Cowering because of a minor setback is unbecoming. Just because it involves James Brownstone, it doesn't change that." He walked toward Makkora, smiling at her magical display. "I'll admit my servants underestimated Brownstone's defenses and made mistakes. I won't deny that, but it's not as if I traveled to Earth and attempted to seize the boy, despite how efficiently that would have solved the problem."

Cerj frowned. "If the humans realize who was behind the attack, it will create difficulties that will doom our future efforts. They already have an innate distrust of our kind. And they have surprising ways of dealing with even powerful magicals."

"I don't fear their toys," Kalath replied. "And the violence of the child's caretaker only proves the correctness of our actions. I lost many good servants to that witch. A child who grows into power surrounded by such vicious individuals will necessarily be arrogant and uncontrollable. That arrogance will spill out until he's preying upon those around him. His advanced growth is another sign. We've been operating under the assumption that we might have decades to deal with the problem if it's the boy, but we might only have years before he can access his full potential. Delaying out of concerns of secrecy might end with both worlds destroyed. We can't take the chance the prophecy is wrong."

Makkora flicked her wrist, and her conjured recording disappeared. "It doesn't matter now, does it? Don't you see? Your actions have already doomed our efforts. We had our opportunity, but now James Brownstone is aware that someone has an interest in his child. That man killed hundreds of humans to avenge his *pet*. There is no way he'll let this go. He'll hunt us now, and that means his servants in his agency are hunting us, as are the Drow. Elements in the United States government might be participating, beyond the local city authorities." She narrowed her eyes and looked down at the ground. "Brownstone will not stop. He will not be persuaded to abandon his pursuit until we are destroyed, or he believes we are destroyed." She waved her hand and summoned an image of Brownstone in his armored form. "He's a perfect killing machine, now given a righteous purpose. It might be better to sleep again and hide from him after this failure."

Kalath bared his teeth. "Perhaps using speech is making it difficult to understand me. Should I send the thoughts directly? We have no time. The boy will come into his power soon. His growth might be accelerating. If we wait, we die."

"If James Brownstone destroys us, we won't be able to test or stop the child as necessary," Cerj offered, his voice calm. "We must consider that possibility."

"True, but he doesn't know who was responsible." Kalath sighed. "Sometimes I think spending so much time in these forms limits our thinking, as useful as it is in conjunction with our spells for hiding us from our enemies. We've been proceeding as if we're afraid of James Brownstone, as if he can't be stopped even by us despite all our power, resources, and age. He is a fearsome creature, but is he truly stronger than the three of us?"

"We can't deny his power." Cerj gestured toward the image of Brownstone near Makkora. "He has proven it repeatedly against powerful foes. His strange armor is unlike anything on Earth or Oriceran. Even we might not be able to face him in direct battle, and while he lives, the child will live. We will accomplish nothing if we are destroyed. If the child is the subject of the prophecy, we at least need to survive to confirm it and pass it on to others to save the worlds."

"I agree," Kalath replied. "Which is why we shall first take care of James Brownstone."

"But how?" Makkora shook her head. "Do you intend to send your servants to attack him again? What good will it do? I doubt any of us will be able to surprise him again for years, not until he's satisfied that those behind the attack on his home have been destroyed. We can't send him to the World in Between either. That failed against the other of his kind who attacked Oriceran before."

"I will do whatever it takes to stop Brownstone." Kalath scoffed, a derisive sneer contorting his face. "He should be destroyed anyway. His child might be a future danger to Earth and Oriceran, but he's an existing danger. Everyone relies on his restraint, but he's a killer, waiting for an excuse. We should have destroyed him years ago."

Cerj shook his head. "No."

"No?" Kalath raised an eyebrow. "Are you saying what I think you're saying?"

"We're not even sure that Brownstone's child is the child of the prophecy. This was supposed to involve minimal exposure, not open and continued warfare against the Brownstone family. Your plan has moved from the reasonable to the questionable, if not the outright foolish."

Kalath roared with all the fury of his true form. The cave shook. Pebbles and rocks shook loose from the roof and walls. Makkora and Cerj didn't move. Both stared at Kalath with faint looks of disgust. He didn't care. They would be made to understand.

"He is not stronger than us," Kalath bellowed. "We can destroy him. He is a child with a strong weapon compared to us, nothing more."

"I refuse." Makkora folded her arms. "This goes beyond James Brownstone. If we start a war with him, others will be dragged in. Blood will be spilled, including more innocent blood. For all we know, those actions might be responsible for pushing the child into the prophecy. Have you considered that possibility?"

"Open conflict with James Brownstone will inevitably lead to the discovery of our involvement," Cerj added. "And that will lead to questions about other manipulations we've been involved with concerning both Earth and Oriceran. Our enemies will multiply, and chaos will follow. We will perish."

"Those are nothing more than pretty words to cover cowardice." Kalath lifted into the air, his eyes blazing with fire. "You are cowards, and you shame your kind."

Makkora shook her head. "We are thinking about all the relevant factors and everything that must be done. You're proceeding as if we're sure Thomas Brownstone fulfills the prophecy. If we can't confirm that fact, it makes no sense to start a war we might not win. If you truly care about the worlds, you have to accept that."

Cerj frowned. "You seem more motivated by a hatred of James Brownstone than the prophecy, Kalath. Perhaps you are the one who is afraid. Are you so worried about that creature that you'll throw away your wisdom and lash out at him?"

"Do what you want," Kalath snarled. "You can cower in caves like some dwarf, but remember, we're all bound by the Ancient Pact. If you harm me, you will suffer the same harm. If we ignore this problem and you're wrong, you will have doomed Earth and Oriceran."

Makkora took a deep breath. "I will help upon one condition."

"I will do nothing to aid this insanity." Cerj scoffed and vanished, his last words lingering in the air.

"Ignore him, Makkora," Kalath replied. "I'm glad to see that you're not forgotten your duty. What's your condition?"

"I refuse to fight him directly, and I also intend to explain our reasoning to him directly."

"You think you can talk him into giving up his son?" Kalath laughed. "And you think *my* plan's unreasonable?"

"If you're determined to fight him, it's our only chance." Makkora shook her head. "I think it's at least worth attempting, but tell me. What plan do you have to defeat James Brownstone should I fail?"

Kalath nodded. "There are certain eventualities I've long since considered and relevant countermeasures I've prepared, including ancient magic that even my greatest servants and you don't know about. Remember, all we need to do to win is ensure we have someone as powerful as James Brownstone."

"And you can do that?" Makkora's brow lifted in earnest curiosity. "You have someone as powerful as a Vax?"

"Not yet, but I will soon enough."

CHAPTER NINETEEN

Someone lightly knocked on James' front door. He rose from the recliner, not worried. In the days since the attack, the constant presence of Drow and bounty hunters from the agency ensured no one would get another shot at taking Thomas. The LAPD drones lingering in the area added further security. He knew the LAPD AET didn't want to get between him and someone who messed with his family, but they might help slow down John if he showed up with a bigger army.

"It's open," James called.

The door opened. Zana stood on the other side, holding a small paper cup half-filled with lemonade. James couldn't help but chuckle at the sight of the armored Drow warrior with the drink. One of his neighbors felt bad for the Drow, insisting James wasn't doing enough to keep them hydrated, especially when it'd been unusually warm the last couple of days.

James narrowed his eyes as he looked past Zana.

William Altieri stood on his porch wearing an oily smile that only true criminals could achieve.

What the fuck? The only shit more annoying than random wizard kidnappers showing up is a random mobster showing up. He better not piss me off more than I am. I can punch him through the wall and have the Drow fix it.

"What the fuck are you doing at my house, Altieri?" James rumbled. "You don't come near me or my people without my fucking permission."

"I didn't mean to offend you." William sighed and adjusted his tie. "May I come in, Mr. Brownstone? I wanted to touch base with you regarding the recent unfortunate incident."

Zana eyed the mobster with suspicion and looked at James. "Shall I kill him, Mr. Brownstone?"

William blinked, his smooth cool lost at the threat. He looked at Zana and James, panic building on his face.

"Nah. That won't be necessary." James grunted. "Yet. And if anyone needs to kill him, it'll be me. Let him in and close the door behind us."

Zana nodded, giving the mobster a cool appraisal before ushering him inside. William was visibly relieved as he surveyed the living room.

"Huh. It's a lot more normal than I expected. But I don't know what I was expecting. Everyone knows you don't like to live it up, but this could be any—"

"Get to the fucking point," James growled. "I'm not in the best mood this week, and I really, really feel like hurting people."

"Of course," William replied. He rubbed his top lip. "The short version is that I've been selected as an unofficial ambassador to you, Mr. Brownstone, on behalf of all *family* men and other similar organizations in greater Los Angeles. We were all disturbed to hear of the attempted kidnapping, and we have, per your previous orders, been doing our best to look into things. We don't like the idea of outsiders coming into our city and threatening children."

"Oh." James sat back down. "That's what this is about?"

"Yes." William nodded toward the door. "I was also prepared to offer a mixed group of volunteers to provide additional protection for your boy, but now that I'm here, I don't think there is much we can offer between the killer elves and bounty hunters you've got."

"I don't need more guards." James grunted. "What I need is the identity of the fuckers behind this, so I can find them and kill them, preferably after beating the shit out of them."

"I understand. I totally understand." William headed to the couch and gestured to it. "May I take a seat?"

"It's a free country."

William sat. "We've done our part to check on the police department, in case there was some bullshit going on there. From what I've learned, they couldn't get any DNA matches off the blood, and the PDA is having shit luck with magical examination. They've been putting in more resources than normal. Everyone seems super-motivated."

"Yeah, that's accurate." James shrugged. "The bastards who did this collected some big-deal artifacts before coming. They were planning to cover their tracks from the beginning. It's not a surprise they haven't left a trail even if it's annoying as fuck, but I've also got my government contacts looking into it. I'm not gonna turn down help from anyone, but I don't think you'll be able to help, so don't strain yourself."

"Why is that?" William asked. "My family might mostly be legit, but there are plenty out there who aren't ready to leave the alley, you know? They might hear something."

"I'm pretty sure the fuckers who did this aren't from around here." James resisted the urge to tear more fabric from his recliner's armrest. Pauline and Alison had both needed to fix it several times in the days since the attack. It wasn't his poor chair's fault.

"Sometimes that works to our advantage," William replied. "Out-of-towners don't realize they can't just ask anyone for help and say the wrong things, but I pledge you, on the graves of my father and mother, that if we get any information about this, we will handle the bastards."

"No." James ground his teeth. "You don't handle it. You send it to me, and *I* will handle it. You understand? This is my family, and I need to be there when it goes down."

"Of course, Mr. Brownstone. We will all do our best to help you make an example of those disrespectful sons of bitches."

James nodded at the door. "Thanks, but if that's all you got, get the fuck out. I'm not in the mood for much else."

William stood. "Of course. Don't worry, Mr. Brownstone. You'll get this guy, and you can send him to Hell to join the Harriken." He waved and headed toward the door. After he opened it and stepped out, Zana watched him, her eyes narrowed, but the effect of the suspicious glare was undermined by her sipping from a paper cup of lemonade.

Everyone's helping me. That's good. We'll find these fuckers. I just hope Shay can turn something up at the warehouse.

Two hours later, Shay stormed in and slammed the door behind her, her face red. "Motherfucking pissant son of a bitch bastards. It's bad enough they played me, but then they had that fucking final punch in the stomach."

James looked at the kitchen to make sure Thomas wasn't there, but the boy was still napping. "What the hell happened?"

Zana emerged from the kitchen. "Is everything all right?" Her eyes darted back and forth as she sought an enemy to kill.

"No, it's not all right, but we were right," Shay shouted.

Zana looked to James for direction. He shrugged, at a loss. At times like this, it was best to let Shay get it out of her system.

Shay threw up her hands in disgust. "I thought we might be. Everything fit, but one part of me wanted to believe we hadn't wasted our time and let those mother-fucking ass-sucking sons of a weasel whore trick us into leaving our son."

"Weasel whore?" James blinked. "How the fuck—"

"Forget the fucking weasel whore!" Shay bellowed. She sucked in a breath and slowly let it out, her eyes closed. When she opened them again, she was quieter and mindful of their sleeping boy. "The Eye of Pluto. I've been examining it, looking for any clues that might help us. I was trying to figure out their angle."

"Yeah. I thought we agreed we were going to have Zana and May check it out."

The Drow woman nodded to Shay. "We were awaiting your direction."

"It wouldn't respond to any of the incantations or rituals I researched." Shay shrugged and scoffed. "I thought it might need a magical, but now I know it doesn't need anything because it turned to fucking dust."

"Dust?" James asked. "It self-destructed?"

Shay shook her head. "Yes, but not the way you think. I've spent years researching that thing, and I've never come across anything that suggests it needs a magical to work. And it's not a fucking banking account. It's not going to lock you out because you used the wrong password too many times." She kicked the wall, leaving a dent. "It was fake from the fucking beginning. It's like I felt. Everything about the damned cave was designed to bait me and keep me interested, but the only thing I don't get is the detail. It was done too well, actual ancient languages, the right crowd, but it was also off in a lot of ways. I don't understand how someone could get so close but leave so many flaws."

Zana cleared her throat to get her attention. "There is one possibility."

James and Shay swiveled their heads to stare at her. The Drow woman walked farther into the living room, a pensive look on her face.

Zana bowed her head. "It was our failure for not intercepting the smugglers earlier."

"The smugglers?" James asked. "They set up the cave?"

"No, that's not what I'm saying." Zana lifted her head.

"We still have our people trying to track down all the artifacts that were involved. We know they used the Dagger of Kaladon during the initial attack."

"Alison mentioned that," Shay replied. "But there's something else?"

Zana nodded. "We didn't think it would be relevant, but now I see that it might be the Many Flower."

"What the fuck is that?" Shay looked to the side. "I've never heard of that artifact."

"It's not an artifact in the normal sense. It's a magical flower. With the proper preparation and ritual, you can use it to learn truths about people and those close to them." Zana raised her hand, and a flower with alternating red, blue, purple, and black petals appeared. "It was bred using magic by a gnome with an obsession for both peace and gardening a thousand years ago. He felt misunderstanding was the cause of all conflict and hoped to create a tool that could help with that. First, he tried magic that read people's minds, but that was too invasive, too alienating, so he came up with the Many Flower instead."

James frowned. "What? He made a spy flower, and that was supposed to help?"

"It wasn't intended as such. It was supposed to be used in the spirit of love and reconciliation." Zana wrinkled her nose. "One would expect less naiveté from a gnome, but ignoring that, when he found that it was being misused and it had unexpected side effects, he stored it, unable to bring himself to destroy it."

"How does it work?" Shay asked. "And what's that have to do with the fake cave?"

Zana lowered her hand, and the flower vanished. "One

bears the flower on their person and empowers it with the positive feelings of people who know that primary subject well. You then inhale its scent during a ritual. The stronger it's charged, the more truths it can reveal about someone. And not just them, but those close to them. It's not like it can reveal everything and anything. It reflects things of intense interest and passion. It's not something you can use to learn deep, secret intricate battle plans and the like."

"Because the damned hippie gnome didn't want that," Shay concluded. "He wanted peace and love and boring shit."

James scrubbed a hand over his face. "In other words, some fucker working for that John asshole or his master has been sniffing around my friends to power up their little spy flower."

"That's what I would suspect." Zana snorted, her lips curled in a sneer. "Those cowards knew they could not face you directly, so they led you astray using a carefully crafted distraction."

"Wait." Shay folded her arms. "You mentioned side effects."

"Yes. Heavy use of the flower can lead to insanity."

"Shit." Shay blinked. "Is that something everyone knows about it?"

"Yes," Zana replied. "It's well known to people who study that type of thing. I doubt anyone could traffic in the flower and not know about that."

James grunted in irritation. "This all means that fucker wasn't lying about being dedicated. Somebody working for him or his master was willing to risk frying their mind to get information to use against us." He pulled his phone from his pocket. "I think it's time to ask around and see if anyone's been talking to our friends."

"Damn it." Shay rubbed her chin. "There are always assholes chatting up my students or other professors. I don't think anything of it because I've gotten used to everyone wondering what it's like to be James Brownstone's wife and asking weird questions."

"So, we know how they might have done the shit with the cave." James' grip tightened on this phone. "But we still don't know why they're going through all this trouble."

Zana frowned. "To prove your weakness, I would presume. If they can't defeat you, your wife, or our queen, harming your child would be almost as powerful."

Shay shook her head. "There's something more to this. Nobody expends that much effort, lives, and magic into trying to kidnap a kid just to embarrass someone, especially when said someone is famous for his unwillingness to forgive people and for blowing up buildings."

James nodded at the door. "I've got to talk to my wife about private shit."

"Yes, Mr. Brownstone." Zana bowed her head and hurried out the front door. She closed it behind her.

James appreciated that the Drow didn't act offended when he did things like that. He was leery of having them around without Alison, but they showed him nothing but respect, unlike the old days when they were obsessed with killing him on behalf of Queen Laena.

Shay frowned. "Why did you kick her out?"

"What if this is a Nine Systems play?" James asked. "If they can't get me, they might have figured getting my son is the next best thing. We know those fuckers would be willing to burn a city to the ground if it meant they could get me."

"What did the old man and the alien spook patrol say?" Shay replied.

"They said no one's detected any unusual Nine Systems Alliance activity." James stared at his phone as if an alien would call him any second. "From what they've told me, the Alliance is backing way the fuck off because they're still trying to explain away that little merc assassin they sent to Earth, while also trying to convince the government to give back the ship I helped them get."

Shay furrowed her brow and considered the idea. "I don't think it's them. Sure, the Alliance has started to play with magic, but that's a long fucking way from stockpiling things like the Dagger of Kaladon and the Many Flower, and there's no way they're going to collect a group of loyal wizards, witches, and elves to do their bidding. No. This stinks of Oriceran and Oriceran alone."

"That's good," James rumbled.

"Good?"

James looked up at her with a hungry grin. "If they're on an alien planet or ship, I can't get them, but we can get to Oriceran. We just need to keep pushing and find them." He held up his phone. "Time to make some calls."

CHAPTER TWENTY

"Fuck, I'm sorry, James," Trey offered on the other end of the call. "I never even thought it could be something like that, but now that you say it, it makes sense. I should have popped her ass right there."

"Don't worry about it," James replied. "And never take someone down in Jessie Rae's. As for the other shit, it's not something I would have thought of. This is why I hate all this magic crap. It's never straightforward."

"If there's anything I can do, let me know."

James sighed. "I will, and you've already helped me, just by confirming my suspicions. Talk to you later."

"See you, big man," Trey replied. "I'll always have your back."

James ended the call and turned to Shay, sitting beside him on the couch. "Between Trey, Maria, Tyler, and my priests, there are an awful lot of attractive women suddenly chatting them up, asking them about me in these last couple of weeks. The women acted the same from what I can tell, but they didn't all look the same."

Shay nodded. "It'd be trivial for a witch to change her appearance. The only thing I don't get is if they were trying to target you with the flower or me."

"Probably both," James suggested. "Their best shot at getting Thomas was getting us both away from him. Pauline killed almost all the first group of fuckers by herself. If it'd been both of you, they would have been dead before everyone showed up. If it was me, they wouldn't have had a chance."

"It sounds like we've done a decent job of linking the Many Flower and Dagger of Kaladon to the kidnapping attempt." Shay drummed her fingers along the couch armrest. "I'll pass that along to Alison and see if it helps with any of her leads."

Alison tugged her brown hood forward to cover more of her face. She'd already used a spell to make her look like an auburn-haired Wood Elf, but the extra protection of the hooded robe wouldn't stand out in the crowded inn. Various humanoid races mingled at the tables, pounding back drinks. It didn't look that different from a bar on Earth, as long as you ignored all the pointed ears, wings, wands, and occasional creature made of stone or giant caterpillar.

She headed toward a corner, where a gnome in a black silk suit and top hat sat, a long cane over his legs. He gave her a toothy grin. He matched the description of her contact. It'd been hard to set up the meeting, especially with Zana and others of the Royal Guard demanding to accompany her.

Their preferred investigative solution involved threats and violence. While it might be unbecoming of a queen to slum in an inn to get information, no other Drow queen had ever possessed her extensive security and bounty hunting background. Rasila was working her own contacts, but for now, they both agreed she should focus on the governing of the Drow while Alison attended to her personal family matters. The Drow saw it as a straightforward case of necessary vengeance.

The gnome lifted a small cup and took a sip, waiting patiently. Alison maneuvered past a table of loud, drunken male Arpaks, all stretching out their wings to compare wingspan and bragging about their size. She rolled her eyes.

It doesn't matter what species. Guys always have to whip it out and compare.

Alison arrived at the table. She reached into her sleeve and pulled out a small silver coin embossed with a series of interconnected circles. She tossed it on the table. "You Gidel?"

She wasn't surprised when he lifted his hand and the background noise from the inn vanished. There was a smug confidence to his face she wanted to slap off, but she wasn't there to knock sense into a gnome. She was there to get information.

"Yes, I'm Gidel." The gnome gestured to a stool on the other side of the table. "Please join me, Queen Alison."

She narrowed her eyes. "I'm not—"

"Please." The gnome pointed more insistently at the

stool. "I'm not a fool. Did you really think one of the Drow queens could meet with a suspicious gnome without someone finding out?" He pulled off his top hat, revealing a bald head, and bowed his head. "Or at least a suspicious gnome finding out?"

Alison took a quick look around the room. No one was paying any attention to her. She could have a shadow blade and shield up in seconds. Even if they got the drop on her, she could portal away and heal herself.

"I'm not going to try to kill you if that's what you're worried about." Gidel set his hat back on his head and twisted it into place. "Given the state of all things Brownstone and Drow, I think attempting to harm you now would be an exercise in utmost folly, but I do question why you came to me instead of sending one of your many loyal subjects."

"Because I'm used to checking things out myself, and my subjects lack nuance." Alison leaned forward, her gaze fixed on the gnome. "Besides, this is personal. Someone went after my brother and almost killed his nanny. They violated my dad's neighborhood with artifacts and spells. That's not something I can let stand as either a Brownstone or a Drow queen."

Gidel rolled his eyes. "Typical Drow thinking. Strength isn't everything."

"No, but it helps keep assholes away from little boys."

"I'm certainly not the only one who might be able to figure out that you're not a Wood Elf." Gidel picked up his cup and took a sip. Now that she was closer, Alison could see the drink inside was a dimly glowing azure liquid she didn't recognize.

"You're afraid of someone knowing you helped me?" Alison asked.

"I don't know yet who was involved in the attack." Gidel set his cup down. "When risking one's life, it's good to weigh the dangers, wouldn't you say?"

"Being owed a favor by a Drow queen and James Brownstone isn't a bad thing. You let that fact be known, it might make you safer by itself. We Brownstones always watch out for people who help us."

Gidel folded his hands on the table, his gaze appraising. "As I said, I don't know who was responsible for the attack."

"But I've heard you know something about it." Alison frowned. "If you're just talking out your ass, tell me now. I've got better things to do."

Gidel raised a hand. "Now, now, Your Majesty. I never lie about what I know and don't know. That's why all sorts of people come to me for information."

"Get to the damned point."

"While I don't know who was responsible for the attack, I do know someone who has information related to it," Gidel explained. "I don't know the nature of the information, other than it relates to the attack. That much I've confirmed with truth magic."

Alison scoffed. "There are ways to beat truth magic."

"Yes, but I'm a careful gnome." Gidel snapped his fingers, and a worn, folded cloth map appeared in his hand. He offered it to Alison. "This leads to a secluded clearing in a forest near here. I'll arrange a meeting in two days at noon at the location, per the contact's suggestion, but that's far as I'm willing to get involved."

"You expect me to go to a random clearing?" Alison rolled her eyes. "That screams ambush."

"A not unlikely possibility," Gidel conceded. "But my contact didn't mention requiring that you come alone. Bring your entire army if you feel like you need it. I can't guarantee you won't be attacked, but I also don't care if you end up killing this person. They're no friend of mine, merely a source of information."

"You're a real trustworthy guy, aren't you?" Alison scoffed quietly.

Gidel nodded. "You can trust someone who is honest with you about what they'll do even if it's despicable, and I've been nothing but honest." He stood and pulled white gloves out of his jacket. "Now, Your Majesty, I must depart. I have a meeting to arrange for you. Please do keep in mind if they try to kill you, I did warn you."

Alison chuckled. "I can appreciate a straightforward gnome, even a despicable one."

Gidel doffed his top hat and wandered away from the table, whistling a low, mournful tune. Alison didn't trust the gnome, but she was dubious of any ambush that began with the challenge of bringing her entire army. She didn't care about the risk. They finally had a lead.

CHAPTER TWENTY-ONE

James sat on a large rock in the center of the clearing. He was surprised by how normal the trees around him looked. None of them were moving or trying to eat him.

Zoe's fucked up my perception of what plants are like when magic's involved.

Beyond the witch's influence, almost every one of James' trips to Oriceran had involved visiting the Drow, who lived in a far starker, more mountainous territory. His current location could have been any random forest in the United States, as long as he ignored the four-legged birds flying overhead and the rabbit with antlers that bounded by. For some reason, they didn't bother him. He'd fought and killed strange animals on Earth, but he'd expected the flora to be more exotic.

I wonder what shit's like on Nine Systems Alliance planets. Do they have a bunch of crystal cities in the sky, or do they all live in weird, sad cities where the poor people live underneath while assholes eat fancy pastries above them?

Whispy kept a steady, quiet background stream of recommended threats. If anything, the symbiont seemed more shaken than James by the attempted abduction of Thomas. It was obvious he had plans for the boy, including additional modifications, but he would never be straight-forward about what they entailed. He'd long since stopped serving his primary Vax programming, so James was treating the bizarre biomechanical symbiont as a Tiger Mom. Some people got little Lisa into Harvard, and some symbionts turned children into super-soldiers stronger than anyone on the planet.

James would have preferred not to have to listen to Whispy until he needed him, but the risk was too great. When Alison contacted James about her lead and suggested he accompany her to the meeting, he wasn't going to risk getting blown up without being bonded, even if the symbiont hadn't witnessed enough blood spilled to satisfy him after the attack on the house and constantly made that clear in James' thoughts.

Increase efficiency of search for threats to offspring, Whispy sent. *Exterminate with maximum power.*

Alison leaned against a tree, one of her legs up and her foot flat against the bark. She didn't wield a shadow blade, but the speckled shroud marked a shield. James wasn't the only one worried about an ambush.

Part of him also worried about taking her away from her duty, but the other, bigger part of him was proud that she was doing everything she could to protect her brother. They might not be biologically related, but that didn't matter. It was what family did that was important, not DNA.

Alison put her fist to her mouth and cleared her throat. "Remember, Dad. If someone tries to kill us, don't *kill* them. We'll need to interrogate them. We're still in the information-gathering portion of this investigation."

"I'll fuck them up," James rumbled. "I'll beat them until they can't move, then you can do your magic shit to them, but if they're involved in trying to take Thomas, I can't let them live."

"Understood, and that sounds like a good plan. I just want to make sure we find the person ultimately responsible for all this. It doesn't do us any good if all we kill are lackeys." Alison dropped her foot and sighed. "I always knew something like this would happen. Ever since that crap that went down when he was born, I've been worrying about it. I just never imagined it'd end up in such a weird, elaborate scenario."

"Yeah, can't say I saw this coming. I thought it'd just be some dumbass local gangster thinking he could get leverage over me by going after the boy. Pauline would have been more than enough for anyone like that." James stood and cracked his knuckles. "My community outreach activities were originally about convincing fucking morons to stay out of LA, but they'll be useful to remind people about this kind of shit, too."

"When Thomas is older, you might consider sending him somewhere." Alison shrugged. "A place where he'll constantly be safe, and he can learn to control his abilities."

"Where? The School of Necessary Magic? He's not a magical." James glared at a pink lizard crawling up the tree as if it were responsible for the attack on his son. "You needed somewhere to learn how to control your abilities, and I couldn't help you with that. If he's more like me, the best place for him to be is at home."

"Maybe not there, but it's not an impossibility." Alison stepped away from the tree. "They teach magic there, but they also have shifters and a couple of other races who can't cast any spells. Sure, Thomas isn't technically *magical*, but he's different, and we don't even know what powers he might come into."

Bonding with offspring will maximize genetic maintenance and potential, Whispy insisted.

Yeah, I'm sure you'd like that, but it'll be a long time.

James grunted in irritation. "He also might not have any powers. I need Whispy."

Alison gave a light shake of her head. "No, you don't. You're more powerful with Whispy, but at this point, you regenerate even when you're not wearing him. And you've always been stronger than a normal human. Who knows what will happen to Thomas?"

"He's growing fast, sure, but he's not regenerating. He's stronger than a kid his age, but not superhumanly strong." James scratched his eyebrow. "I don't know what we'll do in the future. For now, we just need to make sure that whatever is happening with this bullshit is over soon."

He wasn't convinced the school was the best place, but he didn't want to irritate Alison. She'd ended up having to fight dark wizards at the school and in a major battle. In more recent years, they'd been in the news for other dangerous events. Sending Thomas there, even if they would accept him, might be a risk.

Something rustled in the bushes. Father and daughter spun toward the sound. James yanked out his .45. He'd already loaded it with anti-magic bullets and brought along spare magazines. Alison summoned a shadow blade and circled around toward the noise from the opposite side. He reminded himself to shoot whoever it was in the legs.

"Come the fuck out with your hands up," James rumbled. "If you make any sudden movements, you're dead. You understand?"

"No, no, no," came a high-pitched voice. The bustles rustled again, and a rat-like creature wearing a hunter-green vest covered with brass buttons emerged. It walked slowly forward, its arms in the air in surrender.

"A fucking Willen?" James narrowed his eyes. "Geeze. Just what we need."

Alison sighed. "You need to leave. We have nothing for you to steal."

The Willen's whiskers twitched, and its beady eyes darted around. "No stealing. Just taking what's been left behind. Not here for that. No, no. Not here for pretty little things. That's true. Not here for them at all." He gestured around him. "Not many pretty things in the forest that I'd like."

Alison pointed her shadow blade at the Willen. "If you try to hypnotize either of us, you're not going to like what we do to you. We've had a bad week, and it's put us on edge. We're waiting for someone, so you need to get out of here."

He bowed his head, his whiskers drooping, and rubbed his claws together. "So rude, Brownstones. So rude when I've brought you information. Good information to help you."

Minimal adaptation potential, Whispy offered, his thoughts thick with disdain for the creature in from of him.

Yeah. These guys aren't the badasses of Oriceran, but it's not crazy, what he's saying. They can get good info from hiding and being rat-like.

"You're the contact?" Alison's shadow blade faded to nothing. "You're the one Gidel sent me to meet?"

"Yes, yes, yes. Gnome with a top hat and cane." The Willen mimed the shape of the headwear. "He was asking around, and I heard things, so we traded, pretty little things for pretty little words. I got the better deal." He chittered in excitement. "Things last forever. Words stop being important soon."

The Willen kept jerking his head around like he wanted to run away at full speed. James wasn't surprised. It took a lot of balls to stand near two obviously tough pissed-off people. Whatever this encounter was, it was no prelude to a battle. An army of Willens wouldn't be able to accomplish much against either James or Alison.

"Then spill it," Alison demanded, folding her arms. "You just made it clear you've already been paid, and Gidel has his own arrangements with me, so don't try and squeeze me for more payment."

"I have pretty little words for you, Queen Alison." The Willen tilted his head. "Information I think you want, as does the Granite Ghost from the City of Angels."

"What info?" James growled.

The Willens shrank back, his tail rigid, then crouched, his tongue flicking across his teeth. He trembled.

Alison sighed. "Just give us what you have for us, and this can all be over."

"My cousin on my uncle's side has a friend who was sniffing around," the Willen replied, still trembling. "His mother's cousin heard about something big happening, so she heard about it, and then passed it along to the other cousins to share with people who cared. We can all earn good pay in different places for the same words. Excellent plan, right?"

James' jaw tightened. He resisted the urge to yell at the Willen and tell him to get to the fucking point. Scaring the creature might be satisfying, but if he knew anything useful, they couldn't let him leave.

"The information was about people collecting artifacts, a group," the Willen continued. "A group who serves something ancient, powerful, and terrible."

"We know all that already." Alison frowned. "That's not helpful."

The Willen held up a single clawed finger. "But did you know they came to talk to me the other day? One of them. A wizard in a gray robe. He had something he wanted me to pass along if a Brownstone came asking. I was surprised he knew that I knew, but I didn't question it. Sometimes it's best not to question things. Whatever this is, it won't hurt me. It'll probably only hurt you."

"What did he say?" James ground out, his voice a barely concealed cauldron of compressed rage. "What did that fucker say?" he shouted.

"That's it, Granite Ghost." The Willen's whiskers twitched, and he offered a toothy smile. "It was specific. Oddly specific. Since I don't want you to hate me and hurt me, I want to say this message is not so pretty. It is an obvious trap."

Alison scoffed and rolled her eyes. "Oh, great. Of course, it is."

"What the fuck ever." James sneered. "I won't blame you if shit goes south, rat boy. Trying to trap me is a good way to die, so don't worry about it. They won't be alive after to bother you about it if that's what you're worried about."

"This gray-robed wizard said someone he serves wants to speak to the father of the boy called Thomas, who lives in the City of Angels." The Willen motioned to James. "To you, I believe, Granite Ghost. This person will be near the entrance to the Cold Sorrow Pass in exactly three days at midnight, where the three trees are fallen to form a shape. If you want information about the boy, you must come." He waved his hand and tail. "That is all." He scurried into the undergrowth before James realized what was happening.

"Hey, you fucking rat, come back here!" James shouted. "We're not done with you."

"It's okay, Dad." Alison stared into the distance. "We got what we need, which is an invitation."

"Where the fuck is Cold Sorrow Pass?" James shrugged. "Do I look like an Oriceran tour guide?"

"I know where it is. It's in a treacherous mountain range a couple hundred miles from here." Alison shrugged. "It's infested with all sorts of nasty creatures. Hunters go in there for rare animal parts for potions, that sort of thing."

"They trying to kill me off by feeding me to monsters?" James snorted. "Like that shit's gonna work. I'm not impressed with those fuckers."

Alison held up a finger. "One, it could be exactly what it sounds like, a legit source of information. Somebody on Team Kidnapping might be afraid now that the effort failed. They might want to sell out their friends." She held up another finger. "Or it could be a trap. Probably is, but if we show up with our forces, we can—"

"No." James shook his head. "I'm gonna go alone. If I'm armored up, I'll win. Simple as that. If it's in the middle of nowhere, I can go all-out."

Alison scoffed. "You don't know that, Dad. This is Oriceran. This isn't someplace where the magic's leaking back in slowly over the centuries. Magic is strong here, and the beings and creatures who live there have been able to hone their power without hiding in kemanas and little hidden coves. Even you might have trouble."

James shot her a grin. "Like I had trouble when I kicked Laena's ass? Like that Vax had trouble when he came and fucked up an entire town and carved a path of destruction across Oriceran?" He slapped his chest. "If anything, I'm the one with an advantage. Whispy can soak up the background magic, so I can go extended advanced or even Forerunner if I need to."

Alison grimaced. "Forerunner? Dad if you do that, the government—"

"Fuck the government," James growled. "They didn't stop a bunch of kidnappers and assassins from showing up at my house. I'm not gonna go out of my way to violate my agreement, but I'll do what I need to protect my family and my son."

"I should go." Alison placed her hand over her heart.

"I've got a better foot in both worlds. They might be less willing to try something if it's a Drow queen."

"No fucking way." James clenched his hand into a fist. "I'm not risking you too, and we can't go in with an army. They might leave. Besides, you're not thinking about a third possibility."

"What's that?"

James grunted. "That this is another attempt to distract us. If I go alone, we can make sure there are plenty of strong people protecting Thomas, and I have the smallest chance of getting killed. Like I said, If I do need to get a little hot, it's better that I do it in some mountain range on Oriceran than around a bunch of people's houses."

Alison folded her arms. "I suppose that makes sense. I don't like it, but it makes sense."

Exterminate those who threaten the offspring, Whispy insisted. *Destroy with maximum force.*

We've got to find them first, and part of that means talking to whoever sent us this elaborate invite.

James nodded. "It sounds like we have a plan."

Alison sighed. "Or you're walking into a trap."

He shrugged. "Purposefully walking into a trap is a plan."

CHAPTER TWENTY-TWO

The wind howled through the narrow mountain pass. Oriceran's two moons were full, their light surprisingly bright. James maintained low-light vision with his armor in extended advanced mode as he stood in the center of three massive fallen trees. He had no idea how long the trunks had been there, but they were covered in holes and pits ranging from tiny to large. Insects, both familiar and odd, such as glowing, chirping beetles, crawled through in pairs.

Alison had delivered him via portal and planned to come back in an hour to check on him. He'd suggested not scrying just in case that frightened off their contact.

Assuming the fucker doesn't run when they see me like this.

James chuckled. His armor had originally been born of rage, but his control and integration with Whispy had advanced to the point of rendering that kind of emotion unnecessary, especially on Oriceran. If the damned Vax who came for him had been paying attention, they would have realized the implications instead of coming to Earth and getting their asses handed to them.

He turned at a bright flash. A beautiful pale woman stood a couple of yards away in a white robe. She threaded her pale, slender fingers together. With her pointed ears and silver eyes, he assumed she was some sort of elf, but you couldn't always tell on Oriceran. It was just another way Earth's sister planet annoyed him.

"Good evening, Mr. Brownstone," the woman offered quietly. "I'm pleased that you came. I was worried that you wouldn't, given the circuitous nature of the invitation, but I thought some distance between the offer and you would help you come to the right choice."

"Who the fuck are you?" James asked. "That's my first question."

"Someone who has questions about fate," the woman replied. "So, I'm helping to put them to the test."

James growled. "Why can't anyone on this planet ever give a fucking straight answer? It's always some fate shit or deep ancient secret or other bullshit. You're not so special. You're no different from humans. Just because you add magic, it doesn't change shit. It's not like I could build myself a cell phone. That's effectively magic."

The woman smiled softly. "I suppose that's true from a certain perspective, but I will note that in my case, there are ancient, powerful rituals binding and limiting me. They prevent me from taking certain actions that I might feel appropriate, but I can deliver a message, especially since someone wanted you to hear it while also concealing themselves."

James raised his arm blade, but he didn't advance on the woman. "No one's attacking me, so this isn't an ambush."

"No." The woman shook her head. "Consider it more a challenge." She turned her palm upward. A scroll tied with a thin string appeared in a puff of smoke. "This is a magical link. With it, those who aid you can open portals to a place normally protected by powerful wards, but only for twenty-hours starting one week from now at twilight. If you try to go there now, you'll find nothing, and he'll know you tried."

"The fucker responsible for sending those bastards after my kid?" James growled. "He's getting ready, isn't he?"

She nodded. "Your true foe is an ancient being, thousands of years old, with more power than you can fathom. He's not evil. Misguided, perhaps, but not evil."

James scoffed. "Lots of gnomes are old too. Is this another crazy-ass gnome with delusions of grandeur? I've met Oricerans in my day who pretended to be monsters and demons."

"I'm not at liberty to describe his true nature." The woman sighed. "But he's far more impressive than a gnome, I assure you. If I accomplish anything here, I will hope to impress that in your thoughts."

"I'll fucking kill anyone who fucks with my family," James snarled. "That's all I care about. Everyone on Earth seems to get that, but I guess the lesson wasn't spread across Oriceran."

"I understand your anger." The woman placed her palms together and bowed her head, a haunting look in her eyes. "I would wish you luck, but I'm honestly not sure that is wise."

"You afraid of this guy?" James asked.

She shook her head. "He can't harm me for the same reason I can't harm him, but I should tell you before you go to face him that his actions aren't motivated by malice."

James growled and smashed his foot into a nearby trunk. Glowing beetles streamed out, fleeing the angry giant.

"Malice?" James bellowed. "He sent people to kidnap my son. They almost killed my nanny."

"There is a prophecy," the woman announced, lifting her head. "A prophecy about a child born of two worlds who will bring destruction to Earth and Oriceran." She pulled her hands apart. "A child born of two worlds. Destruction comes in his wake. He will consume Oriceran and Earth. The threat hides in the land that opposes demons."

"Is that supposed to impress me?" James crunched a splintered piece of wood under his armored foot. "Anyone can make up shit like that as an excuse."

"It's not an excuse," the woman insisted. "It's a true prophecy. Unfortunately, the only way to test if your son is the child of prophecy is to perform a ritual that will cost his life."

Destroy all threats to offspring, Whispy screeched.

James roared, the noise echoing through the pass. Animals and birds hidden before scattered, fleeing the perceived threat. The woman didn't move. She stared at James mournfully.

"Why the fuck would I ever allow that?" James snarled.

"If he died, but you knew he'd destroy the worlds, wouldn't that offer some comfort?"

James stomped toward the woman until he was right in front of her. He towered over her slender frame. It'd be trivial to slice her in half.

"This isn't the story of Isaac, and you're not God, and even that ended with a substitution." James growled. "I don't give a shit what a bullshit Oriceran prophecy says. I know all about how they've been wrong. You people think you're so perfect with your magic, but you've fucked things in ways humans never have."

The woman continued looking at his eyeless helmet, no fear in her eyes, only pity and sadness. "And what if you're wrong? What if the prophecy is right, and your boy grows into power and misuses it?"

"Then he'll have to answer to someone worse."

"Who is that?" the woman asked.

"Me."

The woman sighed and stepped back. She knelt and set the scroll on the ground. "Everything I've said is the truth. You'll have to make a choice—"

"I've chosen," James interrupted. "I choose to come in a week and kill the fucker responsible."

"So be it." The woman vanished.

Keep this shit up, and it won't be my son destroying the two worlds.

CHAPTER TWENTY-THREE

Two days later, James sat at his kitchen table with Shay, Alison, Maria, and Trey. Alison had arrived after his meeting with the informant as scheduled without trouble. He'd returned to Earth, then called Maria and Trey to explain the situation and asked them to come for a meeting. He couldn't order them, only ask as a friend.

Alison held the scroll. "It's some sort of magical artifact with a sympathetic link. I suspect the location is some-where near where you met the woman. If there is some-thing ancient and powerful holed up there that's using magic to hide, that might explain why that area has an unusually dangerous reputation."

Maria wrinkled her nose. "They let random mountains be overrun by dangerous creatures on Oriceran? You have all those magical armies. I don't get why that would be a problem."

"It's…different over there. You have to remember that." Alison shrugged. "Different races have their lands and kingdoms, but a lot of the area is far wilder than people on

Earth realize. When magic's everywhere, it changes things. Adds wonder and danger in a way humans can never fully appreciate. Here be dragons is a real thing over there, and you're starting to see that here, too."

Shay snorted. "With our luck, there's probably a dragon behind all this shit."

"Big fucking deal." James grunted. "I've killed a three-headed dragon before, so I don't care who or what it is—dragon, gnome, elf, or giant rat. I'm going to fight that fucker, and I don't give a shit who it pisses off, whether it's our government or King Oriceran. Whoever's behind this shit is all but spitting in my face by telling me to come after him, so I figure, why not take up the bastard on his offer?"

Alison set the scroll in the center of the table. "Rasila has been conducting backchannel diplomacy on our behalf. Basically, the word is if we keep it reasonable, everyone's willing to look the other way, especially since it seems like the fight isn't going to be anywhere near a major populated area, and whoever's responsible started it by attacking Pauline and Thomas."

"What does 'keep it reasonable' mean?" Shay asked with a frown.

"No strategic-level magic or strategic-level anything." Alison nodded at James. "I'd suggest Dad keep it to extended advanced mode. Any of my people who come along won't use major rituals. We can't risk the Great Treaty. It wouldn't just be this current threat then. It could easily end up with large swaths of Oriceran targeting us."

James gripped the edge of the table so tightly the wood cracked. He let up when Shay glared at him. "Fine. We get together some people, and we go kick the fucker's ass. If I could beat Laena with extended advanced, even when she was all high on souls, I can finish off whatever gnome or elf or fucking super-turtle who's at the other end of the rainbow this time."

Zana stepped into the kitchen and bowed her head. "My queen, I have news."

"Go ahead," Alison replied.

"Her Majesty, Queen Rasila, has asked me to pass along relevant intelligence to your family." Zana took a deep breath. "She's found evidence that suggests Kalath might be behind the attack."

Alison scrubbed a hand over her face. "Oh, for fuck's sake. Now things are starting to make sense. Thanks, Zana. I'll call you if I need anything."

Everyone turned toward Alison as the Drow warrior departed. Alison sat staring down at the table for a moment, nibbling her lip in deep thought.

"Who the hell is Kalath?" Shay asked, breaking the silence. "Is he a big deal?"

Alison looked up. "Let me give you a little background. After I became queen, Rasila gave me a crash course on major potential threats to the Drow. That way, we could better coordinate and watch for them. She divided them into high, moderate, and low possibilities, but also divided them into high, moderate, and low threats. Kalath is low-possibility but high-risk threat."

"Who the fuck is he?" James rumbled.

"A dragon, an extremely ancient one," Alison replied. "He's been involved in a lot of things throughout Oriceran history, some major, some minor, most only suspected. The thing is, he goes to sleep for long periods of time. Has his minions do his bidding—wizards, witches, elves, that sort of thing—and they wake him up only for the important stuff. He isn't supposed to be awake right now."

"I don't give a shit about some arrogant old dinosaur." James snorted. "I've killed dragons before."

"No." Alison shook her head. "You've killed small dragon-like creatures on Earth. You haven't faced an Oriceran dragon who has been mainlining pure magic for thousands of years, Dad. Not only that, but Kalath has also been known to work with other dragons. He might be as powerful as you."

"So what?" James slammed a fist on the table, leaving a dent and earning another glare from Shay. "The Vax who came to LA could have destroyed this whole planet. I fucking beat them. I can beat a dragon, even if he's old."

"And if there's more than one?"

"There was more than one Vax." James pushed his feet. "This changes nothing. I'm not afraid of a dragon. I'll just toss off a prayer to Saint George before I start the fight."

Trey whistled. "Damn, big man. I thought you had balls, but they are so big, they might as well be motherfucking planets."

Maria furrowed her brow. "You might be able to beat a dragon, but I don't know if the rest of us can."

Shay inclined her head toward the scroll. "A dragon might be behind all this, but we can't be sure we'll be facing one right away. This master has operated through pawns this entire time. This meeting he set up for James is probably just about setting a trap so he can send those assholes after Thomas again once we're over at Oriceran fighting another set of assholes."

"Then we make sure Thomas isn't here," Alison suggested, rubbing her chin. "We can have Pauline take Thomas to the Drow's lands. If I'm there, along with Rasila and our warriors, we can protect him. No assassin will be able to easily slip in, and even a major attack force like the one that attacked Pauline would be outgunned."

"What if the dragon shows up and decides to lay waste to your capital?" Maria asked.

Alison shook her head. "Dragon, or not, I think whoever is behind this will be far more circumspect about a massive frontal assault on the Drow lands than messing up a random LA neighborhood. Attacking a Drow city is a declaration of war that risks the Great Treaty and might tempt us to use strategic-level magic. Other races wouldn't stand by idly and allow it, even if it meant going up against Kalath. Still, we can't be sure. He already outmaneuvered us once by dividing us, but if the goal is to ultimately get Thomas because of the prophecy Dad was told about, I want to make sure the boy's got an army guarding him."

James lowered himself back into his seat, calmer now. "It sounds like you're saying this Kalath can be killed."

"Of course he can, Dad. He's a dragon, not a god. But he's also an ancient dragon who might be able to take on an entire army. I'm not sure you can take him on by yourself, and having a few bounty hunters on your side might not be enough."

"No, it'll be enough." James gave her a predatory grin. "If it's one-on-one and I don't have to worry about anyone else, I can fucking end that lizard."

"You don't want to join in on the attack, Alison?" Shay asked, looking surprised.

"I want to protect my brother," Alison replied. "And Thomas is going to be scared. Having Pauline will help, but I think having Pauline and me there will keep him calm."

"It's fine." James nodded slowly, the plan starting to form. "The Drow, Alison, and Pauline can protect Thomas. Me, Shay and whatever Brownstone forces who want to volunteer will show up and meet the dragon."

"I'll still send warriors if they're willing to volunteer."

Maria chuckled and shook her head. "This is going to be interesting. I'm going to help kill a dragon before I retire."

Trey clapped once. "Always a fun and deadly time with James Brownstone."

Shay gave the scroll a cool look. "That dragon asshole is cocky. He thinks he can win."

"Yeah, he does." James nodded. "So let's teach that reptile how us mammals do shit."

CHAPTER TWENTY-FOUR

An army of men and women stood in the sprawling yard outside the Brownstone Agency's main building. Obstacle courses filled the area behind them, along with a commanding and windowless black building, Fort Shorty. Years of modifications and technological upgrades had transformed the once-modest training area into the ultimate bounty-hunting simulation center.

Fort Shorty was one of the reasons not many other bounty hunters had joined the facility's namesake in death on missions. A man or woman who worked for the Brownstone Agency might come in with their own experience, but most had never had access to the level of equipment and training provided by the company. In truth, the Brownstone Agency didn't just train bounty hunters, it effectively trained an army, and now it was time to deploy that force.

Maria stood next to James as he surveyed the bounty hunters. "This is pretty much everyone, James, both from

LA and Vegas. The others are deep off the grid on vacation, or handling important family matters."

"That's okay," James replied. "We can field a decent force if a fourth or a third of the guys agree."

Trey nodded to one side of the formation, comprising the Brownstone bounty hunters from Las Vegas. A redheaded witch, Victoria Stone, Trey's right-hand woman, stood near the front, her hands folded behind her back. The wizard Ramon, another Vegas magical, watched James with an excited smile. Other bounty hunters, magicals and non, mostly looked curious. No one knew why James had called them in, but when the big man called, you didn't ignore him.

He stepped forward. "As most of you already know, my house was attacked recently. Magical forces attempted to kidnap my son. My nanny was almost killed. She tore the attackers a new asshole, but she was overwhelmed by simple numbers. She's okay now, thanks to Keller."

Murmurs and curses filled the air. Anger flashed in the eyes of the Brownstone employees. To disrespect James was to disrespect them. It was a transitive property of blood vengeance.

"We've learned that there might be an ancient Oriceran dragon behind all of it," James continued. "And to get to the fucking point, he's pretty much given me the time and place he wants a showdown. I might be semi-retired, but when a dragon sends fuckers after my kid and he tells me he wants a fight, I figure I'll give him one."

"Brownstone represents!" yelled a man from the back—Carl, one of the OGs with Trey's boys. The man had graduated from street punk to one of the best snipers in Los Angeles.

"An ancient dragon?" Victoria asked, worry playing across her face. "There's going to be a dragon showing up to fight you on Earth? That can't be right. The PDA would shit itself, and the Army and Air Force would be all over that."

James shook his head. "Not on Earth, on Oriceran. Look, I'll keep it simple. We expect to walk into a major battle, not just with this dragon, but with his little bitch-ass servants, almost all magicals. He also has been known to use Zain mercs. We don't know if this whole thing is a misdirect, so Thomas will be secured in a safe place with an army guarding him while I take a force to a remote location on Oriceran and fuck shit up." He motioned at the crowd. "I've got friends in the government pulling strings for me, and my daughter's doing shit on her end in Oriceran. We're in the clear for this as long as we don't nuke anything or shit like that."

"Brownstone's gonna nuke his ass!" shouted Daryl, another OG.

Scattered laughter broke out in the crowd. Not everyone looked amused. Many looked surprised or worried. James couldn't blame them. It wasn't every day your boss walked in and explained he wanted you to go to war against a dragon.

"And I'm going to be straight-up with you," James continued. "This dragon wants to test my son as part of some doom prophecy shit."

Trey laughed. "The dragon's causing some doom

prophecy shit. If he hadn't thrown down to begin with, you wouldn't be after him.

"I don't know about no prophecies." Lachlan shrugged near the front of the crowd. "And no offense, James, but do this dragon and his mercs have bounties?"

James smiled. He remembered when Lachlan was a little bitch who wanted to quit the agency. Most of Trey's boys had transitioned from gang members to bounty hunters with ease, but Lachlan had needed extra work to whip into shape. Now he was one of the best.

"No," James replied. "They don't. I'm not gonna sit here and say you have to do this shit. This is a bounty-hunting agency, not my own personal army. I'll provide bonuses for anyone who wants to participate, and it's strictly voluntary. If necessary, I'll just go with the people who've already agreed." He motioned to the crew behind him, consisting of Trey, May, Keller, and Maria. "But I think we're gonna need more people. I have a feeling this bitch dragon's gonna do his best to hide. Like I said, this is personal, and if none of you want to risk your lives for my kid, I'm not gonna be a bitch and hold it against you."

Lachlan fluffed his lapels and stepped forward. "No way I'm staying behind when I can tell my girlfriend I helped beat down a dragon and his friends."

Victoria pulled out her wand, grinning. "I haven't been to Oriceran in years. It'll be nice to be able to do magic more freely."

Isaiah raised his fist in the back. "We're all family here, and anyone who fucks with one of us fucks with all of us. I say we go and show this dragon bitch how we Brownstone bounty hunters do things."

More cheers and calls to volunteer rose. James smiled. He'd stepped back years ago, but even in his heyday, he never felt he did enough with the employees, leaving a lot of it to people like Trey and Maria. He'd been a man who wanted to solve all his problems by himself, but who sometimes accepted that, no matter how powerful a man was, he needed help.

Maria stuck her fingers in her mouth and whistled loudly to cut through the raucous crosstalk. She glared at the crowd with an intensity only a woman who'd spent her entire life corralling strong, boisterous men could master. The crowd quieted, stray comments leaking out over the following moments until finally silence returned. Everyone watched her, waiting for her to continue.

"This crap is taking too long," Maria shouted. "Let's make this easier. Anyone who *doesn't* want to volunteer, raise your hand. Like James said, we won't hold it against you."

She surveyed the crowd, waiting for people to opt out. After thirty seconds, no one had raised their hand. They looked at each other, faint disapproving frowns on their faces as if daring someone to give up.

I don't give a shit if it's peer pressure. It's still voluntary.

"Okay." Maria smiled at James. "That makes things easy. It looks like everyone's coming. Is that going to be okay with the government?"

James nodded. "We'll have some of the Drow Royal Guards to help with the portals and also the attack." He turned to Maria and lowered his voice. "I never thought everyone would volunteer."

"Having more people for an attack shouldn't be a problem." Maria shrugged. "The more people we have, the easier it'll be to cut through any cannon fodder. The way this Kalath's been hiding makes me think he won't be in the front waiting for us."

"But that means we're taking all the Brownstone Agency people away from LA and Vegas," James replied. "Shit could happen. Criminals might think it's playtime."

Trey laughed. "Yeah, don't worry about it, James. We all keep the punks in line, but it's not like the cops and the PDA aren't still around. I think we can all be gone for a day or two without our cities falling apart."

"Huh." James chuckled. "Yeah, that makes sense. I'll leave organizing everyone to you. If you need me to okay additional equipment, let me know. We'll be going up against strong magicals, so I want every last man and woman equipped with anti-magic deflectors and anti-magic magazines."

Trey grimaced. "Damn, James. Everyone? We're definitely going to have to source some more. That's a lot of money."

"I've got plenty of money. Most of it is sitting around doing nothing." James headed toward the building. "Get it done before we head to Oriceran."

CHAPTER TWENTY-FIVE

James nodded in satisfaction as he surveyed the gathered army. He was already in his extended advanced armor, though he hadn't sealed his helmet yet. People always found it unnerving to talk to him when he lacked facial features.

His people stood in Drow territory atop a remote plateau tucked away among mountains a decent distance away from the capital. Although most of the arrivals were waiting professionally, some found themselves entranced by the two moons hanging in the sky or the unusual birds. For most of the army, this was their first trip to Oriceran.

James hadn't been impressed during his first trip to the planet, or the first trip he could remember. At the time, he'd been focused on fighting. His next trip had involved a similar problem. The more he thought about it, the more he realized that almost all his trips to Oriceran had involved him tracking someone to beat down or kill.

Could be worse. I figure this indicates I'm meant to stay on

Earth. Fucking dragon, if you're so old and wise, haven't you heard of the Harriken?

The black-suited rank-and-file bounty hunters represented the bulk of the Brownstone army. All wore anti-magic deflectors around their necks and were armed with assault rifles with anti-magic magazines. James had had to stop by three banks in person to explain why he was transferring millions of dollars out of his accounts.

Maria stood in the middle of a circle of power armors. The Agency didn't have a huge number, but between their railguns, heavy rifles, and rocket launchers, they could be damned effective. Magical shields could be impressive, but simple, technological destructive power could close the gap.

A small number of bounty hunters, like Trey, possessed their own artifacts, both offensive and defensive. Most of those artifact bearers were leaders in the company, so it wasn't difficult to organize the other hunters around them. The company's small number of witches and wizards were interspersed among the non-magicals, including Ramon, Keller, May, and Victoria. A large squad of rock statues stood next to May, ready to bash in the heads of anyone opposing the Brownstone army. She walked past the statues, casting last-minute enhancement spells.

Drow warriors stood in a tight formation off to the side. James was surprised when Alison announced they would be sending so many warriors with him on the final battle, but she assured him the bulk of her forces would remain near the capital to protect her people and Thomas should Kalath or his forces launch a more direct attack.

I hope this shit doesn't start a war, but there's no way I'm standing by and letting my son be threatened.

All secondary casualties are irrelevant, Whispy insisted. *Protection of the offspring is paramount.*

I'm glad we agree. Soon, we'll get to kill a lot of fuckers.

Yessssss.

Shay tightened the straps of her backpack and her tactical vest before double-checking her pockets and belt. She'd brought along her standard defensive artifacts and weapons, but she'd also dug deep into her artifact warehouse to find toys she hadn't handed off to Alison or Lily. Not one to ever ignore the practical, she'd also made sure to bring plenty of grenades.

"It's been a long time since I've led this many people into a fight." James looked at the army, taking in everyone's expressions: the laughter, the frowns, the fear. "This is a lot bigger than when we took on the Council, and this shit isn't even about bounties. It's kind of weird when I think about it."

Shay clipped a grenade to her belt. "Remember, everyone who is here volunteered. No one's forcing you to do anything, so don't overthink it. Right now, we have a job to do, and that'll eventually involve fighting a dragon."

"I know, but I'm still wondering if I shouldn't have handled this shit on my own." James shook his head. "This is fucking dangerous. This might be the most dangerous thing they've ever been involved in."

"You think a bunch of Drow warriors and professional bounty hunters don't know things are dangerous?" Shay rolled her eyes. "They're not grade-schoolers. Get over yourself, James. Sometimes friends and family risk themselves to help others. If I, of all people, have learned that lesson, you can get it through that thick, barbeque-obsessed brain of yours. They *want* to help. They *want* to protect Thomas. And, shit, some of them just want to prove they're lethal on not one planet but two."

"I can't and won't let the dragon have our boy," James rumbled. "The truth is, I don't care who I have to kill or sacrifice to protect him. I don't force anyone, but I don't have it in me to push them away. He's my son, and I will destroy everything to save him."

Shay patted her stomach. "I'm the one who housed the little punk for nine months. I'm with you. I don't give a shit what happens today as long it ends with this Kalath in bite-sized pieces. If King Oriceran or the State Department wants to bitch us out later, it's fine. It'll work out. It always does, if only because they're afraid of you." She shrugged. "It's not like the Fixer showed up to threaten us. That's got to mean something."

The Drow contingent broke formation. The unarmed conjured shadow blades. Others drew their weapons and shouted in alarm.

What the fuck? Is Kalath ambushing us?

The Brownstone bounty hunters drew their guns and rushed toward the Drow. The power armor squad whirred to life and bounded to support the Drow. May's statue army remained back, the witch surveying the scene, but Victoria, Ramon, and Keller all charged forward with their wands out.

James crouched and jumped. He sailed into the air and landed with a loud thud next to the Drow. "What the fuck is going on?" he growled.

"Someone's opening a portal," a Drow warrior explained. She frowned. "The magic doesn't feel like ours."

James extended a blade from his arm. "Then someone's ready to fucking die ahead of schedule. Let's give them what they want."

A swirling portal appeared, lacking the dark tinge often seen with the Drow. James expected a gray-robed wizard or Zain to emerge. Even a massive dragon would haven't been a surprise. What he didn't expect was an attractive blonde Light Elf in clinging dark blue leggings and a matching tank top. The Drow blinked in surprise, looking at James for direction.

"Nadina?" James retracted his blade. "What the fuck are you doing here?"

The Light Elf wrinkled her nose and let out a long sigh. She looked down at her clothes, and then around at the armored Drow and the suited bounty hunters. "I kept asking myself, 'What should I wear to a major battle?' And I figured there was going to be a lot of running and jumping, so I figured why not this, but now I feel like I made the wrong choice." She shrugged. "There was that incident with us, but it's honestly been a long time since I've done this sort of thing."

"Forget the fashion." James shook his head. "I'm not going to a barbeque cookoff."

"No, you're not." Nadina smiled. "Just because I'm a pitmaster, it doesn't mean I don't keep my ear to the ground, especially when it comes to you. I heard you were gathering an army, and I also heard that despite the news reports playing down the incident at your home, someone came for your son." She held out her hand, and a flickering flame appeared. "I told you before, James. I'm not defense-less, but if it wasn't for you helping me, I might have ended up dead. I owe you for before, and I think this is a way to pay you back, as both a friend and a pitmaster."

James raised his hand and circled with his finger to tell his men to disperse. "Nothing to see here. Everyone go back to getting ready. I'll figure out what to do with her."

The Drow eyed the Light Elf with suspicion but walked away. Some muttered quiet insults under their breath. Nadina rolled her eyes.

Lachlan laughed. "Damn, Nadina. Can I get your auto-graph? And you're looking hot in that outfit."

Trey glared at him. "There's a time and a place, brother. Do you really think this is the time *or* place?"

Lachlan's shoulders slumped. "But it's Nadina!"

She shot him a warm smile. "After this is all over, I'll be more than happy to sign autographs and pose for selfies."

Lachlan perked up and lifted his chin to offer Trey a smug look. He adjusted his tie before nodding to Nadina and motioning for his team to come with him.

James sighed. "I don't think you get what's going on here, Nadina. We might be going up against Kalath. You heard of him?"

Nadina winced. "He's awake?"

"Supposedly." James shrugged. "I can't guarantee your safety. I can't guarantee anyone's safety. Everyone here is a volunteer, and they understand the risk."

"I'll leave the dragon to you." Nadina shook a finger. "But I'm sure there's something else I can help with. I think you forget that I'm far older than I appear, and I'm trained to be able to defend myself. Since you brought this entire army with you, I suspect you think you'll be running into someone or something else before Kalath."

Shay came over, eyeing the new arrival with skepticism. She glanced at James and Nadina, shaking her head. "Somehow, it always comes down to damned barbeque with you!"

"I'm not gonna turn down help as long as they know what they're getting into." James nodded slowly, a smile creeping onto his face. "It's like you said, Shay." He raised his voice. "Okay, everyone, it's time to saddle up." He pointed to the sky. "Looks like twilight to me, and we have a date with a dragon."

Portals opened in front of the different squads. They performed last-second weapons checks and smoothed their features. No one knew what waited on the other side of the portals. They might arrive in an immediate battle or be forced into an annoyance game with a flying reptile who should have stayed asleep.

High adaptation potential, Whispy announced. *But adaptation is secondary objective.*

What? Since when do you not care about us getting new exposure?

Primary objective is the elimination of all who threaten the offspring. Recommend maximum application of force for efficient termination of all targets, regardless of species. Longer engagement time risks enemy forces escaping to present a future threat to the offspring.

I got it, James thought. *Kill them all, and do it fast.*

Yes. For the offspring.

James sealed his helmet. The last time he was on Oriceran, he'd fought a queen, and now he was fighting an ancient dragon. At the rate things were going, he might find himself facing King Oriceran in the future.

I tried to live a quiet life. I tried to stay out of shit, but fuckers keep coming at me. Prophecy? Who gives a fuck? Time to bust up some prophecies and make some legends.

James threw back his head and roared in defiance. The Drow raised their weapons and cheered. The Brownstone bounty hunters joined in with their own shouts and cheers. It was time for the army to face their foe.

CHAPTER TWENTY-SIX

James was the first to step out of a portal. No enemies stood on the other side. No magical enemy attacks fell from the sky. No deadly traps sprang and pulled him into the rock and dirt. The area was similar to the mountain pass where he'd met the informant, with scattered rocks and trees. But unlike before, a large narrowing canyon led up to a gargantuan cave.

This dragon is a little on the nose. Or is this another way of trying to be intimidating?

The first group emerged from the portals, all taking a moment to sweep the area and get their bearings. They visibly relaxed once they'd accepted there would be no immediate fight. The warriors and bounty hunters spread out into their pre-determined formations.

Shay pointed at the sky with a slight frown. "It's more green than blue. That's...different."

"Just like at the house, from what Pauline said," James replied. "But the Drow have the Dagger of Kaladon now. How can Kalath be using it?"

"He's not, but that doesn't mean he doesn't know how to do it without an artifact. If he's as powerful as Alison said, he's learned some tricks over the years, and he has more magic to work with over here." Shay murmured an incantation, and an argent sheen surrounded her body. "Without the scroll, we would have never been able to find this place, I bet. That means he's decided the best way to handle this is to clear the playing field."

"Fatal mistake." James grunted. "I guess even ancient dragons can screw up."

"When it comes to you, yes." Shay patted her small backpack. As long as the Drow could focus on the scroll, they could use it to open portals, but James decided his wife should be the one to carry it. He was confident he could win, but if too many people got hurt, they might need to retreat. Volunteers or not, he didn't want to throw their lives away.

We've got a good, well-trained group here. We can do this. If Kalath comes, I'll just tell them to let me handle him.

Drow, bounty hunters, and power armors continued to stream out of the portals, some stomping on the ground in a coordinated fashion, their attempt at purposeful intimidation, but there was nothing to frighten. James didn't see any animals, not even any bugs. If the magic around the area was similar to the Dagger of Kaladon, animals wouldn't have been affected, but they might be smart enough to avoid any areas with large magical reptiles.

For all I know, Kalath flies around eating sheep when he's awake.

Nadina shivered upon exiting the portal. "The magical

power here is impressive. I haven't felt this much in a while."

"Not too late to turn back." Shay smirked at the elf. "This is more a bounty hunter-warrior thing, not a pitmaster thing."

"I always pay my debts." Nadina opened her mouth. Overlapping melodies came out, and a glow surrounded her body. Bright orbs of white light winked into existence and orbited her head. "I imagine although we won't be able to talk about it immediately, it will eventually be useful to my brand to be associated with this."

"Useful to your brand?" Shay scoffed. "Seriously?"

"A woman can do the right thing and still benefit from it." Nadina winked.

The last stragglers emerged from the portals, and the Drow closed them one by one. The light din of conversation slowly died out as the army awaited enemies or direction.

James pointed to the cave in the distance. "I'm guessing our boy lives there."

A booming voice sounded from around them. "I greet you, brave warriors. It takes courage to face a powerful foe, and I've learned that you already understand you're not facing a common enemy. I am Kalath. I have lived while generations of your kind have withered and died. No one here is greater than I."

Shay rolled her eyes. "Likes to be theatrical, doesn't he?

"I know that James Brownstone has been told about a prophecy that might apply to his son," Kalath continued. "His son might be one who threatens both worlds. It was for this reason alone that I sent my servants to take him. If

James Brownstone agrees to turn over his son, no more people have to suffer. There will be no more unnecessary deaths. It's the logical thing to do—to sacrifice the one to save the many."

Lure and exterminate primary threat, Whispy demanded. *Destroy with full power if necessary.*

Don't worry. We're not leaving until he's dead.

Trey stepped toward the growling James and shook his head with an easy smile. "Can I take this one, big man? I might be able to give a little better speech."

James nodded slowly. "Go ahead," he managed to get out between growls.

Trey coughed to clear his throat before he shouted. "I'm guessing you can hear me all the way back there, Kalath. You probably already know who I am since you sent your witch to chat me up so you could do some weird-ass spy magic on James and Shay. I know you think you've got all sorts of reasons for what you're doing, and you know what, they probably seem great to you, but all I know is that James Brownstone is my friend. He helped lift me up when my own society was ready to toss me aside and wait for me to die." He gestured to the bounty hunters. "He built the Brownstone Agency and has helped turn LA and Las Vegas into some of the safest big cities in America." He nodded at the Drow. "He took on a blind half-Drow girl who wasn't his own and showed her the love she needed until she became a queen, and every time some crazy-ass homicidal magical motherfucker showed up, who was there to take him down? James motherfucking Brownstone, not you, Mr. Big Dragon."

A cheer erupted from the bounty hunters. The Drow

shouted their approval and stomped the ground. May smirked and flicked her wand. Her rock statues stomped in unison with the Drow.

"You are a child, Trey Garfield," Kalath replied, pity in his voice. "You know nothing of the dangers that confront our worlds. What I do, I do for millions, if not billions."

"I might not know all that, but I know that James Brownstone has saved Earth before, and there are billions of people on Earth." Trey looked at James, a hint of uncertainty on his face. He knew James' secret, but not everyone in the agency did. James nodded back. If people wanted to ask questions later, they could figure out the answers then.

"James Brownstone is not his son," Kalath answered. "His son will bring calamity to both our worlds."

"You don't know that!" Trey yelled. "You admitted that. You're going to kill his son as a test? You're fucked up. You think because you're a thousands-of-years-old superdragon that his son's life doesn't matter. That our lives don't matter?"

"No, foolish human!" A loud roar shook the area. "I do this because I value your lives more than you. Now, you will give me the child, or you will die here for nothing but defending the child of a monster who will grow into a monster."

"There's only one motherfucking monster dying today, you scaly bitch," Trey shouted, "and that's you." He pulled his artifact gloves out his pockets and slipped them on. "Because we're here to help James Brownstone beat your ass. No one is being coerced. We all agreed because we believe in him more than you."

James smashed his fist into his palm. The impact was so

strong, it echoed around the area. "You made a big deal of luring me here, Kalath. Stop wasting our time. The only chance you're gonna have to get at my boy is to go through them and me."

"So eager to die, Brownstone?" Kalath replied. "Then do so."

Bright portals rapidly opened and spread across the canyon. They accompanied another thunderous roar by Kalath. The Brownstone army spread out, everyone readying their weapons or spells. May's statues jogged in front of the rest of the army as the vanguard. They were ready to become dragon slayers.

CHAPTER TWENTY-SEVEN

The first wave of enemies rushed through the portal and onto the battlefield. James had been expecting Zain, wizards, witches, or elves in gray robes. A kilomea or some crazed dwarves with magical spears and hammer wouldn't have been out of place, given his luck the last year. None of those emerged.

Instead, dark panther-like creatures with six legs bounded through some of the portals. Giant scarlet wasps with eight sets of wings streamed through others, spiraling into the air. Faceless wooden giants stomped through some, each holding a long pike. Sunlight glinted off the strange whorled metal surfaces of the weapons. James didn't know if they were magical, but it wouldn't hurt to assume as much. What was there bothered him less than what wasn't.

What the fuck? Where are the wizards? Where are the Zain?

Force composition irrelevant, Whispy responded. *Terminate all enemies and defend the offspring.*

If the gray robes aren't here, they are somewhere else. That's probably not good news for my guys, but you're right. If we just kill every fucker in front of us, that'll solve the problem.

The panthers shrieked, sounding more like bats than cats. James wasn't impressed. They rushed forward, outpacing the rest of the enemy land force. Wasps continued to appear from the portal and head into the air. Their massive swarm dotted the sky, but they seemed uninterested in making immediate attacks on the Brownstone army.

A decent distance separated the two armies, but it was obvious after the opening seconds that numbers were on Kalath's side. There was no let-up in the monsters and giant automatons coming from the portals. Even in a best-case scenario, this wouldn't be an easy fight.

You're gonna get your favorite, Whispy. Lots and lots of killing.

Maria's voice bellowed from her armor's loudspeaker. "Everyone proceed as we planned. Remember your fall-back positions, and that if the dragon comes out, we leave him to James."

Some of the Drow looked disappointed at that command. James chuckled. He wasn't sure if he should be impressed by their willingness to take on a dragon or contemptuous of their desire for a battle they almost certainly couldn't win. As for him, he wouldn't allow himself to entertain the possibility that he wouldn't win. This wasn't about him. It was about his son and that left victory as the only acceptable outcome.

Maria raised her railgun and aimed toward the closest panthers in the approaching force. The other power armors, already spread out on both sides of the Brownstone army, targeted different components of the enemy army, with half aiming at the burgeoning swarm in the sky. Keller and Ramon stood near the back with most of the other Brownstone magicals, performing almost synchronized wand movements while they chanted to fuel a ritual they'd discussed during the operations planning. Pulsating arcane symbols carved through the skies above them, growing in number and stacking in horizontal layers. May's statues strode forward, a wall of solid rock in front of the army.

Fuck. I remember when it was just me opening an app and finding some bounty to drag in. Now I've got all this shit. So much for Keep it Simple, Stupid.

Destroy the enemy, Whispy insisted.

Yeah, yeah. That's coming. Keep your tendrils on.

James jogged after May's statues. He had no idea how long the fight would last. Keeping his big moves and abilities in reserve until he needed them seemed prudent. Six-legged panthers and wooden giants were a minor obstacle blocking him from his true target. If Kalath was half the badass everyone kept saying, it might not be as simple as cutting his head off.

Is there enough magic around here for me to go modified Forerunner?

Yes, with reservations, Whispy replied. *Length of modified Forerunner mode before possible interface damage unknown. Recommend reserve use until primary power source available.*

Makes sense. The few times I used it before, the fights didn't last long. I'm sure I'll get pissed off before this is all over.

Then easier transition into Forerunner will be possible, Whispy replied.

Shay, Trey, May, and Victoria kept pace with James, the latter witch bathed in golden light from the illuminated glyphs covering her suit, her wand tight in her right hand. The Drow warriors sprinted along with his group, shouting and cloaked in their shields, their blades of metal and shadow ready to be unleashed with eagerness on the enemy.

I keep thinking it's weird where Alison ended up, but a Brownstone leading a bunch of warriors isn't that strange.

"Give them hell!" Maria shouted.

Her railgun screamed to life. Her initial shot reduced several wasps to a fine red mist. The others nearby got the point, their movements becoming erratic, but they stayed in the air and away from the armor. Additional railgun rounds, rockets, and bullet torrents ripped from the other power armors with a focus on the ground targets. The attacks shredded panthers and blew giants in half.

The other bounty hunters strode forward at an almost sedate pace as they opened fire next with controlled, careful bursts. Each man or woman picked their own target, but the large number of hunters firing created a constant crack like a single monstrous machine gun that cut down many of the advancing enemy.

The first panther creatures to survive the Brownstone wave of death reached the frontline and one of May's statues. Two leapt on top of a statue and ripped at it. Their claws and teeth gouged out stone like it was soft flesh. James didn't want to see what they could do to a person.

A line of conjured shadow crescent spells blasted from the Drow and sliced through the nearby panthers and giants. Aided by Maria, the rear bounty hunters' gunfire continued to suppress the wasps above them despite their superior numbers. James had worried about airpower, but right now, being in the air didn't accomplish anything but make the wasps obvious targets.

A wooden giant rammed his pike through a statue, which exploded in a shower of rock shards. Other statues pummeled the giant. Each blow knocked a huge chunk off the enemy, and they managed to pulverize him before a panther and giant returned them to their roots as well. May muttered under her breath in frustration and moved her wand in an intricate dance. The rubble from the first statue swirled to form a replacement.

I've seen her control a lot of statues, but how long can she keep that up?

One of the panthers leapt toward the distracted James. He sliced the creature in half without stopping his forward jog. Its blood splattered him, and the two pieces bounced off his armor. The constant, relentless gunfire and explosions from the Brownstone army continued to mow down the advancing enemies. The Drow and James shredded the small number of survivors who made it through, but as they closed in on the portals, they had less time for their fire support to take out their enemies.

Trey sighed and pulled his gun. "Damn, big man, you're not even letting me get close enough to do my thing. Zoe's going to complain later."

"If it makes you feel better, I'm not trying hard." James removed four of the six legs of one of the panthers with one swipe before finishing it off with a free head operation on his next.

"Not trying hard?" Trey put rounds into an advancing

panther and scoffed as the creature rolled to the ground. "All these years, and you still need to work on your people skills. Look out!"

One of the giants stabbed James. The spear bounced off, and James decapitated the wooden soldier and sliced his body in half. Trey winced and gazed at James, his head half-turned, his expression laden with anticipation.

"No big deal." James shrugged. "I'm not gonna blow up."

Maximum adaptation already achieved against existing attack type, Whispy reported.

I doubt our old dinosaur has anything all that special out here. He's relying on raw numbers. Can't say I'm impressed. I was expecting badass wizards with nice tricks, not the rabid six-legged kitty brigade and evil scarecrows.

White fireballs blasted from the interlacing mystical symbols floating around Keller and the others. The rapid attacks produced a stream of explosive magical death. The fireballs arced as they flew over the battlefield, some heading into the sky to consume wasps in bright explosions. Others crashed through the ranks of the enemy army, leaving scattered charred bodies and blackened wood.

Good job.

It'd been a long time since James had witnessed his wizards crack out that kind of ritual spell. The Los Angeles and Las Vegas authorities took a dim view of fireball machine guns being used, even against dangerous enemies, but in the hidden mountains of Oriceran, there was no one to get hurt other than the horde. There was absolutely no reason for his bounty hunters to hold back like they were constantly doing on Earth.

Victoria stood near James, chanting with her wand outstretched. She barely moved, and her eyes were half-closed. He would have preferred more direct and immediate monster killing, but he knew the witch had something special in store.

Shay reached into her pocket and pulled out what looked like a tiny origami bird. She rubbed its wings and uttered, *"Yati almawt min alsama"* before tossing it in front of her. The paper bird sprouted feathers and grew as it flapped into the air, where it became a massive black-and-gray bird of prey casting a huge shadow over the battlefield. Its sharp hooked book and talons looked like they could shred James' F-350.

When the hell did she get that?

The gigantic bird dove toward the enemy, raking the panthers with its claws. Its first run gutted three. A mighty bite snapped a giant in half, although it speared the bird's side. The monstrous bird bled droplets of bright white light rather than blood, but the wound only enraged it more, leading to another pass and more enemy casualties.

Shay supported her conjured friend by opening fire with her pistol. Rather than the coordinated bursts of the bounty hunters, she sent careful, deliberate headshots against the panthers. Despite their danger and size, her bullets penetrated with ease. The wounded monsters fell to the ground with shrieks, tripping their brethren and setting Shay up for easier follow-up shots that added more red to the already blood-soaked ground.

Victoria finished her spell. A massive golden beam erupted from her wand and carved through Kalath's front rank, weakening with each it passed through until it merely scorched the last in the line. The attack had obliterated the initial enemies with ease and Victoria nodded, a satisfied look in her eyes. Monsters and automations rushed to fill the gap, which made them easy targets for Drow spells and bounty hunter guns. Bravery and an indefatigable nature were no match for mass death-dealing.

James cut down two giants who had survived the gauntlet. The enemy forces might vastly outnumber the Brownstone army, but there were so many bodies and so much wood strewn about that the reinforcements were stumbling over them. Kalath's forces were being slaughtered.

What's he doing? It's obvious he can't win this way. But we can't make much progress here either. Maybe the magicals will need to close the portals, but can they win against Kalath?

A power armor rocket barrage vaporized a group of wasps. Every time one of the winged monsters tried to dive, a fireball or bullet stream ended its attempt. They weren't accomplishing much but dying.

The enemy portals remained open, feeding new monsters onto the battlefield. The Keller and Ramon-led bombardment alternated between striking the enemy and blasting the portals. They were scorching the ground and kicking up a thick cloud of dust, but the portals didn't close or falter.

A May rock statue grabbed a panther by the neck and squeezed until the bones cracked with an audible pop, and the creature's head slumped. A giant avenged his ally by impaling and exploding his killer a second later, only for Drow shadow crescents to converge on the wooden giant and cut through his leg, arm, and center of his chest. He fell, and his own spear impaled him before he burst into a cloud of wood chips.

Magic-canceling spears, maybe? Who the fuck knows?

Nadina raised her hands, making careful, quick movements. She opened her mouth, and harsh, dissonant notes escaped. A bright lance of pure light appeared and started growing. The normally docile pitmaster ignored the carnage around her, including James punting a panther into the air and slicing open its stomach as she continued growing her lance until it was over ten feet long. When she released it, James thought she was going for the wasps, but the spell exploded in a bright flash and released dozens of smaller lances. They riddled the enemy line to pierce the panthers and giants.

Damn. I should have been trying to recruit her for the agency all these years instead of just talking about barbeque. She fought well before, but she's got a lot more up her sleeve than I realized.

Victoria timed another beam attack to hit the same area. It was effective, but the mountains of corpses blunted the full strength of her attack. This beam didn't penetrate as many enemies as her first had. She arguably accomplished more clean-up than tactical dominance.

Shay ejected her magazine and slapped in a new one. "I think he might just be trying to run us out of ammo and energy. These assholes aren't even getting close, and you're not going all out. If he's got any sort of limits, we'll easily win."

"Having a limit and pushing someone to their limit are two separate things," James replied. "I probably can't survive being thrown into the sun, but telling someone I have 'limits when it comes to hot things' isn't useful information."

"I'll keep that in mind."

Shay's bird continued raking the flanks of the enemy. It had accumulated wounds, producing a surprisingly beautiful trail of glittering light, but the creature only flew faster and attacked with greater intensity. A wasp managed to survive the deadly skies to dive-bomb James. He grabbed it by the thorax and threw it down on the ground. It turned, but he crushed its head with his fist.

"Fucking dragon hiding behind bullshit monsters he probably ordered from fucking Oriceran Costco," James rumbled. With a growl, he snatched up the body of the wasp and threw it into another low-flying wasp. The two collided, and the living wasp spiraled out of control, not able to recover before a Drow leapt into the air and gutted it with a spinning shadow blade attack.

Fuck. What is *your limit, Kalath?*

James could only imagine what would have happened if the dragon had used this type of attack against his home. It would have been impossible to explain away. The Oricerans would likely be outraged, even if they didn't care for James, but that didn't mean it couldn't happen. Every monster they killed here would be one less Kalath could use against his family on Earth.

"Eat this, assholes." Shay yanked out a frag grenade with a grin. She pulled the ring and hurled it like an Olympic champion into the enemy line. The explosion shredded clustered panthers but didn't do much more than scorch an advancing giant. A Drow near Shay finished the giant off with a black orb that exploded with blue-purple flame to blast the giant apart.

Everywhere James looked, his forces were slaying panthers, wasps, and giants, but their rate of emergence from the portals appeared unchanged. Overwhelming force was a good strategy only when you were sure the enemy didn't have unlimited resources.

"This shit's endless." Trey stopped to reload and shook his head as new monsters scrambled over the piles of corpses filling the battlefield. "I've already lost count of how many of those things I've killed."

The rearguard bounty hunters and power armors continued their steady advance toward the frontline. The rapid fireball ritual continued spitting death but stopped on occasion, allowing the enemy horde a brief moment to advance. Bullets and explosives filled the gap before it resumed spewing magical death.

"The endlessness might be the point," shouted May, wiping sweat off her brow. "Even on Oriceran, magicals will strain themselves and have to give up. Everyone else will run out of ammo."

"We just need to win before then." James grunted and kicked half a wooden giant out of the way. "How long can Kalath keep this shit up? We haven't even lost any people."

Half the portals disappeared. James grunted in satisfaction. It looked like Kalath was already losing the war of attrition. The portals reopened, but this time behind and to the sides of the Brownstone lines, the steady stream of monsters otherwise unchanged.

"Shit," James rumbled. "That could be a problem."

CHAPTER TWENTY-EIGHT

The panther creatures, wooden giants, and massive wasps now rushed at the Brownstone army from all sides. Maria and her power armor squads broke into groups without orders to engage the new arrivals, the instant results that only careful training could provide. The other bounty hunters instinctively turned to face the enemies closest to them. Their attacks remained as effective, but the lack of concentrated fire was allowing more enemies to close the distance.

Fucker. Did he lure us in on purpose?

A giant stabbed at Lachlan. The bounty hunter spun to the side, and the spear ripped through his suit. He hissed in anger and emptied half a clip into the giant. The now-hole-filled attacker collapsed. Lachlan smirked in victory before a panther sideswiped him. He screamed in pain and fell, blood soaking his shirt. His fellow bounty hunters filled his attacker with bullets until it stopped moving.

Carl rushed over to pull him back and give him a

healing potion. "Stay with me. You can't go out because of something weak like that."

Every man and woman in the agency had at least one healing potion. They were expensive, but James had been purchasing them in bulk from Zoe since the founding of the agency. A healing potion couldn't save someone who was dead, and even with his generosity, there was only one guaranteed medical intervention per bounty hunter. They didn't have enough support magicals with the group for general healing. They couldn't allow the enemy to continue to close in.

Fuck. The anti-magic deflectors aren't gonna do shit against basic strong claws. That fucking dragon just wanted to fuck with us. He is probably throwing those kinds of creatures at us just because it'll dull our edge.

Screw you, Kalath. You're going down no matter what.

A Drow warrior cried out as a giant pierced her shoulder with his spear. Thankfully, and unlike the statues, she didn't explode. Shay and Trey gunned down the giant and the Drow collapsed, clutching her shoulder. Other Drow formed a half-circle around her facing out. James was confused by their lack of aid until shadowy tendrils extended over the wound to seal it.

A group of giants caught Shay's bird on a swoop. They impaled it from different directions and pushed the spears deep into its body. The bird let out an ear-splitting cry before disappearing in an explosion of glittering sparkles.

"Well, shit," Shay muttered. "I'm not gonna find another of those for a while, but he did a good job."

James nodded before thrusting his blade through a

nearby panther. "I'm beginning to think nuking the place isn't a bad idea."

The rapid fireball array switched targets, now concentrating on pounding the portals and the wasps in the air. There was too much of a risk of hitting their own people with the change in the battlefield deployment. Keller had specifically highlighted that risk.

Victoria took short, ragged breaths. Sweat matted her hair to her forehead. Her powerful beam attacks were impressive, but they were taking all her strength. She tossed her wand into her left hand and drew her pistol. Knowing when to use magic vs. non-magical tools was what separated professional survivors from the foolish magicals who ended up dead.

Maria and a squad of power armors closed on James' location. She swept through the nearest line with a stream of railgun fire, creating a cloud of dust, blood, fur, and wood. "James, we're going to get pushed back like this. If this is Kalath's home turf, we can't be sure he can't keep spewing shit at us for hours or days like it's some World War I crap. We're going to get overwhelmed. I've been radioing the other power armors. We're going to coordinate an attack. You can break through then. You need to get into that cave, find that dragon, and tear him a new asshole."

James grunted. "You want me to leave you all out here while you're being attacked?"

"We'll fight as long as we can to keep your escape path clear," Maria replied. "Remember, Alison's watching us, too. If necessary, she can reinforce us, but we'll do our best in case he decides to send some of these monsters to the capital."

Shay jerked her gun from left to right to put bullets into the brains of charging panthers. "That sounds like our best plan other than using magical nukes. Fuck the Great Treaty."

"I'll watch your back, big man." Trey grinned. "Just like the old days. You're tough, but you could get buried in these critters."

Victoria nodded. "I'll come, too."

Nadina finished launching another bursting light lance and smiled. "I feel like I haven't done enough, so I will as well."

"Thanks, everyone, but Trey, I think it was more me watching your back." James cut through the spear of a giant and then sliced it from head to legs.

"Ouch, big man."

"Whatever works."

May fell to one knee. Her statue army continued to fall to the enemy, and she continued to summon them back as quickly as possible. Kalath wasn't the only one who could make a play using attrition. "Have you considered, James, that they're stalling for another reason? That the goal here isn't to simply overwhelm us with numbers?"

"Then what is the fucking goal?" James asked.

"I'm sure you already noticed it, but there are no gray robes here, no Zain." May forced herself to stand and glared as two of her statues smashed a panther's skull. "The only things here are mindless monsters who probably have no more thoughts or souls than my statues. If the gray robes aren't here, where are they? From what we saw at your house, they had a decent number, and one of them is probably worth thirty of these monsters."

Shay frowned and tossed another grenade. "They're getting ready inside, I'd bet."

"Fuck," James muttered.

Shay reached into her backpack and fished out the scroll. She handed it to May. "You guys will probably need to escape more than us."

May took the scroll and tucked it into her belt. "Be careful."

"Maria, clear the way," James ordered. "Shay, Victoria, Trey, and Nadina, you follow me, and we make a break for the cave. From the looks of it, the portals are all opening this way, which means once we break through, it's harder for them to follow us."

"Power armor squads, get ready to execute the plan," Maria ordered. "Mr. Brownstone needs pest control on his walking route."

The cessation of the power armor rockets, rifles, and rail guns was noticeable even among the chaotic din of the unfolding battle. The seeming disengagement of the power armors emboldened Kalath's forces, and they attempted to press the attack, but the tired but still stalwart Drow stepped up their attacks. Thin shadow crescents carved through enemies, and dark orbs and lances exploded around them. The Brownstone Agency bounty hunters continued their fire, with many now resorting to the grenades they'd previously saved. Enemy after enemy fell in a bloody or burned heap, their temporary advantage turned into another defeat.

I'd almost feel sorry for them if they weren't mindless monsters.

"Here we go!" Maria shouted. The power armors fired simultaneously to form a deadly tapestry of railguns, rockets, and rifles aimed at a narrow lane between two of the portals. The combined volley swept through the area, blowing the monsters and constructs to pieces. Explosions shifted the parts and debris, spreading them evenly. They'd plowed and tilled the field.

Without hesitating, James charged into the newly cleared breach. Shay, Trey, and Victoria ran alongside. Nadina brought up the rear, an overly delighted look on her face.

She's enjoying this shit way too much. I hope I haven't corrupted her.

Monsters stormed out of the portals on either side of their area, but Drow and power armor suppression fire stopped them from getting a swipe at James' insertion team. Soon, James and the others were behind the enemy lines and sprinting unmolested toward the cave.

Now that James and the others were clear, the remainder of the Brownstone army could spread out their attacks again. Carl, along with other snipers and the power armors, picked off emerging monsters who tried to turn and head after the new vanguard. The Drow continued slicing and tossing off deadly spells near the front, with the support of May's statues. Her creations had dwindled in number, but the witch wasn't done yet. She stood, a determined look on her face.

James closed on the cave, not running at full speed to keep the others with him. While he wasn't worried about facing an enemy he couldn't defeat, traps, and convoluted magic could mess him up. It'd be helpful to have a tomb raider, two magicals, and a man with a good eye for detail. Keeping people alive might come down to seconds, given the situation unfolding outside the cave.

The group kept running until they hit the cave mouth. Orbs of bright light appeared near the roof of the cave, illuminating the entire area. Rather than an irregular natural formation, a polished floor covered the entrance, leading to narrow hallways with open obsidian doors. The loud noise of the battle sounded in the distance, but it no longer overwhelmed.

Kalath's booming voice returned. "I'm impressed that you could rally so many people, James Brownstone. You're a far more impressive creature than I realized."

James growled and spun at the entrance, shifting his gaze from door to door. "You still going to hide? Aren't you tired of being a cowardly little shit?"

Kalath laughed as one of the doors swung open. "I'll make it easy for you, but this means nothing. I'm not afraid of you. Coming here will prove a fatal mistake for you."

"I'm sure that kind of smack talk makes you seem like a big deal on Oriceran, but on Earth, it's weak shit."

James and the others rushed toward the door. He kept expecting portals to open, but nothing happened. The only noise was his group's heavy, resounding footfalls.

If he's not opening portals, that means he's got people here already. Or does it mean he's at his limit with the portals outside?

Combat capability of enemy forces is modest, Whispy sent. *Internal forces are unlikely to be significantly stronger.*

This shit isn't about winning. It's about him slowing us down. May was probably right.

"This whole assault is proof of everything I've been saying," Kalath offered. "You're an inhuman monster, James Brownstone. You wear a human skin, but you're not human, now are you? You're nothing but a killing machine that revels in mass slaughter."

James scoffed. His group passed through the doorway into a long, narrow hallway with a couple of forks. Wisps of glowing light appeared, flowing toward the end of the hallway. It could be a trap, but at this point, he didn't want to waste time second-guessing himself. Kalath had gone out of his way to invite him. On some level, the smug dragon must want to finish it. James would be happy to oblige.

"Is that the best you got, you dinosaur fucker with a bad breath problem?" James shouted. "I came to terms with what I am a long time ago, so give it the fuck up. You're embarrassing yourself."

"You've come to terms with the evil you've done? The blood you've spilled? That makes sense for a ruthless killer."

James chuckled. "The only person I confess my sins to is my priest. Given what you're trying to do, I don't want to hear a bunch of shit about blood being spilled. Fuck you. This isn't about me. This is about you coming after our son."

Kalath let out a long sigh. "And yes, the mother should be considered, too."

Shay smirked and pulled out her dagger. She activated the flame before speaking. "I don't know about dragons, but human mothers protect their children. You're not going to guilt-trip me into letting you kill my son, you arrogant flying fossil-fucker."

"All your ranting doesn't change that you're a ruthless killer who plays at being a teacher," Kalath replied. "You think a love of knowledge and your family absolves you of your crimes. It's pathetic. Delusional in a way that only humans can be. The fact you hide it is proof."

James didn't worry about Kalath revealing anything. Victoria and Trey already knew about Shay's background. Nadina's amused expression didn't change. Anyone who hung around James Brownstone would eventually figure out there was a reason he'd ended up with Shay. For that matter, anyone who talked to Shay for more than a couple of minutes sensed the lethal potential barely concealed beneath the surface.

Everyone had something they didn't care to share from their past. It just so happened that Shay didn't want to volunteer the information she used to kill people for money. It was more of an embarrassment than a dark secret.

Destroy the primary threat to the offspring, Whispy insisted.

He is close, and I promise you I'm not leaving the room he's in until you get your wish.

"Shove a diseased cow up your ass, dragon boy," Shay shouted. "You think I'm impressed just because you used magic? I don't care about your Many Flower or whatever other bullshit magic you used to scope me out. You're not going to get into my head, especially when you started this shit by coming after my boy. We're going to find you, and James is going to carve himself off a new trophy."

James nodded, smiling under his helmet. His wife could stand up for herself. It didn't matter if she was dealing with a mob boss, an ancient dragon, or an annoying dean. She refused to take anyone's shit.

A brighter light shone at the end of the hallway. They continued running forward without any interference. James' confidence grew with each step. All he needed to do was get to Kalath, and he could end it all. He wasn't what he once was. Whether it was arrogance or simple recognition of the truth, he didn't think there was an enemy he couldn't beat if he went all-out.

"Don't you see?" Kalath asked. "You have James Brownstone, who is a tool of conquest and an inhuman monster paired with a woman who chose to become a killer, a monster who is very much a human. You play at different disguises, but you're both vicious killers in your hearts. Don't you understand that means you'll raise a vicious killer? Whether you believe in the prophecy or not, it's inevitable."

Nadina, Trey, and Victoria remained quiet as they hurried along with determination on their faces. James didn't know if Kalath thought his revelations would influence them, but he didn't miss the dragon's pointed ignoring of their backgrounds. He was familiar with Trey's and Victoria's, but he was curious if Nadina had some hidden darkness.

What the fuck am I doing? It's not the time for that kind of shit.

"If you know all that shit about our backgrounds,"

James replied, "you shouldn't have been stupid enough to fuck with us. Vicious killers don't take kindly to people screwing with them. The most dangerous monsters on this magic fucking planet are gonna rip the heads off people who fuck with their young."

The group hit the end of the hallway and entered a massive, sprawling chamber of polished white stone with an open doorway across the room. For the flight-inclined, the ceiling opened to the sky. The lack of furniture and the size pointed to it being a place where Kalath took his true form.

Is he gonna face us here?

A string of portals opened across the room. This time man-sized spiders crafted of gemstones skittered out, their legs ending in sharp barbs. Within ten seconds, groups of sapphire, ruby, emerald and onyx spiders spread out in front of the portals and cut off access to the other side of the room.

Maybe not. Always a new trick with this fucker.

"I'm not impressed." Shay snorted in disdain. "He's got the Chalice of Arachne. I bet Victoria or Nadina could do the same if they got their hands on that artifact. I think our dinosaur boy is all talk, no walk. I'm sure most of what he's accomplishing is because of artifacts rather than his own power."

No wonder everybody's so impressed with dragons on Oriceran. They're just a bunch of Wizard of Oz *bullshitters.*

"Does it matter?" Kalath replied. "You wield artifacts, human, as does Trey Garfield. Now you doubt me because I retain the use of more powerful artifacts?"

"Sure, we use artifacts." Trey lifted a gloved hand. "But

we don't talk smack about being the ultimate being, and we don't think that gives us an excuse to play god."

"All this resistance, and I'm trying to save you. It's wearying dealing with lesser beings. Your thoughts and feelings are so short-sighted."

Shay scoffed. "I'm so sorry, O great scaly one, that we were born human."

"No, I don't care how you dress it up." Trey shook his head. "In the end, it comes down to the same thing. You're trying to murder Little Brownstone." He grinned, his teeth pearly-white. "And I have to say, fuck you. That's not happening, even if it is short-sighted."

Spiders continued to crawl out of the portals, but they'd yet to attack. The thickening swarm obscured the exit door.

Victoria raised her wand and narrowed her eyes. "James, don't waste time with this crap. Let us handle pest control." She smiled at Trey. "Let's make a bet, Trey. We'll count up the number of spiders we destroy. The net difference is the number of days the other person gets free lunch."

Nadina clapped. "How delightful. For every net kill you have over me, I'll offer you a free meal at one of my restaurants." She shook a finger. "I wouldn't want to embarrass you by being better at your job than you."

"Oh, now it's *on*," Trey replied. "I'm going to waste more spiders than you, Nadina, and then I'm going to go back to Earth and cook a better brisket."

She laughed and winked. "That would be wonderful."

"Pretty fucking awesome."

James leaned toward Shay to whisper, "I'm gonna grab

you and jump. Maybe this is the way it's supposed to be. We're his parents. The spiders haven't attacked yet. The dragon's making a point, so let's make our own."

Shay nodded slowly and stowed her gun and knife. "None of you die. Martyrs make great saints but lousy friends. And I hate when people make bets they weasel out of."

"Yeah, dying's not high on my list of things I'm looking forward to doing anytime soon." Trey pounded his fist into his palm. "I'm going to die old and alone in my bed, after my favorite meal, and long after my great-grandkids are born."

Victoria twirled her wand in her fingers. "I'm insulted that we're being attacked by summoned garbage, and I'm beginning to think this dragon's just a tad arrogant."

"It's unfortunate we couldn't resolve this with a cook-off." Nadina raised her palms. "Though I am starting to suspect that James is getting the better end of me owing him." She smirked. "Even if I forced my way along."

James scooped Shay up in his arms. "Is that it, Kalath? I thought you didn't want me going forward, but is your plan to strip us away from everyone? Fine. Enough bull-shit. We're coming for you."

"Hurry, monster," Kalath offered, his voice low. "Or those you claim to value will die. Or don't you care? It's just more bodies. Will you give them a building named after them to justify it? Do you even think about Shorty?"

Trey's face contorted into anger. "Find that mother-fucker, James, and end him. For all of us, and our boy Shorty, who doesn't deserve to get done like that."

The spiders scampered toward the group. James

grunted and jumped high into the air, the lack of a ceiling freeing him of worries. The spiders didn't change direction. He landed with a loud thud near the exit and set Shay down.

She pulled her gun and inclined her head toward the door. "You heard the dragon. Let's go. You know what they say. Cut off the head of the snake, and the body dies. This just happens to be a really big snake."

"Yeah." James spared a final glance toward his friends, who were about to be surrounded by a giant gemstone spider swarm. He followed Shay through the door.

Shit. Kalath's right. People are willing to do crazy shit for me. I better make sure I deserve it. No, I better make sure my family deserves it.

CHAPTER TWENTY-NINE

"How did I go from being a cop to being chewed on by the Devil's cats?"

Maria gritted her teeth as one of the panther creatures pounced on her. He raked his claws across her armor, leaving deep marks. She slammed her arm into the monster, knocking him off before shoving her railgun against his head and vaporizing it at point-blank range. Her breaths came fast and ragged. The attack was close, too close.

The army's position was precarious. A group of panthers had pierced their group's flank, ripping into some of the agency bounty hunters and sending them to the ground in sprays of blood. She'd laid down covering fire, eliminating the monsters and allowing other men to pull back the wounded. They were there to help James end the threat, but that didn't mean letting people die.

Unfortunately, all their technology, skill, and magic didn't prevent wounded from piling up. Even with the extra rounds loaded into the back of Maria's power armor, there was no way she wouldn't run out, and she'd already burned through far more ammo than she'd expected. The power armor enhanced her strength, and she could smash and stab the enemies into submission, but if she took a couple more bad hits, she might have to bail.

I'm supposed to be retired, but instead, I'm on another planet fighting hordes of magical monsters. I am really, really too old for this crap.

"Damn it." Maria hissed as a giant stabbed at her. She backpedaled to avoid the enchanted spear, unsure of what it would to the power armor. One of May's statues knocked his head off from the back. "Thanks, May."

"I'm doing my best, but I don't know how much more I can do," the witch replied. Blood trickled down the side of her face. A jagged tear ran through her suit from an earlier close encounter with one of the monsters. They'd quickly learned the claws of the panther creatures went through almost anything easily, including magical shields. Preparation didn't help when you hadn't prepared the right way.

Thanks to the portal reorientation, the enemy had them pinned in on all sides. That initially made concentrating their fire more difficult, but the one advantage was that their increasingly small defensive square also was starting to reverse that. They simply needed to survive until then.

A fountain of flame erupted from the ground beneath a group of advancing panthers. A pale Keller sauntered forward, his wand pointed at them. The rapid-fire offensive ritual he'd been helping coordinate had broken down after one of the other wizards was mauled. They'd stabilized the poor wizard's condition, but he remained unconscious.

Keller, Ramon, and the others had subsequently spread out to support the others. Their wands might never run out of ammunition, but the strain of near-constant magic use was taking its toll. There was a reason magicals on Oriceran still bothered with weapons.

Maria downed some wasps. That was the one type of enemy that was barely reinforcing itself, suggesting that Kalath's power wasn't limitless. The problem was the Brownstone army wasn't James. They had limits too.

He can win. If he gets to the dragon, this will all be over. We just have to survive in the meantime.

"We might have to retreat to the capital," Maria announced.

A nearby Drow glared at her. "If we leave, the enemy will overwhelm the queen's father and the others. We can't flee now. Our warriors will have fought for nothing, human."

"Getting overwhelmed is the damned problem." Maria fell silent before sweeping her railgun in an arc and downing a cluster of advancing giants. "We'll hold for as long as we can, but we need to make sure someone who can open a portal keeps breathing, or we could start having a lot of dead bodies pile up." She shook her head. "Why didn't I retire when I had the chance?"

May managed a weak grin. "If you survive, at least you'll have a great story for your retirement. Tyler's going to be furious."

"He already is. Me volunteering for this crossed a line in his mind. He told me when I get back, we're going on vacation and hiding from James for a long time."

"Then you have something to look forward to." May

lifted her wand and closed her eyes, chanting rapidly. Pieces of nearby destroyed wooden giants lifted from the ground and flowed together to create something new. The shape was different than their original forms but obviously humanoid. The new giants turned and tackled panthers, crushing them before other monsters shredded them back into simple wood.

"Just keep it up," Maria shouted. She killed two panthers and a wasp in rapid succession. The kills flowed together, each blurring into next. There was nothing but screams, shrieks, loud noises, and death.

A Drow warrior stumbled toward Maria, coughing up blood. He held his hand over the huge hole in his upper chest, murmuring quietly until shadows spread to cover it. "When we win this battle, we will become legends."

"I'm sure that's what King Leonidas said at the Battle of Thermopylae," Maria replied. "And he certainly did become a legend."

The Drow grinned at her. He turned as his flesh knitted itself. "Then let us face our enemies and earn the same end as King Leonidas!"

"Oh, shit." Maria groaned.

Last time I use an Earth reference with these guys.

Trey threw a right hook that connected with an onyx spider. Cracks shot through its body. He followed up with another punch. The blow shattered the spider into dozens of pieces due to the power of his artifact gloves. They had allowed him to routinely bring in level fours and fives without the aid of a magical.

"Yeah! That's what I'm talking about." Trey danced back. "You fuckers haven't gotten to see me use my magic gloves yet. Do you know how much my wife has fine-tuned these things? You see me, Kalath? You see me representing for Las Vegas and LA? I don't need no army of freaky spiders to fight my battles for me because I'm one-hundred percent a badass human, not some pussy bitch-ass dragon who hides in the mountains because he's afraid of Brownstone and his boys."

"I don't think you're going to win a smack-talking war with an ancient dragon, Trey. If that was all it took, no one would care about dragons." Victoria gripped the center of her wand like a hilt. A golden shaft of light extended from the tip. She swung at a ruby spider charging her and sliced it in half, nodding with a smirk. "But we should try to push through and give James some support."

"Is that going to be possible?" Nadina jumped away from an emerald spider. "These spiders seem rather insistent on trying to kill us."

The spider leapt forward and struck an invisible barrier. She smiled and cut through the air with her arm. A bright light followed the path of her arm and sliced the spider.

"Why aren't any of these fuckers tossing poison or shit?" Trey yelled. He smacked one spider into another before decapitating a third with an uppercut. "I was thinking the same thing outside. They have all sorts of monsters, but the guy shooting the other guy at range is going to win. Is he afraid to use his wizards and witches because we're winning?"

Victoria twirled her wand sword, ending the lives of two more gem spiders in a single slash. "Who knows? I don't know if we can call this winning. These things aren't coming out in the same numbers as the monsters outside, but we're not gaining any ground here. I'm reduced to this."

"Reduced to this?" Trey batted a jumping emerald spider out of the air and then crushed its head. "Damn, Vic, getting all prissy-pants. Sorry you have to hang out with us mere peasants who get their hands dirty."

"Bite me, Trey."

He grinned. "You'd like it too much."

Victoria sliced through another spider. "Your ego has increased faster than your skill."

Nadina cried out in pain as a sapphire spider impaled her thigh with its leg. She shouted a spell, which came out half in a human-intelligible language and half like a tortured song in her native language. Invisible blades converged on the spider and chopped it to pieces. No matter how much damage they did, the creatures never cried out or screeched. Their deaths were marked only by the thuds of their body and the clatters of their chunks as they fell to the floor.

"You okay, Nad?" Trey asked between fending off a spider with a series of jabs, his brow furrowed with concern. Nadina might have more moves than any of them had realized, but she didn't fill her days by going after dangerous men and creatures. Being skilled in battle was as much about experience as power.

"Considering you do this sort of thing a lot, I'm beginning to have serious doubts about your lifestyle choices." Nadina placed her hand on her leg and murmured a quiet healing spell. "The excitement of constantly risking my life is starting to wear off."

Trey laughed and backhanded an enemy so hard, its head cracked in four places. "Nah, you got it all wrong, pitmaster."

Victoria hissed as she hacked at a still-moving ruby spider missing its leg. "How's that, Trey? It seems like she's got it exactly right."

"Come on, Vic." Trey punched the same spider again and again until its head exploded in a shower of gem fragments that bounced off him. "We go after bounties, but it's not like this shit all the time."

"Just most of the time." Victoria grinned. "I think my life was safer when I was a bodyguard, and that was people who thought people might have reason to come after them."

"That's what it means to work for James motherfucking Brownstone, the Granite Ghost, and the only dad I know who'll take on a dragon for his kid. You face the danger with him, and you come out stronger on the other end."

Nadina's wound closed and left a hole in her now-blood-splattered pants. "You should consider working for James in his restaurant. It's probably safer. Why not face the danger of an angry customer?"

"Where's the fun in that?" Trey bounced on the balls of his feet. "I never thought magic would mean much in my life. It'd just be another thing I mostly saw on TV. I was just a punk piece of shit who turned to a gang to make something of himself." He punctuated his sentence with a one-two blow that obliterated a spider's head. "And now I'm married to the world's hottest witch—no offense, Vic—and I've got awesome artifacts that let me hunt all sorts of born magicals. I might not have been born into magic, but I can't imagine any other life."

"I was born into a magical existence, and I think I prefer barbeque," Nadina replied. She swept through the air with her arm as soft notes escaped her throat. Pieces of the dead spiders lifted into the air, swirling in a dazzling, glittering cloud. The cloud pelted the living spiders, not injuring them much, but slowing their progress and giving the three more time to prepare attacks.

"Nice. Good move." Trey smiled. "And don't worry. The big man will find Kalath soon and end this shit. We just need to hold on."

"If we can't go forward, should we pull back?"

Victoria frowned. "All that means is we'd be leading a stream of spiders to reinforce the other monsters."

"That's right." Trey bobbed his head. "Let's keep taking these eight-legged fuckers down."

CHAPTER THIRTY

Alison frowned as she sat in another of her pointless conference rooms at another equally pointlessly long rectangular table watching the Brownstone army's battle against the outside monsters. It was taking tremendous magical power to maintain her scrying window, and her attempts to follow James and Shay inside failed. She wasn't surprised after seeing Shay hand the scroll to May. The strategy made sense, but she was worried about the mounting wounded and shrinking defensive lines of the Brownstone army.

She sighed and turned to Zana, sitting beside her. "I think we need to prepare to evacuate the army. Dad's already inside, which means he'll be able to get to the dragon and end this, but our forces are getting torn up, and they're on the verge of collapse. I need you to gather the reserve force and defend the evacuation of the force. It's all up to my mom, Dad, Trey, Victoria, and Nadina now."

Zana stood. "Yes, my queen, as you desire." She headed out of the room just as Rasila walked in through a different door. She nodded at the scrying window. "You wish you were there, don't you? And you regret being here."

"Yes." Alison slammed a fist on the table. "I was convinced it was a feint, but now my friends and people are getting hurt while I'm sitting here watching safe. I'm seeing men and women I grew up with getting ripped into and stabbed." She ground her teeth. "I could be helping. I could be fighting. This is about my family and my brother. I should be doing more."

"I understand your frustration, Alison," Rasila tilted her head and stared at the window. "But I also overheard your orders to Zana. Those brave warriors you worry about will soon be safe." She offered Alison a thin smile. "But if you believe there has been no deception, then let us both lead the army to reinforce them. Fresh Drow warriors, led by their queens, will run through whatever reserves the dragon has. We will send a signal to Oriceran that all allied with us directly or indirectly are under our protection."

"You just want the glory." Alison snorted. "It's not the same thing."

"Glory is a currency all its own, my fellow queen." Rasila clucked her tongue disapprovingly. "You are wiser than your years, and certainly more powerful, but you have much to learn. Purity of motive is nice, but often unnecessary. We…" She frowned.

Both queens snapped their heads to the side, the same magical sensation responsible. A non-Drow had passed over wards they'd set up in the palace the night before. It'd been part of last-minute suggestion by Alison just on the off-chance that an enemy managed to infiltrate the palace looking for Thomas. It was one of an array of wards they could quickly put together as they tried to account for different types of countermeasures and artifacts.

Alison jumped up. "Impossible. There's no way they could be this deep inside the palace already."

Rasila conjured a shadow blade and a shield over her body, an eager grin spreading over her face. "They could if they are worthy foes." She jogged out of the room. "You should be happy. You anticipated the enemy's strategy, and now you will be able to personally destroy those who would harm your brother."

Alison followed Rasila out into the hallway and summoned her shadow blade. "Happy that someone managed to penetrate deep into our palace? I wanted everyone to be safe, not invite a bunch of dragon-worshippers into the heart of our lands."

"Think only about what is important—that you will be able to defend your brother and your palace from the minions of a dragon." Shadow wings grew from Rasila's back, and she lifted into the air. "What is a Drow queen without strength? And how does one prove strength if they don't fight worthy foes? If anything, having the enemy pierce our defenses and then defeating them will better prove that strength."

Alison shoved magic into her back for her own wings and joined Rasila in zooming down the wide hallway. "Sometimes I think you're so normal, and then I remember you're not. There's always some scheme in that head of yours about showing off. You're like the socialite from hell."

"I'm perfectly normal for a Drow," Rasila replied with a huge smile. "You're the one who is abnormal by our standards, but I think that is why you'll continue to make an excellent queen."

"Secure the exits and entrances!" Alison shouted to a passing Drow man. "We have intruders. Likely wizards, witches, and perhaps Zain. Send reinforcements to the guest quarters. You're authorized to kill any intruders who don't immediately surrender."

The Drow's eyes widened, and he pivoted on his heel to rush back the way he'd come. The queens continued their flight. Alison would have preferred to have portaled right to Thomas, but the queens had warded most of the area extensively against portals to cut down on another sneak attack. Their security measure was backfiring. They should have been observing the action in a room closer to Thomas, if not in the same room, but she'd worried about frightening her already worried little brother.

How did these assholes get in? More fucking artifacts? That damned dragon and his people are too prepared. I'm not going to let them take Thomas, and I'm not going to force Pauline to risk her life again. Rasila's right. Sometimes a queen just needs to throw down.

Alison's husband, Mason, a powerful life wizard in his own right, was also keeping an eye on Thomas. His long history as a bodyguard and security contractor meant he was prepared to protect the boy against hostile threats, but it shouldn't get that far. This was Drow lands and the Drow palace. Drow should be able to defend it.

I've internalized Rasila's propaganda more than I realized.

Alison and Rasila stopped abruptly and hovered in the air. A large group of men and women in gray robes strolled down the hallway in the opposite direction, already wrapped in lightly glowing shield magic around their forms. Wands marked witches and wizards, interspersed with a smattering of Light and Wood Elves. Alison was grateful there were no Zain.

"How dare you?" Alison shouted, quivering with righteous indignation. "You assholes dare come at my brother again in my own palace. You've invited one thing, and that's death."

The infiltrators spun around, raising their wands and hands. They spread out but kept their focus on the two Drow women as they settled back onto the ground and released their wings. Alison coiled shadow magic around her legs. This wasn't a problem she wanted to talk her way out of, and the sons of bitches standing in front of her weren't going to get one last chance to surrender. Sometimes a woman just needed to decapitate a man to make her point.

A bearded wizard smiled. "Now, how can this be? We had hoped not to face you directly." He shook his head and nodded at a blonde witch near him. "I told you, Vina. Even the best artifacts have their weaknesses."

"We shouldn't linger, John," Vina replied with a giggle. Her eyes were unfocused.

I wonder if she was the one who was responsible for using the Many Flower. You lost your mind, bitch, and soon you're going to lose your life.

"You've come for the boy, I presume?" Rasila asked. She kept an easy smile on her lips, although it didn't reach her eyes. "I'd ask how you knew he was here, but I'm presuming your master provided you with the appropriate tools. I applaud your loyalty, but in this case, Alison is right. Your violation of the Drow can't be forgiven. You will pay with your lives."

"No, you don't understand." John lifted his chin and sneered. "My master gave me a task, and I executed it by gathering everything I needed. All the while, you arrogant fools have blocked our efforts, blocked the efforts of a great being. A Drow is nothing before our master. You're a squabbling race of foolish warriors who let themselves be led by a corrupt queen for centuries."

"Your great master is a fucking lizard who wants to murder my brother," Alison shouted. "I don't give a crap about any alleged prophecy. If you want Thomas, you'll have to go through me, and my track record is almost as scary as my dad's."

"And what of you, Queen Rasila?" John asked. "Kalath could be a mighty ally to you, the greatest you could ever hope to gain. Aid us, and we'll rid you of this half-human co-queen. You will help defend Oriceran, and you will attain the throne for yourself. The Drow will rise to greatness, feared not because of a capricious nature, but because of true strength."

Rasila threw back her head and laughed so hard it was almost a cackle. "You foolish, foolish little wizard! You really think I want to *depose* Alison? I serve as her co-queen only because she insisted it would be best for our people. I would gladly and *have* offered to bend knee to her. And you offer me the chance at betrayal?" She sneered. "You have no honor. You have no true strength. I thought you might be a worthy foe, but you hunt down a child at the direction of a being who claims greatness yet cowers and hides behind servants and monsters. What sort of master leads from behind?" She spat on the ground, her entire face contorted in disgust. "Alison, your father will soon kill their master. There's no reason we need to keep them alive, is there?"

"No, there isn't." Alison smiled. "Congratulations, *John*. You get to die in service to your cause and master. I'm sure there can be no greater honor for a fanatic like you."

John shouted an incantation and a fireball blasted from his wand. Alison released the coiled magical energy around her legs and launched herself forward. The wizard's attack zoomed past her and exploded against the back wall. She brought back her shadow blade and sliced at the wizard. Her blow landed but didn't sink through his thick shield.

Rasila brought up her hand. Four dark purple orbs winked into existence, spinning. She thrust her arm forward, and they flew toward the group. They exploded in succession against a different wizard, ripping through his shield and scorching his face and chest. He fell to the floor, gasping for breath.

"Pathetic."

Vina snickered and pulled a golden rapier from beneath her robe. She ran toward Rasila. "I will kill a queen!"

Alison pointed with her free hand and deposited a thin layer of shadow magic, using the wall as an anchor. She thrust her blade at a nearby witch, then banked off a nearby wall before shoving her conjured weapon through the witch's shield and heart. The witch's eyes widened in surprise before she coughed up blood.

John launched another fireball, but Alison shoved the dying witch into his path. The fireball crashed into her before she fell on him. He growled in frustration and pushed her off. Alison pivoted and tossed shadow crescents at the closest invaders. The blows staggered them. Her follow-up series of hacking strikes against one of them ended with his throat cut.

I'm really feeling Dad right now. I'm so tired of these assholes not getting the damned point!

Vina stuck her rapier into the wall. The blade sank in as if entering water. She sprinted toward Rasila, her eyes wide and her mouth parted in ecstasy. The Drow queen held out her palm, feeding a burgeoning and crackling arrow composed of wisps of purple-black shadow. Her expression dripped disdain for the charging witch.

Alison shoved an explosive orb into a nearby wizard. The explosion flung them both back, but while her shield held, his was done. She summoned another shadow crescent, and the tenebrous blade sank deep into his chest. His blood spurted over the ground and the nearby bodies as he tumbled back.

People shouted in the distance. The buzz and crackle of spells sounded. An alarm spell let out a low, deep tone. There were more battles going on, but none were in the direction of Thomas' room.

"Damn it," Alison muttered.

They must have planned to distract us with the other groups and then go after Thomas. We screwed up their timing. I trust my people to beat down their second-stringers.

Rasila scoffed and released her arrow. It sailed toward Vina, but the witch slashed through it with the golden rapier. The spell vanished in a hiss of dark steam. She grinned and skipped toward the Drow.

"Afraid yet?" Vina asked. "Do you know what it's like to face death?"

"I've faced death countless times, you insane witch." Rasila smiled and released her shadow blade. "But that cancellation is convenient, isn't it?" A purple glow suffused her hand. "I'll need to be a little more careful, then. Don't worry. You'll die soon enough, and I'll try my best *not* to remember you."

Alison gritted her teeth as John nailed her with two fireballs in the back. She ignored the pain and relieved his penultimate living ally of their head before turning to face him. Stopping to heal would take time she didn't have.

"You've lost already, wizard." She glared at him. "You lost the second you went after my brother. You're so obsessed with prophecy. Then I'll offer a prophecy of my own. He who goes after a Brownstone suffers a beat-down. So it is written in the stars."

A crimson glow surrounded John. "I didn't want to have to use my master's greatest gift. It's unique and irreplaceable." He glared at Alison. "But you've forced me to. You've stopped nothing. We're all prepared to die to serve the master."

Alison jogged back. She lifted her hands and funneled a mixture of light and shadow magic in front of her into a long spinning lance, dark lines liberally sprinkled throughout. "That can definitely be arranged."

Vina circled Rasila with a smile. "You're going to have a very short reign."

She thrust the rapier at Rasila, but the Drow didn't dodge. Instead, she met the blade with her body. It ran right through her chest and stuck out the back. Alison's

MICHAEL ANDERLE

eyes widened, but she didn't stop feeding her spell. John laughed triumphantly.

What the fuck is Rasila doing? Is it an illusion? No, I have to trust her. There's no way she'd lose to some second-rate insane witch.

The witch cackled. "You've given up. I applaud you for facing reality, Queen Rasila."

"No." Rasila gritted her teeth and pushed herself farther along the blade. "I didn't give up. I respected your weapon and made sure you didn't hit anything vital."

She clapped her energy-covered hands on either side of Vina's head. A violet shockwave blasted from them, blowing chunks out of the roof, wall, and floor along with vaporizing the witch's upper body. What was left of her fell to the floor. Rasila fell to her knees and yanked out the rapier with a wince.

John turned toward Alison, his jaw clenched. He brought back his fist and ran toward her. She released her spell, and the spiraling lance burst from in front of her and struck John square the chest. Dark purple and white lines of energy crackled from the impact point. The attack tore through and carved out most of his upper chest. He mouthed final words of defiance, no lungs to give voice to his words before falling backward. His glow faded.

Alison released her shield and ran over to Rasila. She knelt. "How bad is it?"

"Oh, I've had worse." Shadowy tendrils spread over her wound. She hissed in pain. "Hmm, but not by much. I might not have done that if I knew it was going to resist normal healing." She stood with Alison's help. "I think I'll need to take some time off, and you'll be full-time queen for a while, but I'll survive."

Alison sighed. "Anything to get me to do more work?"

"Of course."

Drow warriors led by Zana charged around the corner and skidded to a halt. Zana surveyed the carnage, a knowing look in her eye.

"The other invaders are dead, my queens," Zana reported. "Wizards, witches, a small number of other Oricerans, and a group of Zain."

"Good," Alison replied. "Now, go evacuate the army."

We did our part here, Dad. Now you do yours.

CHAPTER THIRTY-ONE

James and Shay arrived in another chamber even larger than the last. Unlike the polished white stone of the previous room, the natural jagged rock of the mountain surrounded them, complete with deep grooves and scratches. It was if something massive had clawed out the room piece by piece. Though bright, only a single light orb illuminated the room, leaving deep pockets of darkness throughout.

Is that what dragons do? James wondered. *He could have used magic to dig this out, but was he making a point to himself. Now it's our turn to make a point to this fucker about what it means to go after a Brownstone.*

"I don't care what Alison says," he rumbled. "I've killed a three-headed dragon, so how bad can a dragon with one head be? Anyone who hides that much has got a reason to hide, and it's not that he's an unstoppable badass." He looked around. "And where's all the gold? I thought this was some super-ancient dragon."

"Gold?" Shay laughed. "Don't believe everything you

read. It's not like old rich men lay around in their money all day on Earth. Most dragons don't have much use for gold."

"Sure, guys don't do that because they have banks, and what about Scrooge McDuck? He swims around in it." James shrugged as if mentioning a cartoon duck made perfect sense in the middle of a dragon's lair.

Shay blinked at him. "First of all, he's not human. Second, he's not even real. I don't think we can use Scrooge McDuck as our baseline for the behavior of wealthy humans."

"You sure?" James shrugged. "Maybe there is some Oriceran duck guy they based him on. There are so many legends and shit on Earth that are true in one form or another. I'm just saying there could be a duck out there swimming through all his money."

"I think it's unlikely, James. Let's stay on task."

James nodded. "Yeah, where are you, Kalath? We came all the way here. Fuck, you invited us here, and now you're being a rude son of a bitch and hiding. Come out and face me. Destroy me, because if you want Thomas, you'll have to take me down first."

Light clapping sounded from the shadows. James and Shay turned toward the source, both raising their weapons. A man in a gray robe stepped into the light. James didn't recognize him from the attack, and he'd memorized the faces of every man and woman there. Something about the confidence in his stride convinced James this wasn't a lackey, but Kalath had played too many tricks, and he couldn't be sure.

Kill the enemy, Whispy shouted. *Destroy the ultimate threat to the offspring.*

At this point, I plan to kill any fucker around here who doesn't work for Alison or me.

"How can such a powerful creature be such an idiot?" the man asked, shaking his head in disgust. "The only reason you're not a real threat is that you lack intelligence."

"Only my wife's allowed to call me an idiot," James replied. "And I think the real dumbass is the lizard who goes after a man's son when that man is known to not take kindly to people fucking with him."

"Don't you realize what you've done?" the gray-robed man snapped. "Don't you realize you've walked right into my trap? Everything is by my design. Your arrogance will be your undoing, James Brownstone. You've eliminated the few lingering worries I had about that."

James snorted. "What trap? I'm supposed to be worried because you've got a billion weird-ass six-legged panthers and gem spiders? My people can handle those. But let's be clear. You're Kalath, right? The big, bad dragon? If you're not, and you run your ass out right now, then you don't have to die."

"No, I will *not* run." The man bowed with a flourish. "This is the form I use most often as of late when dealing with lesser races, but yes, I am Kalath. I was the architect of the attack on your son, but you don't understand the full scope of your mistake."

Shay pointed her gun and her flaming knife at him. "Then why don't you explain it to us, O great scaly one? We're curious to know what you were thinking before you die."

"You think I'm not aware of the threat you represent, Vax," Kalath replied with a sneer. "You're a killing machine from another world. You adapt to attacks, magical and non-magical. You spent years as a bounty hunter fighting all manner of magical beings, adapting to their diverse powers, honing your abilities to be able to slay anything that might come your way." His gaze flicked to Shay. "And you, the tomb raider, the collector of artifacts who was trying to flee her bloody past. A murderer with delusions of being a scholar."

Shay rolled her eyes. "Are we really going to do that bullshit again? I'm betting I've killed far fewer people than you, Mr. Jurassic Old Fart."

"I just wanted to provide context for our conversation." Kalath gave her a thin smile. "I worried that time might be running short. There were some underestimations and mistakes, and I realized once my loyal servants' initial attack failed that there needed to be adjustments to the plan. It was a careful balance." He stroked his chin. "I realized if I challenged you directly, you would be too arrogant to back away, but I also realized that if you met too little resistance, you would be paranoid. All the other tools I have employed are in service to a greater plan."

James grunted. "You trying to say you've got me in a trap? Because from where I'm sitting, you're here, and I'm here, and I'm ready to kill you. When I'm ready to kill an asshole, I usually do."

"Make that both of us." Shay glared at Kalath.

The dragon shook his finger. "I will admit the adaptation worried me. I've had my servants collecting information about you since the other Vax attacked Oriceran. He defeated even their last-ditch attempts to send him to the World in Between, and once I realized what you were, I only cared about finding ways to neutralize you in case you ever interfered with my plans. I didn't realize then the importance of my planning and how it would relate to the prophecy."

"Gee, I'm touched," James replied. "I love my fans."

"Everything my servants found and every spell and arti-fact I used to learn more pointed back to the same truth: James Brownstone is effectively indestructible." Kalath sighed. "I'm sure your killer tomb-raider wife helped expose you to all manner of artifacts through the years as well. So, that presented me with the problem of how to get you here to my place of power and kill you. I couldn't hope you would be so stupid to walk in here without your armor. Even you're not that arrogant."

"Yeah, pretty much." James sliced through the air. "I figured you might try to blow me up or shit like that. So, can you fuck off and die, or is this one of those things where you're gonna bore me to death first?"

Kalath smiled. "You don't realize the true wisdom of my plan. You're secondary. The boy is everything, and now you've walked right in here and given me exactly what I need to destroy you while my most loyal minions grab the boy. You've already lost, James Brownstone.

Terminate the threat to the offspring, Whispy shouted. *Destroy, kill, annihilate, obliterate.*

"You son of a bitch," Shay snarled.

James let out a low growl before forcing a chuckle. There was no way he was letting some stupid dragon manipulate his emotions. Kalath had admitted he was afraid of James. Working on his nerves must have been part of the trap.

"What's so amusing, James Brownstone?" Kalath asked.

"You." James took a couple of steps toward him. "You have a stupid plan like turning into Mr. T. Rex and swallowing me? That shit's been tried, and I've cut my way out."

"I'm surprised you're not more worried about your son."

"You think we didn't know you might be trying to make sure Shay and I weren't there? We saw through that shit right away." James pointed his blade at Kalath. "He's safe. He's surrounded by an army of fanatical warriors and his sister, one of the most powerful Drow queens ever. My nanny by herself beat your people's asses. What do you think a Drow queen or two is going to do to them? Those Drow are aching for a fight." He scoffed, injecting every last morsel of contempt he could into the sound. "Alison and her people can beat whoever weak-ass pieces of shit you've sent their way. You know what? They probably already went after Thomas, and she killed them. Sorry you're losing so many people lately. Your HR department must hate you. I know it can be hard to replace experienced employees. You do what I did and outsource that shit."

Kalath's eyes glowed briefly. "I worry about you, James Brownstone, but I also respect you. While I command greater magic in scope, I suspect in terms of raw destruction, our abilities might be evenly matched, so I've come up with a better plan. I don't wish to implement it, so I'm going to reach out to you one last time, and get you to do the right thing. Because despite what you think, I'm not evil, and you could serve a greater good."

"A greater good that involves turning my son over for death?"

"I know that you've heard the prophecy. Don't you understand the implications? We're speaking of the destruction of both worlds. You can't be assured your child won't be dangerous. Are you willing to put family before all?"

"Yeah, I am." James wanted to charge his cannon and blast the bastard's head off, but he suspected it wouldn't be that simple. "That's your big plan? Guilt-trip me into letting you murder my kid as part of a test?"

"It's a simple calculation. The lives of many for the life of one boy. Even you should be able to understand that."

"Bullshit." James shook his head and lowered his arm. "You sound just like the fucking Nine Systems Alliance nutjobs. They were so *sure* that I was gonna be a bad guy that their agent came after me and hurt a lot of people, and then they were prepared to kill thousands of innocent people who had nothing to do with me to stop me, the alleged bad guy who was in the process of saving the fucking planet. There comes a point, asshole, when all your murderous bullshit isn't for the greater good anymore. It's just more murderous bullshit."

"This isn't the same situation." Kalath waved a hand. "Those space creatures were operating off assumptions based on your species. I am acting on the power of prophecy."

"Oh, yeah, that's so much better. Prophecy? More bullshit. You might be some super-ancient dragon with his claws into everything on Oriceran, but you don't know the future for certain." James gestured to Shay. "You wouldn't have been able to know she'd change from a killer to a professor. Fuck, if you actually knew the future, your lackeys wouldn't have lost outside my house. You would have anticipated Alison's dead man's switch system. You act like you're a god, but you're just a lizard who thinks too highly of himself."

Shay nodded, the anger on her face from before replaced by determination. "I might not be you, Kalath, but I've studied a lot of prophecies in my time, both as a tomb raider and as a professor. Most are made-up crap, but I'm guessing a dragon isn't going to be so easily fooled by those. But not being fooled is not the same thing as being unable to make a mistake."

Kalath's nostrils flared. "If you'd let me check the child, we could confirm things. Then you would know."

"By letting him die? Even if you do confirm Thomas is the child in your prophecy, that doesn't necessarily mean anything." Shay shrugged. "Sometimes prophecies are a matter of interpretation, which is why all the panicked whining about the end of Oriceran from before turned out to be false. Have you ever considered that the destruction your prophecy refers to might relate to the destruction of a social order or something like that? Thomas might be destined to be a hero who unites the two worlds and unifies magic and technology."

Kalath nodded. "Of course, I've considered such possibilities."

Shay blinked, stunned by the revelation. "Really?"

James growled. "If you get that, why are you still coming after Thomas?"

"A possibility isn't a certainty," Kalath replied. "There's a non-zero chance that he's the child of prophecy and the prophecy will end with the destruction of Earth and Oriceran, and I refuse to take the risk. Thomas Brownstone must die for the good of all."

Extended interrogation irrelevant, Whispy insisted. *Destroy the primary threat.*

Fuck it, Whispy. When you're right, you're right.

"Enough of this bullshit. Negotiations have broken down." James whipped up his cannon. Green sparks formed into pulsing lines of energy gathering around his blade. "I don't give a shit who you are. You come after my boy, you die. How's that for simple?"

Kalath shook his head. "A pity you're such a fool."

"A pity you fucked with the wrong kid, asshole."

A bright light consumed the room. The inherent protection of the helmet prevented James from being blinded, allowing him to realize it was less that there was a bright light and more that bright white coloring was the only thing left in the world.

"Shay?" James asked.

She didn't respond. He looked around, but he couldn't find her.

Well, damn it. One last trick, huh? I hope that fucker didn't send me into some different dimension.

CHAPTER THIRTY-TWO

"James?" Shay called.

She squinted as color returned to the world around her. It'd be embarrassing if they ended up getting taken out because the dragon blinded them, but it was something he would do. All her years of being a killer and a tomb raider had taught her that sometimes the most effective way to take someone out, even someone powerful, was the simplest and most direct. People spent far too much time preparing countries for the more elaborate.

But that wasn't right. She wasn't blind. Kalath hadn't used a flare, and though she was standing in a cave, she wasn't in the same cave as before. Rather than a vast chamber with a light orb, she now was in a gloomy darker area lit only by flickering torches and the dim light from her flaming knife. Huge stalactites and stalagmites stuck out from the floor and roof of the cave. Both features were so long it was as if she was in the closing mouth of some great rock beast. She fought a shiver at the idea of being in some giant dragon's mouth.

"Did he shove me in a portal?" Shay murmured. "This isn't what the World in Between looks like."

"I don't know, did he?" came a familiar voice.

Shay ducked behind one of the stalagmites and swept the area for the source. "Oh, for fuck's sake. You've got to be kidding me. Fucking dinosaur."

She spotted herself, same dark hair, same backpack, same tactical vest and weapons standing about twenty feet away. It wasn't a mirror image because her doppelganger wasn't crouched behind the rock. The flickering light revealed the other Shay was smirking.

Damn, do I really look that smug?

The doppelganger didn't have a silver glow from artifacts, but a quick check revealed that neither did Shay. She theorized that whatever weird illusion or pocket reality had been generated might have inherent anti-magic properties. It didn't matter. She'd started her career without artifacts and could fight without them, even if she had to fight herself.

"Welcome, Shay." The doppelganger waved her knife. "Now you finally get a chance to take on someone truly bad. You can kill the one person in your life who most deserves it."

Shay snorted. "Oh, I get it now. That's what Kalath had planned all along. I thought it'd be something else, but I am a short-sighted lesser being."

"You really think you have this figured out?" Shay's double shook her head.

Shay nodded but stayed hidden. "Yeah. I'm guessing that's why he needed the big speech. There's some sort of artifact. Shit, the more I think about it, it's probably powered by both magic and all the feelings of those people fighting. I've read about these kinds of things. I bet the entire damned room was an artifact. If he can't beat James, then he'll use James to beat James. It's halfway clever, but only halfway."

"Interesting." The doppelganger crouched and rolled behind a stalagmite. "All that knowledge and it's wasted on a vicious killer. What happened to you, Shay? Whatever happened to the woman who used to say she wasn't an assassin but a killer and that anyone who didn't get up close to kill their victim was a pussy? Aren't you ashamed that you went from that woman to being so domesticated? You teach children at a university. You go to meetings and have coffee."

"Is this the part where I'm supposed to say I wish I was the same woman? Fuck that woman, and fuck you, if you're supposed to be that woman. That woman who had no friends? Fuck, one of that woman's friends tried to murder her in her own damned kitchen for money because of some drug-dealing cartel. If you're a magic copy of me, then you know the reasons. My life was a dead end. No. I was already dead. I'm not going to tear myself up for shit that happened before, but if I kept on like I was going, I was going to end up dead, and no one in the world would have given a shit. So I've moved on and found something better. I've got friends and a family and a job I love. And I still do the occasional tomb raid."

The doppelganger laughed. "And you think they care now? That you have people who will miss you when you're gone? Who? The alien freak who is going to destroy the world someday, or your demon spawn who will? Just because you found solace in the arms of a monster, it doesn't erase your past."

"That's weak-ass manipulation." Shay shook her head. "Since you're supposed to be me, I'm almost ashamed of how pathetic it is. Come on, bitch, get to me; tear my soul a new one. Right now, I'm more annoyed than anything. Or if you're Kalath, then fuck you. You're going to be dead soon."

"James Brownstone is a pathetic monster with little emotional depth. He clings to you not out of love but out of the knowledge that no one else will ever love some ugly, pathetic excuse for a human. But that's just it, isn't it? He is a pathetic excuse for a human because he's a fake. He's a Vax, and he always will be one. Someday he'll get angry, and he'll kill you, and he'll lay waste to your world. And in your dying thoughts, you'll blame yourself."

Shay gritted her teeth. It was annoying to hear those things voiced by someone who looked and sounded exactly like her.

I've had just about enough of this shit and Evil Me. Or wait. I'm the evil me, so is she the good me? Whoever she is, bitch needs to die.

Shay squeezed off three shots. The muzzle flash illuminated the slick surface of the cave. Her bullets sparked and bounced off the rock. With a grunt, the doppelganger rolled and returned fire. Both women stayed low and continued to exchange shots, neither landing a shot.

"You're going down," Shay shouted.

"This is pointless, you know," the doppelganger replied. "I'm you. If you think so highly of your skills, then you have to realize that you're not going to beat yourself. You can't think of anything I won't think of.

"Fuck you, bitch." Shay reached for a grenade, but she'd used them all in the first battle. "Damn it." She jerked down as her opponent sent more rounds her way. "I can win. I *will* win."

"Why are you even bothering? Even if you win here, James will fall. He's weak. He clings to his false notions of love, his precious church, all to convince himself that he's worthy of love. But he'll soon realize he isn't, and then he'll want to destroy himself."

Shay snickered. "Save that script for my husband, bitch, but I don't think he'll be impressed with it either." She rolled to new cover, taking another couple shots along the way. Both shots went wide.

She is right about one thing. If she is some sort of magical copy of my mind, then she's going to know my tactics and moves. We could be doing this for an hour and not make headway. Every second I spend fighting her, the more risk there is the fucking dragon being able to do something to our guys outside or James if he's in some other pocket dimension.

"There's nothing you can say that I already haven't thought a thousand times," Shay shouted. "Do you think just because you saying it in that sexy voice and showing my sexy body means I'm going to fall down, crying like a little girl? Give me a fucking break. I'm a killer, remember? A vicious monster? It takes a lot more than that to flay my soul."

They both popped up at the same time and attempted to flank the other. They dodged between rock formations, squeezing off rounds with wild abandon until they both ran out of ammo. Shay ejected her magazine and reloaded.

It's clear she's not reading my thoughts. She just knows how I typically think, which means I can beat her. I will do something spontaneous that defies my normal tactics but doesn't require me to make a clear decision ahead of time. What can I do?

Shay held her breath and closed her eyes. She moved her gun hand back and forth rapidly, counting mentally and keeping her gaze focused in the general direction of her hunkered-down double. When she got to eleven in her head, she released her gun, and it flew off in the darkness, bouncing and clattering off a stalagmite. The other woman turned toward the sound. Shay sprang to her feet and charged her doppelganger, knife in hand.

The other woman turned back. Shay jumped, her blade in front of her. The doppelganger fired twice before her gun clicked empty. A bullet grazed Shay's cheek, and another skimmed her thigh. She hissed at the pain but kept her knife in hand until her momentum brought her to the doppelganger.

"Die, bitch!" Shay shouted.

The blade sank into the heart of the copy. The other Shay's eyes widened in shock while the real Shay ripped the blade out and plunged it again, deeper and deeper, blood spraying all over her. She ripped the blade out one last time before slitting the double's throat and watching with satisfaction as the body dropped to the ground.

"Don't feel bad," Shay whispered. "If the dice had fallen the other way, you might have won, and it's like you said. A real killer gets up close and personal when she takes someone out. She doesn't hide, and she's not a pussy afraid to get a little blood on her." She sheathed her knife and wiped some blood off her face.

I hope James doesn't get taken in by this self-flagellation bullshit. It's too much like the way he used to think.

Temporary neural disruption abated, Whispy reported. *Passive defenses holding. No significant forward risk of neural link disruption in current engagement.*

James grunted and stood. Half-collapsed buildings with windows shattered surrounded him. The burnt-out remains of cars and trucks filled a nearby road, blackened skeletons inside. Fire licked the sky and plumes of smoke obscured the sun. He'd been around enough battlefields to know this one was wrong. There were too many details off, mixtures of recent and long-ago damage. But Whispy's report provided the clarity he needed.

Someone tried to fuck with my head? James asked.

Yes. Temporary severance of neural link and reinforcement of passive defenses minimized intrusion.

Kalath must have tried his big final plan.

A familiar roar ripped through the air. In the distance, a Vax Forerunner in extended advanced mode crouched on the edge of a building, his blade pointed at the ground. There were no other enemies James could pick out even with his enhanced peripheral vision, but the Vax didn't make any sudden movements other than roaring again.

Okay. This isn't LA, and I doubt we got sent back to Earth or anywhere with a Vax. This is some magical simulated shit, I'm betting.

No evidence of neural link overriding primary sensory data, Whispy replied.

So big deal. It's real, but it's not. I'm guessing there's a copy of me over there, but they fucked up somehow. Something to do with that neural link attack.

Kalath had made the same mistake that a lot of people targeting James did. They thought of Whispy as equipment and not as a fully intelligent and self-aware partner, which meant James' copy was probably struggling for control against a now self-loathing symbiont. James was more powerful than a normal Vax because he'd achieved true integration with his symbiont rather than just being a meat puppet.

"Come on, James," shouted Kalath, his voice coming from all around. "Why fight it? You feel the anger all the time, the alienation. You're not of the planet. You know it."

Oh, I get it. The fucker was trying to reach into my head to screw with me.

"So the fuck what?" James bellowed back. "That doesn't mean I'm gonna blow it up. Everyone has shit that messes with them. I bet when you were a little hatchling, all the dragons wouldn't let you play in their dragon games."

"You're a killer. That's all you're good for—a beast who kills other beasts. Your planet would have been far better off if you'd never come."

"Hey, I don't personally slaughter my meat for barbeque," James joked. "But maybe I should start. I can be the farm-to-table guy." He laughed. "Then I would be the beast who kills beasts and grills them and adds the perfect sauce."

"You think you're funny?" Kalath asked. "You still can make jokes after all this?"

James jumped into the air, the massive leap carrying him to the top of a building. "I think you're an annoying fucker who went after my son. You want me to respect you? Fuck that. The only respect I'm giving you is the respect of wasting your ass once this game is over."

Whispy, I'm assuming you can change shit so my cannon can get through my own defenses, right?

Understood. Initiating modifications. Please wait.

The other Vax growled and roared. He hacked away with his blade at the roof of his building, knocking off debris but seemingly uninterested in engaging James. That was all the proof James needed that his copy was struggling with the integration of the symbiont.

You may fire when ready, Whispy ordered.

James lifted his gun and chuckled. The familiar green energy flowed across the blade. All the while, his copy continued his loud one-man war against a roof.

"What do you want me to say, Kalath?" James shouted. "That I'm a bad man and a sinner? I get that already. I believe that already. That's why I go to confession. It's not like I do it because it's fun."

"You're going to raise a monster who is even worse than you," Kalath replied, still nowhere in sight. "How can you be a father? You didn't even remember your father. You'll perpetuate a broken cycle."

James scoffed, the energy on his blade now so bright it bathed the entire area in a soft green glow. "I've had plenty of fathers. They just happened to be priests. Now let's end this bullshit because I've got better things to do than watch myself and listen to you."

A massive green beam erupted from his arm. It shot across the area and blew through the other James with ease. He adjusted his aim slightly finishing the vaporization of his poor copy, but the angle change also carved through the roof, leaving the remnants of the Vax, his legs, mostly, to tumble into the now-open roof of the building.

James ceased fire. "Nice try, dinosaur, but the real enemy stopped being me a long fucking time ago."

Dark holes appeared in the sky and the city. They spread, the blackness growing and consuming everything. James waited for the nothingness to overtake him.

CHAPTER THIRTY-THREE

J ames didn't stay in his urban purgatory for long. The original cave reappeared around him, with Shay standing over him with a frown.

Oh good. I was half-convinced he had sent me off to some distant planet with another Vax.

"You going to sleep all day?" She quirked a brow. "Did your whole world collapse like old-time film burning after you beat your double?"

"Yeah, that's about right." James sprang to his feet. He was still in his armor, complete with his blade. He nodded to Shay before turning toward Kalath who still stood in the distance, now looking far less confident than before. "Is this one of those things where if you die in the dream, you actually die? Was that the plan?"

Kalath glowered at him. "It wasn't a dream, but you blocked half the spell when your wife couldn't."

Shay folded her arms and scoffed. "Don't go filling his head with too much bullshit. I'll never hear the end of it." She leaned toward James. "I'm guessing we're at the limit of what I can do. I'm going to back out, so you can do what you need to do to protect our son."

"This isn't over," Kalath shouted. "Just because you beat my ritual doesn't mean this is over."

"Since you knew all that shit about me being an alien," James replied, his voice lower than his normal bass concentration of implicit threat, "then you should have planned better for it. I'm through with your fucking games, you overgrown lizard. I don't know how much of that shit was about you actually thinking you can beat me and how much of it was about you just stalling, hoping I don't go back to help with Thomas, but it doesn't matter."

"How does it not matter?"

Shay edged backward toward the exit, keeping her attention focused on Kalath, but he didn't glance her way. He continued glaring at James, his face red, and his eyes now reptilian. It was hard to tell at a distance, but James thought he could even spot a slight tremble.

"Because you've lost, Kalath," James shouted. When he spoke next, he lowered his voice. "Because I know Alison will protect her brother. All your little schemes and artifacts and plans meant shit in the end. Because you might have followers and servants, but I've got family and friends. And that's something your bitch-ass probably doesn't understand because you were hatched from an egg in some mountain somewhere and left to eat deer. If I were a good man, then I'd give some big speech about how I understand you thought you were doing the right thing, and we could let bygones be bygones now that my people killed a lot of your people."

Kalath sneered. "Is this what you're going to offer me now, James Brownstone, pity?"

"Fuck no. Because you know what? I agree with you. I'm not a good man. I'm a bad, bad man, and it's about time I showed you what a monster I am."

Shay disappeared into the hallway, leaving James more comfortable with what needed to come next. He'd considered the different possibilities, and despite the dragon's trickery and magic, he wasn't ready to blow him off as a threat. Alison wasn't easily intimidated, and if she said he needed to be cautious of Kalath, he would, but that didn't change one important fact as Whispy highlighted.

Mate has now left primary tactical engagement zone, Whispy sent. *Previously demonstrated tactical awareness suggests she will continue to leave area. Existing forces likely are suffering casualties from subordinate enemy forces. Recommend complete and immediate obliteration of primary enemy to minimize risk to allied forces, mate and offspring.*

You could have just said let's fuck him up.

Very well. Fuck him up. Protect what is ours.

James grinned under his helmet. He'd not felt this close to Whispy for a while.

"You won't win," Kalath asked.

"You did all that research on me." James sidestepped to angle his back away from the exit. "You know I don't let shit go. I tried to in the past, but I figured out something important. I realized that when I let shit go, it just makes people think I'm weak, and when they think I'm weak, they come at the people I care about and me. So there's a new policy. I'm not letting any shit go. If you come at me, if you come at my friends, and especially if you come at my family, you're going the fuck down. That's what it means to be James Brownstone."

Kalath's form contorted, his skin splitting. His limbs expanded, and his entire body inflated like a high-pressure balloon. His snout expanded, and red scales replaced his skin. The entire process took less than ten seconds, but when it was over, a massive red dragon stood in the chamber, his mouth easily large enough to swallow James whole. The dragon roared in rage, which shook the entire room.

His transformation was weird from what Alison and Shay have told me about dragons. Was that more last-minute intimidation shit? Man, this fucker never gives up.

James' expanded vision didn't require him to crane his neck upward to take in all of the dragon, but he did it anyway for effect. "You are a lot bigger than the dragons I fought in the past, but you know what they say—three heads are better than one. Well, fuck, I'm sure some dumbass says that. How about, 'The bigger they are, the harder they fall?'"

Kalath reared back and opened his mouth. A jet of red-orange fire burst from the dragon's cavernous mouth and surrounded James. He could sense the heat under his armor, but it wasn't uncomfortable other than not being able to see anything but fire.

Maximum adaptation already achieved to existing attack type, Whispy reported. *Minimal damage. Regeneration in progress.*

Kalath continued scorching James for what felt like an eternity before closing his mouth and roaring even louder than the last time. "You've not won, James Brownstone. You have no idea of the true extent of my power."

James crouched and growled. "Neither do you, you fucking old dinosaur with a death wish."

Kalath tilted his head. A dark purple bolt of energy blasted from above him and struck James. A fireball followed, then lightning. The attacks continued for a good minute as a colorful array of bolts, orbs and beams erupted from near the dragon and struck James. The blows staggered him back, stripping off some armor. Many blasted chunks of the ground up around him, leaving pits and scoured cracks in the ground, forcing him back, leaving him regenerating and pitted, but no closer to defeat.

Minor damage sustained, Whispy reported. *Regeneration in progress. Balancing in process to maximize regeneration.*

"All that power," James shouted, "but all you're doing is sending shit at me that's too similar to what I've seen before. Right now, I think I need to deliver a message to Oriceran, and that message is don't fuck with my family, even if you're a dragon."

James charged an energy cannon and fired. The green beam headed straight toward the dragon before deflecting and striking the wall. He growled and tried again, but the beam again veered off and headed out the opening of the top of the cave.

Kalath bellowed out a laugh. "So confident, but winning a battle isn't simply about surviving blows. Your capabilities are impressive, but far more limited in scope than mine."

Another deadly stream of varied attacks followed, appearing from different angles, the types never the same. He hissed, some of them stinging. Whispy's high level of regeneration was keeping the attacks from reaching his body, but he wasn't going to be able to do much against the dragon under the constant assault.

James gritted his teeth. He'd asked a lot of people to put their lives on the line to help protect his boy. Even with potions and magic, people might get hurt or die. Pauline had almost died defending Thomas, and if he didn't stop the dragon then and there, the whole cycle would repeat itself, but next time Kalath might not be restrained. Next time, some nuke-level spell might go off in Los Angeles, and thousands if not millions would die. The loud, constant growl leaking from James filled the chamber.

Sufficient background alternative power and primary power for modified Forerunner, Whispy observed. *Do it.*

Fuck my agreements. Fuck the government. Fuck everyone who wants to keep me chained while people go after my family. You're right. Let's do it.

James roared as every part of him felt stronger, energy rushing through. Another arm blade shot out. A bright green forcefield appeared around him and streams of energy now flowed freely around his arm blade, crackling with power. Kalath continued his bombardment, but this time none of the attacks reached the armor, his shield absorbing them.

James raised his arms and released his own hell. A rapid-fire stream of green energy blasts erupted from his arm blades. Unlike the beams, they didn't veer off at the last second, but exploded yards from the dragon's body, the explosion spreading out along an invisible barrier tracing the body of the beast. James kept up the assault, ignoring the constant spell bombardment around him. Sparks and explosions ripped through the chamber. It shook from the combined force of all the attacks on both sides.

Fuck it, James sent. *Rebalance so most of my power is concentrated in attack.*

Not advisable, Whispy replied.

I don't give a fuck. I want this over.

Noted. Preparing.

James' shield vanished. Spell explosions now struck him directly, some more powerful than before and ripping off layers of armor. He ignored the sting of the attacks and continued firing. His blasts were now coming more rapidly and were larger. Kalath opened his mouth to bellow a challenge, the loud noise adding to the shaking of the cavern. James matched the effort with his own loud roar.

An energy blast passed through Kalath's shield and ripped into the dragon's hide, blasting a huge crater in his body. His attacks continued but slowed. Another energy blast passed through, then another. Kalath's attack ceased, but James continued to batter the huge, ancient beast with attacks that would have destroyed entire starships or buildings. Hit after hit landed, incinerating scales, flesh, and the organs underneath. James continued to roar and fire, barely conscious of what he was doing. All he cared about in that moment was killing the creature who had threatened his son.

He wasn't sure how much time had passed when he finally stopped. Smoke and dust filled the cavern, and he'd blown holes clean through to other parts of the cave system. A roasted hole-filled sizzling red mess barely recognizable as anything once alive lay in the center of the cavern. It was like hungry lava piranhas overran the dragon.

Target eliminated, Whispy sent with joy. *Threat to offspring minimized.*

James stared at his latest victim and shook his head. Kalath should have been proud. Even the other Vax James had fought hadn't been able to take that kind of punishment, and if he'd fought them on Oriceran, they might have made easier prey.

"You were harder than most," James muttered. "You made me have to go all the way to win."

This fucker probably has some special artifact that stores his soul or something. I should blow up this entire mountain to be sure, but then Johnston's gonna have a terrible day, and King Oriceran will probably go yell at Alison. What the fuck ever. There's no way he's coming back from that.

James grinned. Even if Kalath had survived, he could just be another creature spreading the tale of the dangerous Granite Ghost. It was time to let Whispy finish regeneration and go find Shay.

CHAPTER THIRTY-FOUR

James had to jog all the way back to the spider chamber before he found Shay. She was helping Nadina stand, and after that, she ran over to wrap her arms around him. Victoria's and Trey's suits were shredded, but the mountain of gem spider corpses in the area proved their intense efforts.

Trey groaned and held the small of his back. "If I never see a fucking spider again in my life, I will die happy. Shit, at this point, I don't even know if I want to see any jewelry."

"Violence isn't fulfilling." Nadina let out a contented sigh and pressed a hand to a side wound. It glowed lightly. "I think I'll stick to cooking."

Victoria tucked her wand into its holster and took gingerly steps toward James. She gestured to a small area with fewer spider corpses. "The portals vanished not all that long ago. You did it?"

James released his helmet and nodded. "Yeah. Ding-dong, the wicked dragon is dead."

"Damn, James. A dragon, man." Trey gave him a weak thumbs-up. "Too bad he didn't have a bounty. That would have been sweet."

James nodded to Shay's backpack. "Your clothes look like shit, and I doubt you can hold much, but Shay's got space." He motioned around the room. "Hey, Shay, are these actually made of gems?"

"That's what the legends say about the chalice." Shay knelt and grabbed a broken hunk of a ruby. "I don't know enough about gemstones to talk about purity. It wouldn't hurt to grab some and find out."

"Good. Let's go check on everyone else, then we can talk about bonus scavenging."

James and his small team emerged from the cavern to find a massive Drow army advancing toward the cavern, Alison at the front. Carnage filled the battlefield, the corpses of the panther creatures and wasps stacked heavy and deep. Blood and body fluids covered almost every inch of the ground. Small numbers of bounty hunters and power armors were among the Drow reinforcements.

Alison sprinted to her parents and looked them up and down. "Are you okay?"

"I'm fine." James inclined his head toward Trey, Victoria, and Nadina. "They got beat up. Where are most of my guys?"

"They're at the capital being treated," Alison explained. "Maria and Zana are helping to coordinate triage. I brought reinforcements, but just as I did, the portals all closed, and the remaining monsters and automatons collapsed and died." She shrugged. "I'm assuming that happened because you took out Kalath."

James nodded. "Yeah. I fucked him up. Casualties?"

"Lots hurt, some badly so." Alison sighed. "But between healing potions and my people, we shouldn't have any fatalities. Some people are going to need several days of healing magic. From what I saw, the monsters just kept coming and coming."

"What about Thomas?" Shay asked, worrying her lip. "That fucking dragon made it sound like he set up a sneak attack for when we were here."

"He did. It failed." Alison snorted. Her face twisted into a scowl. "He sent his gray robe squad. They're all dead. Rasila and I personally took out the lead witch and wizard. They didn't even get close to Thomas. Mason's bitching about how he didn't get to fight."

Shay let out a sigh of relief. "Then it really is over. We fucking won against an ancient dragon." She laughed and threw up her hands.

A portal opened nearby. The Drow pivoted toward it and raised their weapons and hands. Alison summoned a shadow blade, but James didn't close his helmet. He wasn't surprised when the silver-eyed woman stepped through.

"I thought you said you killed all of Kalath's gray robes," James rumbled.

Alison hissed in irritation and raised her blade. "I've never seen this one before."

"I am Makkora," the woman announced.

Alison blinked. "Oh, shit. Just our damned luck." She motioned for the Drow to back up. "We'll handle this.

Don't engage. Prepare to evacuate with the remaining wounded."

Shay, Nadina, Trey, and Victoria walked toward the Drow line, all watching the woman with suspicion but not fear. Part of surviving in a dangerous world was learning to trust one's instincts and the tactical advice of those you trusted with your life. Alison's reaction was enough to signal a powerful and dangerous threat. There was one immediate explanation for what could possibly scare a Drow queen. James was weary but ready to fight again.

Destroy all threats to the offspring, Whispy demanded.

"Who the fuck is Makkora?" James asked. "I've got a good idea, but I need to know for sure."

"This should clarify things," the woman replied. Unlike with Kalath, there was no grotesque transformation. A bright light suffused her body and spread. When it cleared, a silver dragon as large as Kalath loomed over them. This didn't seem anything like the friendly much younger silver dragon Alison had talked about from her time at school. From what James had just dealt with when fighting Kalath, he knew Makkora could wipe out a city with ease.

Age is power, but we can still win.

James cracked his neck. "You here to get payback for your friend?"

Makkora shook her massive head. When she talked, her mouth didn't move, but her words were clear. "He chose his path, partially against my advice. I know you must hate him for what he attempted, but know that he was following a path he thought would help protect the worlds."

James patted his armored hand over his chest. "On

Earth, we have a saying. The road to Hell is paved with good intentions. I don't give two shits about your prophecy. I'm not sacrificing my son because of the *possibility* he might be a dipshit someday."

"This goes far beyond your son being a 'dipshit' as you say, Mr. Brownstone." Makkora bowed her head, a mournful look in her massive eyes. "The Ancient Pacts that bound me to Kalath prevented me from interfering with him directly, but I could have done more to stop him in the beginning. I didn't because the prophecy might not be wrong."

The Drow army watched in rapt fascination and silence as James parlayed with the massive beast. They'd stowed their weapons and released their spells. If a battle was to take place between titans, they were smart enough to not get in the way. Ants didn't have a vote in the elephants' war.

"So, what?" Shay shouted. "Are you going to come at us eventually? Then some other dragon? Do we have to kill every last dragon on Oriceran to keep him safe?"

"Most dragons aren't as involved in such activities." Makkora spread and shook her wings. "And I don't wish more violence. I know that despite his heritage, your husband has ultimately used his power for good, but if there's even a small chance your child will threaten the worlds, it's not something I can easily overlook."

"I don't want to kill you," James rumbled, "but if you're going after my son, that's the only way this ends."

"Perhaps it doesn't need to," Makkora replied.

"Then how does it end?" James shrugged. "My son isn't going to die in some twisted-ass prophecy test."

"I have an alternative suggestion." Makkora lowered her head to the ground, blinking a couple of times. A golden crown winked into existence floating in front of James. It looked identical to the one they'd retrieved from Wyoming.

Shay narrowed her eyes and rushed toward the crown. "Son of a bitch. It's the Eye of Pluto." She glared at the dragon, not showing any fear of the massive creature. "It's the real one."

"Yes," Makkora replied. "I have already invoked its magic, and it can be used to bind. I will bind myself to be unable to harm Thomas Brownstone. It will be almost as powerful as the Ancient Pact that bound me to Kalath, but, in exchange, you, Mr. Brownstone, will bind yourself to protect Earth and Oriceran against any threat powerful enough to destroy them both. I know, in this way, you will stop your son if he is the child of the prophecy. I'll give you time to dec—"

"Deal." James shrugged. "I just want you fuckers to stay away from my son. If I need to spank him in the future to keep him in line, that's my responsibility as his dad."

Makkora lifted a leg and held it over the crown, her size creating a pocket of shadow. "I, Makkora, swear here and now that I will never harm Thomas Brownstone as long as I live, nor send others to harm him."

A brilliant light surrounded the crowd before gathering into a luminescent pinpoint. The pinpoint carved an intricate glowing sigil in the air. It spun in place, speeding up for over ten seconds before shooting toward Makkora's heart and disappearing. She pulled her leg back.

James reached toward the crown. Shay snatched his

hand away and shook her head. Makkora narrowed her eyes.

"You don't have to do it," she insisted. "The dragon already did it. We won. Thomas is safe."

James pulled his hand away from hers. "I'm not starting a new fucking dragon beef when I just finished one. All I need to do is swear I'll do what I was planning anyway." He placed his hand over the Eye of Pluto. "I, James Brownstone, swear here and now to protect Earth and Oriceran if there is any threat powerful enough to destroy them both, so help me God."

The sigil display repeated itself, and the Eye of Pluto vanished. Alison winced and rushed over to her father. She eyed him with a pained look on her face.

"What's wrong?" James asked. "Did it make me look ugly? Uglier?" He shrugged.

Alison pointed at Makkora. "You knew exactly what you were doing, didn't you?"

"I've done nothing dishonorable," Makkora rumbled in response. "I've ended the bloodshed and removed the necessity to spill the blood of a child."

Shay's eyes widened, and she burst out laughing. "Fucking dragons. Too damned tricky."

"What the fuck am I missing?"

Alison shook her head. "Your oath, Dad. You just repeated what she told you earlier. But your oath didn't say you would stop Thomas if he got out of hand. Your oath said you would protect against any threat powerful enough to destroy them both."

"So much for retirement." Shay shrugged.

James groaned. "Well, that shit doesn't happen all that

often. Not more than, what, every few years?" He nodded at Makkora. "As for Thomas, I'm not gonna let my kid turn into an asshole. Not more of an asshole than me, anyway, and I haven't blown up anything worse than a building or two. Maybe a town if you count that cartel shit."

Makkora's wings flapped, the buffeting winds pushing back the small beings below. She lifted into the sky. "Farewell, James Brownstone. Don't hate me for what I've done, but with Kalath gone, additional help is needed."

"This shit is gonna be more like you have to tell me about it, and then I have to go, right?" James asked. "Not I wake up in the middle of the night and sleepwalk toward danger?"

"Yes. For all sakes, fates willing, may your oath never be invoked." Makkora continued higher into the sky. She flew toward the mountains, a majestic sight in white.

Yeah, whatever. I would have just gotten dragged into that shit anyway.

CHAPTER THIRTY-FIVE

"Whee!" Thomas shouted, his arms outstretched above him as he flew down the slide.

Pauline waited at the bottom with a smile for him. Shay and James sat on a nearby park bench. The quiet normalcy of their child playing in a park seemed distant from the exotic dragon-hunting adventure they'd just been through on Oriceran.

I tried to live a normal life. Lord knows I tried, but maybe this is his way of telling me that I can cook all the barbeque I want, but that I've got responsibilities and not just to my family.

Shay stretched her arms above her and yawned. "My sleep has been shit since coming back from Oriceran. I wonder if there's such a thing as portal lag."

"Portal lag?" James offered her a quizzical expression.

"Yes, like jet lag except from portals." Shay lowered her arms. "Or it might just be me still processing everything that happened." She grimaced. "Oh, I forget, another reporter stopped by my office at the college today. They were sniffing around for quotes about the 'James the Dragon Slayer' rumor."

"Yeah, the fuckers are like locusts at the agency," James muttered. "I think Maria retired right away because she didn't want to deal with that shit. Tyler's taunting me about it."

Shay patted his arm. "She was planning to anyway. You can't blame her. Are we still doing the official denial thing?"

"Sort of." James grunted as he remembered his last encounter with a reporter. "I told a couple of them I don't know what they were talking about, but if I had killed any dragons it was only because I had to defend my family."

Shay laughed. "That's pretty much admitting it. I thought you said Senator Johnston told you to deny it."

"He did, but I want some of this shit to leak back to Oriceran. Dragons aren't the only ancient beings over there who might decide they want a piece of us."

"We didn't really talk about it afterward." Shay's smile faded. "The prophecy."

James scoffed. "Who gives a fuck about prophecies? I think a lot of people do dumb shit when they think they know the future. I'll worry about the future when it happens. For now, I'm just going to live my life and raise my kid so he won't be a dumb shit. I'm sure there are prophecies about me out there. For all I know, there's one on my home planet, and that's why they won't come back, or maybe that's why they came for me to begin with."

Shay took his hand and gave it a squeeze. "So, we're just like any other parents, trying to do our best and hope our kid doesn't end on some sleazy talk show talking about

BBQ AND STFU

how his parents drove him into being a coked-out stripper."

James eyed her. "You're more worried about him being a coked-out stripper than destroying Earth and Oriceran?"

"Sure." Shay grinned. "They're both unlikely, but one of those is more likely than the other, and it's not the one that ends in doom. Like I said, just like any other parents."

"Yeah, just like any other parents." James squeezed her hand back. "After everything we've been through together and everything we've done, I know we can handle this as a family. Because we're Brownstones, and when Brownstones encounter a problem, they don't whine about it. They destroy it."

Shay kissed him lightly on the lips. "Don't ever change, James."

Thomas ran back and forth, miming a sword slice and roaring at a laughing Pauline. Shay and James watched him for a minute.

"What are you playing?" James asked.

Thomas stopped running and smiled at his father. "I'm playing James the Dragon Slayer!"

THE END

What can you say when the time has come to end something that you love so dearly?

James Brownstone was a character that I created with a few of my fans in mind. He wasn't going to have a swimmer's build, he was going to be a man's man, and he wasn't going to be all magical.

But he was going to be special.

He was into trucks, barbecue, and the K.I.S.S. principle. His life was exactly the way he wanted it until a young blind girl came into his life. Allison became what we called in the writing business, the "inciting incident."

I suspect that if you asked literary professors, they might tell you I am using the wrong point in his path to call it such. However, for me, the reason I consider it the inciting incident is that she changes his heart. Before, he was no-nonsense, and it was easier to allow others to be responsible for their actions.

In the end, he could not allow what happened to Allison and her mom to go without a response. He accepted the responsibility of not only a young lady but also someone who was going to be a challenge no matter what.

And for that, my heart grew two sizes that day.

The number of times that I've had wonderful conversations with fans of James Brownstone has been significant in the last few years. In fact, we have a whole barbecue location here in Las Vegas (Jessie Rae's barbecue) that has enjoyed many fans coming in to taste the food. I've had Mike Ross, the owner, tell me that the Brownstone books have been the best marketing ever!

Even now, I've been reading reviews on book 21 where fans are aghast that we are ending the series. I wish I could say that we could go on forever, but it's time to close the final chapter.

Does this mean this is the last book for James? No, I certainly hope not. I believe that we have options in the future where you will see James again. For now, Martha and I are not expecting James to have another series of his own. However, he will show up, we promise.

Fans are asking for his children to have a series! I could imagine this occurring. I won't say that we have plans at the moment for this to happen, but I could see those of us working on The Unbelievable Mr. Brownstone talking about it.

Instead of the regular diary entry, I'm going to share the original setup for what became The Unbelievable Mr. Brownstone – WARTS AND ALL.

Here is the original idea, characters, names (for example, Alison was originally Paula).

Don't rip me too hard as we celebrate the end of this

series by 'going back to the beginning... and then a little farther.'

Ad Aeternitatem,

Michael

ORIGINAL START OF THE IDEA OF BROWNSTONE AND THE ORICERAN UNIVERSE.

Tales of the Unbelievable Mr. Brownstone

"If I wanted to stay clean," my voice, guttural and deep resonated in the alleyway, "I wouldn't have come here to make sure this little girl got home in one piece, without any scratches."

I stared down at the two Harriken. They were from the locally dominant Japanese mafia. Both had swords, the shorter variety, worn on their sides. I stood behind Paula who had asked a favor of me when she brought me back my dog.

The only companion I've ever had that didn't run from me when they saw what I looked like, or heard my voice.

Nor, come to think of it, did Paula. But, that could be because she is too young to know danger when staring him in the face.

Once I got down on my knees so she could see my face.

"We don't really care if you stay clean or not, meat bag."

The first murmured, a touch of a smile gracing his face, "We only care that the girl comes with us."

Paula, forgotten when the adults were talking, spoke up, "If you think I'm stupid enough to go with you, forget it! I asked Mr. Brownstone here to help me find my Mom, not to get caught up in some stupid kidnapping. So, both of you can kiss my butt." She folded her arms in front of her and blew out a small amount of blond hair that had fallen in front of her eyes.

"Mr. Brownstone, is it?" the second spoke now turning to his partner, "I don't remember any Brownstone's running the street." He turned back to me, "Are you new in town? Because, if you are, it would be impolite not to let you understand you are in Harriken territory, and we take our territory very seriously. Perhaps we let you go with but a scratch, but if you resist, and I would like you to resist let's be clear, then you will be made a living example of Harriken protection of those businesses around us." He nodded to the buildings back out the front of the alley, "So they know they are getting their monies worth."

Cockbite number one spoke up, "Yes, we haven't provided a physical example of our value in some time, and you," he nodded upwards toward me, easily topping the two Japanese by a head and a half, "will make an excellent example."

I reached down and put a hand on Paula's shoulder, "Little one, you need to get in back of me."

"Fine," she said, exasperated as she walked around behind me, "how is it the little fourteen-year-old can see these two are about to get their butts kicked and they can't?" She turned away from me and walked to an upturned box and sat down facing us, "too much testosteronie." She grumped.

I turned to the young girl, "It's testosterone," I corrected her, "and who is teaching you such large words?"

"I read a lot," she replied.

I turned back to the two, "Ok guys, do we say a few more things or do I just go ahead and beat you senseless? If you leave it with knives and swords, then you both walk away…Well, perhaps you might be carried away, but you will live. If you pull out anything harder? I'll stop playing by GG's rules."

"GG?" Number one smile, "Your grandmother?" He took a couple of steps to his right, giving his partner room to pull out his sword.

"Not my grandmother," I told him, waiting for the second to make a move, "mine."

"And just what," the first continued, "makes you think that we will play by your rules?"

The second reacted damned quickly. I'll give him that. For a slightly gifted human, he was alright. Quick, accurate and determined to take that Wazikashi and slice into my face with it. I pulled my arm up, and the ting of metal hitting metal reverberated off of the walls in the alleyway.

"Hai! You have some sort of armor under your clothes," the first commented, his sword also bouncing off of my other arm with a loud ping this time.

For the next few seconds, the three of us traded blows, blocks, and parries. For me, I wasn't working too hard. These cats were okay; I'll grant them that. But, they weren't even up the scale of danger for me. If I had been hired to bring them in, I doubt I'd get a difficulty adjustment of two for either one of them.

That means I'd get about a hundred bucks, for each. It was going to cost me more than that to fix up my clothes after this debacle.

Humans, unoriginal since 1888. At least the Japanese in this area still had honor.

Oops, spoke too soon. "Now, see," I said as I used my mental ability to pull the pistol out of the guy's hand when he flashed it out of its holster.

I slowly bent it in my hands, "I told you, I would play nice until you did that."

He looked shocked when I dropped his pistol, totally crumpled up to the ground. I paid his buddy more attention until I decided to stop playing. I grabbed his blade when he sent it whistling towards me. His eyes opened wide as I crushed it, the sword's edge not cutting into my hand at all.

"Paula is here, so I'm feeling a little concerned about too much blood," I told the two grunts.

"Why?" Spoke the little devil, "Research shows that by age 18 an American child will have seen 16,000 simulated murders and 200,000 acts of violence. What's the difference if you just off them right now? I'll probably get an abject lesson in the difference between real and simulated violence. I'm willing to take the risk that I can be horribly traumatized by the death of these two jerks right in front of me."

The two Harriken looked at the younger girl, the first one barked, "Would you shut up!"

I casually backhanded him, breaking his jaw as his body

slammed twelve-feet away into a brick wall, "Don't," I told his inert body, "be disrespectful to the young lady."

The other, the lead, looked back at me and then the girl, "If you so much as move a muscle in the general direction of the pistol you are carrying, I will toss your ass up to the height of the roof.

He glanced to confirm the building had three stories.

"Mind you, you won't land on the roof, you will just go splat on the ground right in front of us, and we will see if Paula will find it traumatizing."

He opened his mouth, and I slapped him, blood spurting from his broken nose and cut up lip, "Don't say a word you will regret. I'm in Harriken territory. I don't care. I haven't seen the last of you, you might say. Yes, I have, or I'll kill you next time. I've heard it all before. Now, grab your disrespectful jerk of a friend and start on your way out of this alley."

He hobbled over and grabbed his buddy. He began pulling him out of the puddle he was laying in.

"By the way," I told him as he made it halfway to the alley entrance, "this little girl, and her mother is now under the protection of the Granite Ghost. Tell whoever you need, that I expect to get an answer where she is and delivered safe and sound or I will rip through this area like vengeance walking, and there will be no Harriken to have any territory, do you understand?"

The man nodded and redoubled his efforts to leave.

I looked over at Paula, who was looking around, a slightly unfocused look to her face. "Hey," she looked over to me, "you have quite a mouth on you." She stood up and walked over to me, looking up, "You are quoting statistics? I need to find out what your teacher is teaching you."

"I don't have a teacher, Mr. Brownstone." She started walking towards the other end of the alley, "I'm self-taught." She took four steps to one of mine, "I read through the night when I can't sleep."

"Doesn't your dad tell you to turn out the lights? What do you do, grab a flashlight?" I asked her.

"Didn't you know, Mr. Brownstone?" She asked, looking up at me, "I read braille. I'm blind."

She turned back around, quickly dodging a pile of something in her way, "You can't be blind, I've seen you walk and respond to stuff, like that shit you just dodged."

"That is because it has energy, Mr. Brownstone. My eyes can see the energy and understand what it is. I didn't find your puppy because he ran up to me, I found your puppy because he happened to be stuck and I saw his red energy flare up. I went looking to see what caused the flare up and found him stuck in a hole by the old Stephen's place."

I searched my mind, thinking that name was familiar.

"It's the old mansion that has been empty for the last fifteen years. The Stephen's were Mark and Bethany Stephens. Double-homicide and the house has been haunted since. No one can go in."

We exited the alley and turned left towards my Ford F-150 Raptor with the big-ass FORD letters across the grill. If I rammed somebody, I wanted my truck's imprint across their body. It tickled me to think of someone running around with a big F stuck on their face, or my tire treads running across their chest.

God, I kill myself sometimes.

I opened the passenger's side door, and Paula reached in. I noticed she did a little test to make sure she understood what she was seeing, and then put her hand in the right place on the door to pull herself up into the truck.

I closed the door behind her and walked around to the other side and got in, shutting the door behind me.

"Before we go anywhere," I asked her, "I figured we had your father's permission to do this. Now, I know I'm not an appropriate guardian here, and I should have asked many more questions. But, here goes nothing, does your father have a clue where you are?"

"Yes, he has a clue," she admitted, "not that he cares since he hasn't been looking for my Mom for three weeks, ever since she mysteriously disappeared and the cops left."

"Is he your dad?" I followed up.

"Only because he is married to my mom, he is nothing but a sperm donor." She replied.

I needed to get a handle on how fourteen-year-olds talked. This one was way ahead of the curve as far as I could tell. "Where do you get this stuff from? There can't be that many braille books out there."

"Easy enough, I plug in my braille reader to my computer and surf the Internet. Then, it will either read aloud or if it is information I don't want to share, I will read it using the translator. It will pull up the braille per line, and as I finish one line, it changes to allow me to feel the next line of text."

I had nothing to say to her. She obviously was a capable young woman. "You think your dad has done something to your mom?"

Paula turned and looked at me. It was hard to believe this little girl couldn't see, "Mr. Brownstone, I know he did something to my mom. How?" I just nodded, she seemed to be reading my mind. "Because everyone gives off energy, Mr. Brownstone, even ugly people can be overcome with even uglier energy. When my Mom disappeared, his energy turned black."

I started the truck, the engine roaring to life. Damn, I loved my new mufflers. However, I reached under the dash and pushed a button that implemented a small noise reduction spell around the cab. I needed it in case I wanted to take a business call or speak without raising any voices in the cab.

"I was wondering why you didn't go screaming when you first saw me," I said, turning into the street ahead of a yellow taxi, "I thought you were naïve," I admitted.

"No, Mr. Brownstone, I'm not naïve. If I have any blessing from this, it is that I always see the purity in a person's heart."

Uh-oh, I wasn't sure I wanted her to go anywhere with that comment. I'm in a mean business, and I've done some pretty mean things. I wasn't sure I wanted a fourteen-year-old being on the other side of the confessional, discussing my sins with me.

Then, she shocked me, "and your heart Mr. Brownstone is the most beautiful color I have ever seen."

Notes - The Unbelievable Mr. Brownstone.

Burt Jamison, Father - Is aware of Nicole's gift, and is selling it to the highest bidder. Believes she needs to be separated from her child so she won't 'waste' it on Paula.

Nicole Kirksteward - Carries the blood of the S'raken (dark elves) - has one gift to bestow (like a wish). Can see the future, but is unable to change, so must plan.

Paula Kirksteward - blind but see's energy, very intelligent, see's people for who they are.

Ms. Pontifax - The lady who is in charge of the Girl's School for the Gifted.

Xander Brownstone - Granite Ghost, Magical Bounty Hunter, can change his body between hard and ghost. Has Telekinetic powers.

His dog, Blind Bart (named after a movie character) can see just fine. Brownstone calls him that because only a blind dog could love a man with his face.

Available now at your favorite online bookstores

Two Rebels whose Worlds Collide on a Planetary Level.

On the fringes of human space, a murder will light a fuse and send two different people colliding together.

She lives on Earth, where peace among the population is a given. He is on the fringe of society where authority is how much firepower you wield.

She is from the powerful, the elite. He is with the military.

Both want the truth – but is revealing the truth good for society?

Two years ago, a small moon in a far off system was set to be the location of the first intergalactic war between humans and an alien race.

It never happened. However, something was found many are willing to kill to keep a secret.

Now, they have killed the wrong people.

How many will need to die to keep the truth hidden?

As many as is needed.

He will have vengeance no matter the cost. *She will dig for the truth. No matter how risky the truth is to reveal.*

Get your copy today from Amazon, or your favorite online bookstore.

OTHER SERIES IN THE ORICERAN
UNIVERSE:

THE DANIEL CODEX SERIES
I FEAR NO EVIL
THE UNBELIEVABLE MR. BROWNSTONE
ALISON BROWNSTONE
SCHOOL OF NECESSARY MAGIC
SCHOOL OF NECESSARY MAGIC: RAINE CAMPBELL
FEDERAL AGENTS OF MAGIC
SCIONS OF MAGIC
THE LEIRA CHRONICLES
REWRITING JUSTICE
THE KACY CHRONICLES
MIDWEST MAGIC CHRONICLES
SOUL STONE MAGE
THE FAIRHAVEN CHRONICLES

OTHER BOOKS BY JUDITH BERENS

CONNECT WITH MICHAEL ANDERLE

Michael Anderle Social
  Website:
  http://www.lmbpn.com

Email List:
  http://lmbpn.com/email/

Facebook Here:
  https://www.facebook.com/OriceranUniverse/
  https://www.
  facebook.com/TheKurtherianGambitBooks/

www.ingramcontent.com/pod-product-compliance
Lightning Source LLC
Chambersburg PA
CBHW031615100726
47898CB00006B/1806